AUNT BESSIE KNOWS

AN ISLE OF MAN COZY MYSTERY

DIANA XARISSA

To my cousin Lauren, who is one of the most caring and giving people I know.

AUTHOR'S NOTE

I keep thinking I needn't bother with these notes anymore, as this is book eleven in the series, but then I remember that some people might read the series out of order and start here! If you've done that, welcome to the Aunt Bessie series and the Isle of Man.

Bessie first appeared in my Isle of Man Romance, *Island Inheritance*, but she was the source of the inheritance for my heroine there. Yes, Bessie had just passed away in that book. So I've set the Bessie series about fifteen years before the romance, beginning the series in March 1998. The books have followed on from there, and the characters do grow and develop, so I recommend reading the titles in order (alphabetically by the last word in the title). Every book should stand on its own, however, if you do choose to read them individually.

This is a work of fiction and all of the characters are fictional creations. Any resemblance they share with any real person, living or dead, is entirely coincidental. The Isle of Man is a real and incredibly wonderful place, and all of the historical sites mentioned within the books in the series are real. The events in my books that take place within those sites are entirely made up. The businesses mentioned in the story are also fictional and any resemblance that any of them bear to real businesses is also coincidental.

I've used British (and Manx) spellings and terminology throughout the book, and there is a short glossary of terms in the back to help readers from outside the UK with anything that might be unfamiliar. The longer I live in the US, the more likely it is that more Americanisms will sneak into the texts. I'm sorry about that, and if you let me know, I will try to correct them.

As always, I love hearing from readers. Please use the contact details at the back of book to get in touch at any time. I hope you enjoy Bessie's latest adventure.

CHAPTER 1

"*B*essie? It's Mary," the voice on the other end of the telephone said.

Elizabeth Cubbon, known as Bessie to nearly everyone, bit back a sigh. She was sorry she'd answered the phone now. "How are you?" she asked the other woman.

"I'm fine, but you know how I get before parties. I was hoping you might be persuaded to come over early as we're just down the beach from you."

Now Bessie did sigh. She'd agreed to attend Mary's New Year's Eve party somewhat reluctantly. While she liked Mary a great deal, she wasn't overly fond of the sort of drunken revelry that seemed to be commonplace at such celebrations. Bessie lived alone and she usually saw in each new year with a small glass of wine and a good book. But Bessie knew that her shy friend Mary would enjoy the night more with Bessie in attendance. As soon as the sigh left Bessie's lips, Mary was speaking.

"I know, you're busy and you're going to be here all night. It doesn't really matter," she said quickly. "Forget I even asked."

"I'm just being lazy," Bessie said. "I'm sitting here with a book and a cup of hot chocolate and I don't feel like moving. I do have to get up eventually and come over, though. I suppose I could come earlier than I'd planned."

"I'd be ever so grateful," Mary replied. "Elizabeth has invited a whole houseful of young people and I've nothing much to say to them. We have half a dozen men and women here trying to get everything ready for tonight and George is out somewhere, no doubt inviting another twenty people to the party. I'm feeling completely fed up and I'm just about ready to come over to your cottage and hide until 1999 is safely underway."

Bessie laughed. "You mustn't let yourself get so stressed," she said. "I'll come over and we can have a drink and relax together until it's time for the guests to start arriving. Shall I come at six?"

"Oh, six is fine," Mary replied. "But five would work just as well. Or even four."

Bessie could hear the hopefulness in the other woman's voice. She looked at the clock on the wall and swallowed another sigh. It was half three already. "I'll be there as soon as I can," she told her friend.

"Oh, thank you," Mary said, clearly relieved.

Bessie put down the phone and shook her head. She should have known that Mary would want her to arrive early. It had been years since she'd been to a New Year's Eve party. Maybe this one would be more enjoyable than usual. She climbed the stairs to her bedroom and changed into her black party dress. As it was a special occasion, she took the time to apply some makeup before she combed her grey hair. As she rarely wore makeup, she wasn't entirely sure what she was doing, but she did her best to make her grey eyes stand out.

"It's a smudgy mess," she told her reflection. But it sounds like most of the party will be young people, and they won't pay any attention to a woman in her late middle age, the voice in her head replied.

Bessie shrugged at the mirror and then headed back downstairs. She'd had her free bus pass for many years now, but she was still some years away from receiving a telegram from the queen to mark her birthday. While some people might have suggested that she was getting old, Bessie didn't see it that way. She walked every day on the beach behind the small cottage that had been her home for all of her adult life. If pressed, she would have credited the daily exercise and regular intake of sea air for her continued good health.

Before she headed across the beach to Mary's mansion, she needed to make a quick phone call.

"Doona? It's Bessie. Mary's just rung and asked me to come over early, so I'll see you at the party, if that's okay with you," she said when the phone was answered.

"Are you sure you want to do that?" Doona asked. "It's going to be a long night as it is."

"I know, but poor Mary gets so nervous before these sorts of things. If I don't go and hold her hand, she'll be a wreck by the time the guests start to arrive."

"Surely George should be holding her hand," Doona suggested, naming Mary's husband.

"Apparently he's out and about somewhere. Anyway, he loves big social events. I'm sure he doesn't understand why Mary gets so anxious about them."

"I would have thought, after being married to George for all these years, that Mary would be accustomed to them by now."

"I think she used the children as an excuse to avoid them for many years," Bessie said. "But now they are all grown up and she can't."

"I'm not sure I would count Elizabeth as a grown-up," Doona said dryly.

Bessie sighed. Mary's youngest child and only daughter was in her mid-twenties, but she often seemed to still behave like a spoiled child. She had been living with George and Mary in their Douglas home, but now that her parents had purchased Thie yn Traie, the mansion just down the beach from Bessie's cottage, Elizabeth had moved into a suite of rooms there. This gave her some space away from her parents, but it also meant that she was unsupervised, and she'd already managed to get herself into trouble on more than one occasion.

Doona worked for the local constabulary as civilian front desk staff, so she'd heard about the car that Elizabeth had accidently driven into the gates at Thie yn Traie, about the fireworks display that Elizabeth and her friends had put on without permission, and about the bar fight that had broken out when Elizabeth and her friends had begun spending time at the nearest pub.

"I understand that Elizabeth has a number of friends here for the party," Bessie said.

"We'd better put a few extra men on call tonight," Doona shot back. "Although John and Hugh will be at the party. I suppose they should be able to handle most things."

"Let's hope they don't have to do anything more than have a few drinks and toast the new year," Bessie said fervently.

"Yes, let's," Doona agreed. "I'll see you at Thie yn Traie around seven, then."

"I'm sure I'll be watching for you," Bessie replied.

Bessie had never learned to drive, and it seemed pointless to ring for a taxi for a short journey down the beach. After slipping her black leather shoes into a bag, Bessie pulled on Wellington boots that were far more suitable for walking on the beach in late December. She fastened her warmest coat around her and then headed out towards Thie yn Traie. It was cold and windy, but it was dry, which wasn't usual in the winter months. In spite of the cold, Bessie found herself walking slowly. She took the time to look in the windows of the holiday cottages that were between her home and Mary's.

Thomas Shimmin, the man who owned the cottages, had been busy throughout December giving them all a fresh coat of paint. Bessie smiled to herself as she reached the last cottage in the row. Several paint cans were spread across the floor and Bessie could see that Thomas had only managed to finish about half of the main room in that cottage. Clearly, he'd have to get back to work in the new year. At the bottom of the steps to Thie yn Traie, Bessie paused and took a deep breath.

"It's going to be fun," she muttered to herself as she began the climb up to the mansion. "It's going to be lots of fun." The words repeated themselves over and over again as Bessie made her way slowly up the steps. The stairs climbed for a short while and then there was a short path to where the next set of stairs began. Bessie felt as if she were zigzagging her way up the cliff face as she held on tightly to the handrail. She'd taken a bad tumble down these stairs once, and she wasn't eager to repeat the experience.

When she reached the top, she stopped to take a good look at the mansion in front of her. She knew that Mary had a great many plans for the place, but Bessie couldn't imagine that anything the woman did would make the mansion more attractive. From the beach, only the large great room with its wall of windows was visible, but now Bessie frowned at the building's wings that seemed to head off in every possible direction aside from straight down the cliff face.

Bessie shook her head. The Pierce family had built Thie yn Traie and given it its name. The words were Manx for Beach House and they'd used the mansion as a summer home, never staying there for more than a few months each year. What they'd needed all this space for, Bessie couldn't imagine. Then again, she wasn't sure why George and Mary wanted the huge mansion, either. They already had an even bigger home in Douglas, although Mary was hoping that George would agree to sell that property once they'd remodeled Thie yn Traie.

Surprised that Mary hadn't met her at the top of the stairs, Bessie followed the path that meandered its way to one of the mansion's many doors. She pressed the bell and waited patiently for someone to answer. After a minute, she tried the bell again. At least another minute passed before the door finally swung open.

"The party starts at seven," the young man who'd opened the door said to Bessie. "Come back then and come to the front door." He began to push the door shut in Bessie's face.

"My goodness," she said. "What terrible manners. I don't know who you are, but you've a great deal to learn about answering the door."

The man raised an eyebrow. "Look, lady, I don't know who you are, either, but I do know the party doesn't start until seven."

"Bruce? Who is it?" a female voice called from behind the man.

"Some old lady who won't go away. I told her the party doesn't start for like three hours, but she told me I have bad manners."

5

The woman behind Bruce laughed. "Well, she's probably right," she said.

Now the door swung open further, and Bessie smiled as she recognised Elizabeth Quayle. "Elizabeth, how nice to see you again," she said to the young woman. "Your mother rang and invited me to come over early, as she was feeling nervous, but this young man doesn't seem to want me to come inside."

Elizabeth shook her head, causing dozens of springy blonde locks to swing back and forth. "Don't mind Bruce," she said, waving the man away. "He doesn't know that Aunt Bessie is a Laxey institution."

Bessie wasn't sure she would agree with that description of herself, but she didn't argue as Elizabeth ushered her into the house and took her coat.

"That was smart, wearing your Wellies on the walk," Elizabeth said as Bessie changed into her shoes. "I can't imagine walking on the beach in my shoes, either."

Bessie looked at the silver and black stilettos that the girl was wearing. They must have added five or six inches to the woman's height. "I can't imagine walking anywhere in those," Bessie retorted. "I'd break an ankle for sure."

"You just have to get used to them," Elizabeth said airily. "They match my dress, you see."

Bessie looked at the tiny black cocktail dress the girl was wearing. She blushed as she realised that the dress was more revealing than anything Bessie had ever worn, even to sleep in. Elizabeth had the perfect figure for the low-cut top and short skirt, but Bessie had to think for a moment before she spoke.

"You look stunning," she said.

"Thanks. Mum thinks the dress is too short, but she's terribly old-fashioned about such things."

Bessie simply smiled. She wasn't going to get drawn into the argument.

"It's a party," the man who'd refused to let Bessie in said now. "Short skirts and high heels are a must at a party."

"Where are yours then?" Elizabeth challenged him with a laugh.

The man glanced down at his jeans and shrugged. "If you get me drunk enough..." he suggested.

"Miss Elizabeth Cubbon, this is Bruce Durrant, a very dear friend of mine from one of my attempts at uni," Elizabeth said. "Bruce, Aunt Bessie owns the darling little cottage down the beach from here. You must treat her as if she were your own aunty."

"Of course," the man said, bowing towards Bessie. "I do hope you're the sort of aunty who drinks too much and ends up dancing with the waiters by the end of the evening."

Bessie glanced at Elizabeth and then shook her head.

Bruce laughed. "Maybe that's just in my family," he said. "Anyway, you've come to see Mrs. Quayle, not me. Let me help you find her."

He offered Bessie his arm and Bessie thought it would be rude not to take it. They made their way down the corridor with Elizabeth behind them. As they walked, Bessie noted that her escort was only a few inches taller than her own five feet three inches. That made him much shorter than Elizabeth, at least while Elizabeth was wearing those particular shoes. He was slender and clean-shaven. Bessie assumed he was in his mid-twenties, like Elizabeth, but she wasn't certain as his receding hairline made him look older. What hair he did have was brown and matched his eyes.

They arrived in the room that the Pierce family had called the "great room," and Bessie was pleased to see that the party decorations made the huge room feel warmer and more inviting. A band was setting up along one wall and Mary was in the corner, talking on her mobile.

"I have to go," she said now in a firm voice. "I'll see you later." She pressed a button on the phone and dropped into her pocket.

"I hope I didn't interrupt an important conversation," Bessie said after she'd returned Mary's affectionate hug.

"Not at all," Mary said, shaking her head. "It was just George, being silly."

"Silly? Never mind, it's none of my business," Bessie said.

"He's in Douglas, at the house there, and he wants me to come down there to help him choose a tie or some such thing," Mary said

7

with a sigh. "I've told him I'm far too busy here to be dashing back and forth. He can pick out a tie without my help, I'm quite certain."

"Shall I go and help daddy?" Elizabeth asked. "I'll cheer him up as well, as he's been quite grumpy lately."

"You're more than welcome to try," Mary told her daughter. "Just make sure you're back here well before the guests are due to arrive."

"Everyone I've invited is already here," Elizabeth said with a giggle. "I hope they don't miss me while I'm in Douglas."

"Take some of them with you," Mary suggested. "They've nothing to do here anyway."

"I'm happy to accompany you," Bruce offered.

"Oh, goodness no, you stay here and entertain Bessie," Elizabeth said. "I'll just see if Howard wants to come along, though."

She glided out of the room on her impossibly high heels, leaving Bessie and Mary with a frowning Bruce.

"What am I to do now, then?" he muttered.

"You can take one of the cars and go into Douglas if you'd like," Mary said. "Or take some of the others and go for a short drive around the island. It's really beautiful."

Bruce shrugged. "Maybe," he said. He walked out of the room, leaving Mary frowning now.

"Imagine inviting a whole group of friends to the island and not planning anything for them to do," Mary said to Bessie.

"Is that what Elizabeth has done?" Bessie asked.

"Yes. They all just turned up the other day. She didn't tell me how many were coming, so we didn't have rooms prepared for them all. There's nothing for them to do here and the party is still hours away, but now she is heading down to Douglas to help George and leaving me with them all."

"How many are there?" Bessie asked, concerned.

"Oh, goodness, I didn't count," Mary replied. "There's Bruce, whom you've already met. He seems quite taken with Elizabeth, but she only has eyes for Howard, er, Howard Bridges, who's ghastly, but I never said that."

Bessie smiled. "I shall look forward to meeting Howard, then," she said.

"Yes, well, he's probably not as bad as I think, but he is clearly just having fun with Elizabeth and not at all serious, and that worries me as I'm sure Elizabeth likes him quite a lot."

"Oh, dear," Bessie said. "And who else am I going to meet later?"

"Jeremy Lee, who is lovely, with the sort of old-fashioned manners you never see anymore. Why Elizabeth couldn't fall for him, I'll never know. And then there's Nigel Hutton. He's the last of the men in the party, and he seems to spend a great deal of his time sleeping. I've not actually met him."

Bessie must have looked surprised, because Mary quickly explained.

"They're all staying in Elizabeth's wing of the house and I've had staff come up from the Douglas house to help out. The staff has been running back and forth with food and drinks for the group all day, but no one other than Bruce has wandered out of their little section of the house."

"How nice for them to have their own wing and staff to look after them," Bessie said.

"Yes, well, I did tell Elizabeth that she'd have to deal with it all, but she's, well, she's a little bit overwhelmed at the moment." Mary sighed. "I know I need to be tougher with her, but she is my baby girl. George and I have agreed, though, that she has to get a job or go back to school in the new year."

"I'm sure that will be good for her," Bessie said. "Are there other women in Elizabeth's party as well or just the men?"

"Oh, yes, a mix of both. Sarah Davies is a sweetheart. She's very bubbly and madly in love with Bruce, who doesn't seem to notice. Emma Taylor is quiet and rather fades into the background, but maybe that's because my Elizabeth and Gennifer Carter-Maxwell have such large personalities. Gennifer is spelled with a 'G' by the way, which she seems to think is quite important."

"I'm not sure I'm looking forward to meeting any of these people," Bessie remarked.

Mary nodded. "They can be a bit much," she admitted. "But it's good for Elizabeth to have her friends around her for the holiday. I keep hoping one of them might inspire her to do something with her life, but I have to say, this group probably isn't going to do that. I don't know that any of them do much more than live off of their parents."

"I hope you've invited some people that I will enjoy spending time with," Bessie couldn't help but say.

"Of course I have," Mary said quickly. "Most of the party will be filled with wonderful people from the island. You mustn't worry about Elizabeth and her friends. They'll entertain one another and the rest of us probably won't even notice that they are here."

Bessie bit her tongue. There was no point in telling Mary just how unlikely she considered that scenario. In her experience, young people always made certain that they were the centre of attention, and Bessie was sure that Elizabeth and her friends would try hard to make the evening's party revolve around them.

"Anyway," Mary continued, "Doona will be here, and I've invited John Rockwell and young Hugh Watterson and his lovely lady friend. I know they're all friends of yours. I've also invited everyone who was involved with 'Christmas at the Castle', and I'm really looking forward to seeing them again, although some of them did say they couldn't make it."

Bessie and Mary had both served on the committee that put together the island's first "Christmas at the Castle" fundraiser at Castle Rushen. The event had been a huge success, in spite of the two murders that had marred the festivities.

"I'm sure it will be a wonderful evening," Bessie said, firmly silencing her misgivings.

"But why are we standing here when we could be having wine and food?" Mary demanded.

Bessie laughed and then the pair made their way out of the great room to the large kitchen that was further down the corridor.

Bessie stopped in the doorway and simply stared at the huge number of people who were busily working in the space.

"I know," Mary said. "When you were here last, it was just me, and now we have a veritable army of people in here. But it's only for tonight, or at least only until Elizabeth's friends leave. I really do want to cut back on our staff numbers once we move in for good up here."

Bessie nodded. "But you couldn't possibly do all the food for tonight's party yourself," she said.

"No, and George would never agree to just having a small gathering for close friends," Mary said. "He wanted to invite a great many more people, but I insisted that we keep the guest list to a reasonable number."

Bessie didn't want to ask her friend what she considered "reasonable" for a New Year's Eve party. There was no doubt in Bessie's mind that there would be many more people at the party than Bessie would feel comfortable with.

Mary caught someone's attention. "Can you please open us a bottle of wine?" she asked. "And we'd love to try out any of the food that's ready, as well."

The woman nodded and disappeared. A few moments later she was back with a bottle and two glasses. Behind her, a man in a chef's outfit was carrying a large tray.

"A small sample from tonight's selection," he told Mary, setting the tray on the table next to Bessie.

"I hope this isn't too much trouble," Mary replied.

"Not at all," he assured her. "I've been sending similar trays over to the guests in the west wing all day."

Mary frowned. "Yes, well, thank you for that," she said tightly. She took the tray with the wine and smiled at Bessie. "Can you grab that one and we'll go somewhere quiet?" she asked.

Bessie picked up the tray, which was covered in mouthwatering finger foods and followed Mary out of the room. They only went a short distance before Mary opened a door and led Bessie into a small room that was furnished with a large desk. There was a huge leather chair behind the desk and two smaller chairs in front of it.

"I know this isn't ideal, but it's quiet and there are chairs," Mary said in an apologetic tone. "This was Donald Pierce's office when he was here. They cleared out all of his things, but left the desk and chairs. I hope you don't mind if we hide in here for a short while."

"We have wine and lovely food," Bessie replied. "We can stay in here until midnight, if you'd like."

Mary laughed as she poured the wine. "I really wish we could," she told Bessie. "I don't know if I've ever been in less of a party mood than I am right now."

"What's wrong?" Bessie asked. "I don't mean to pry, of course."

Mary smiled, but it didn't reach her eyes. She handed Bessie a glass and then took a large drink of her own wine. "You aren't prying," she said eventually. "I know that you genuinely care. Things are just difficult right now. I know half of the good people on the island think that George was involved in Grant's criminal activities. George is having a difficult time dealing with the repercussions. He really misses being the life of the party at every social event on the island. No one seems to be inviting him anywhere at the moment."

Bessie nodded and sipped her wine. George's former business partner, Grant Robertson, had fled the island some months earlier as the police began to look into his business practices. The subsequent investigation had brought a great deal of criminal activity to light, but George had been cleared of any involvement. Bessie knew that many people found it impossible to believe that George hadn't known what was going on, however, and the man had suddenly found himself cut off from his previously extensive social circle.

"That's one of the reasons we're having this party tonight," Mary told Bessie. "I knew no one would invite us anywhere, so I thought we should have our own party."

"And your real friends will all be here," Bessie said.

"Yes, unfortunately, not many of the people George thought were his friends will be," Mary said. She finished her glass of wine and refilled it. "George went through the list of replies this afternoon. That's what he was so upset about when he rang. Nearly everyone he invited had some sort of excuse for not coming."

"I'm sorry," Bessie said.

"I'm sure they'll all come around eventually," Mary replied. "But

George is like a small and confused child. He thought they were all his friends and now they've all turned their backs on him because of a little bit of trouble."

"I wish they'd find Grant. I think everyone on the island would be happier if he were behind bars."

"Yes, that would probably help," Mary agreed. "Oh, I'm sorry. George is feeling glum and his mood has rubbed off on me, that's all. I'm usually the one who dreads these sorts of parties while he's usually all excited and eager for them to start. Now he's hiding in Douglas, threating not to come at all and I'm stuck here, wishing we had a good reason to cancel the whole thing."

"You can cancel," Bessie said. "Just tell everyone you're ill. People would understand."

Mary shook her head. "I won't give those people the satisfaction," she said grimly. "We're going to have a party whether they want to attend or not. Besides, Elizabeth's friends are all here and they've been promised a proper New Year's Eve celebration. We're going to do this and we're going to have a good time."

Bessie had to smile at the words that contrasted so sharply with her friend's miserable countenance. "I intend to have fun," Bessie said. "It's been a very difficult year for all of us. We deserve a party."

Mary nodded gloomily and then the two women began to work their way through the tray of food.

"This is delicious," Bessie said when the tray was about half-empty.

"They've done a really good job," Mary agreed. "I don't like the green ones, but otherwise, everything has been really good."

"Oh, I haven't tried the green ones," Bessie said. She picked one up and sniffed it cautiously before she took a tentative bite. "It isn't my favourite, either," she said after she'd swallowed. "But it's still good." She finished the rest of it and washed it down with wine.

"I'm feeling better," Mary said a moment later. "I'm sure the wine is helping, but spending time with you always makes me feel happier."

"Then I'm glad I came over," Bessie replied.

Mary opened her mouth to speak again, but she was interrupted by a knock on the door.

"Ah, there you are," George said as he pushed the door open and walked into the room. "Bessie, you look gorgeous. I hope you're ready to greet the new year in style?"

Bessie rose to her feet gave the man a quick hug. "It's good to see you, George. I'm really looking forward to the party and to the new year. It will have to be better than last year, I'm sure."

"You did have a somewhat trying time of it lately, didn't you?" George mused. "All those dead bodies turning up everywhere."

"Now George, I don't think any of us want to discuss such things," Mary chided gently. "Tonight is all about welcoming a new year with all sorts of wonderful new possibiites."

"Yes, of course, dear," George replied. He gave Mary a hug and then leaned over her to help himself to some of the hors d'oeuvres.

"Don't eat the green ones," Mary said. "You won't like them."

"Spinach?" George asked, wrinkling his nose. "You should have told them not to make anything with spinach."

"Yes, well, you aren't the only person who is going to be at the party," Mary said. "Some people actually like spinach, you know."

George shook his head. "I don't believe it," he said. "It's horrible and slimy."

Bessie laughed. "I don't exactly like it," she told the couple. "But I don't mind it. It's quite tasty here, with whatever it's mixed up with, sitting on its crunchy base."

Another knock on the door prevented the argument from escalating.

"The first guests are starting to arrive," a man in a black suit announced formally from the doorway.

"Oh, goodness, I need to change," Mary exclaimed. "Bessie, I'll be back in five minutes. You can wait for me here or go on out to the great room, it's up to you."

"Oh, I'll wait here," Bessie said, settling back in her chair.

"I'll go and start welcoming guests," George said, his eyes shining. "I love having guests."

Mary looked relieved as she watched the man leave the room. "I think he's feeling better," she said softly. She pulled the door shut behind her, leaving Bessie on her own.

Bessie settled back in her chair and helped herself to more food. "I could get used to living like this," she said to no one. She sipped her wine. She still wasn't really looking forward to the evening ahead, but after some delicious food and half a bottle of wine, she was far less concerned about it. And in a few hours she would be home, in the cottage she loved. No one waited on her there, but really, she wouldn't trade her comfortable life with anyone she knew.

It was more like fifteen minutes later when Mary rushed back in. "I'm sure I'm being a terrible hostess," she said as Bessie rose to join her. "What will the guests be thinking of me, not being there to welcome them?"

"I'm sure they won't have even noticed," Bessie told her. "Everyone will be busy admiring the house and looking at what everyone else is wearing. You can probably sneak in and no one will ever know that you haven't been there the whole time."

"Oh, I do hope so," Mary replied.

As the pair made their way down the corridor towards the great room, Bessie could hear George's voice echoing through the house. In the doorway to the room, Bessie surveyed the small crowd that had already gathered. There were about a dozen people standing around George, apparently listening to some anecdote he was relating. Clearly some of his business associates were still happy to spend time with him. On the opposite side of the room, Elizabeth had her own smaller crowd around her. They were laughing and talking amongst themselves, seemingly ignoring everyone else in the space.

Bessie took a glass of champagne off the tray being carried by a passing waiter and headed towards a quiet corner. She had no interest in talking to either group. Maybe she could ring in the new year on her own, in spite of the crowd.

CHAPTER 2

a short time later, Bessie was relieved to see Doona arrive. As her friend entered the room, Bessie smiled at Doona's appearance. It was clear that she had taken a great deal of time and made a real effort tonight. The woman's brown and highlighted hair was swept up into a twist and her eyes, which were green thanks to coloured contact lenses, had been made up with a heavy hand. Her little black dress showcased curves that were somewhat less generous these days.

Doona had had something of a shock recently when her second husband had reappeared in her life. His murder less than twenty-four hours later had further added to the stress in Bessie's closest friend's life. That she'd been named the chief beneficiary in the man's will was an added twist, but one that Bessie was hoping would ultimately provide Doona with financial security.

In the doorway, Doona glanced around the room and then smiled when she spotted Bessie. "I should have known you'd be in a corner somewhere, watching everyone," she told Bessie after greeting her with a hug.

"I barely know anyone," Bessie replied. "And they all seem to be having a lovely time without me, anyway."

Doona looked around at the two groups that were still segregated. "I don't know anyone talking to George," she said. "But I feel much too old to join the other group."

Bessie laughed. "You feel old?" she demanded. In her early forties, Doona was about half Bessie's age.

"The group with Elizabeth all look so very young and beautiful," Doona said.

"They are all young and beautiful," Bessie agreed. "And I'm sure they're all from very wealthy families, as well."

"So, I've nothing in common with them at all," Doona laughed. "George's friends all look like arrogant businessmen and their gorgeous pampered wives. I've nothing in common with them, either."

"It's a good thing I'm here, then," Bessie teased. "Although we've nothing much in common, have we?"

Doona laughed again. "You're right; at least on paper we don't have much in common," she agreed.

The pair had met at a Manx language class more than two years earlier and had bonded over the difficult language that they'd both struggled to learn. Doona's second marriage had just fallen apart, and she found herself crying on Bessie's sympathetic shoulder quite regularly when they should have been practicing their vocabulary. Bessie mixed compassion with tough love and helped Doona through the worst months of her life. Doona repaid the favour by being strong for Bessie over the past year as Bessie had found herself in the middle of multiple murder investigations.

"But you're still the best friend I've ever had," Doona continued. "I don't know where I'd be now if you hadn't helped me through my marriage breakup and then Charles's murder."

"That's what friends are for," Bessie said, patting Doona's arm.

A waiter came by with drinks and both women took glasses of champagne. Bessie put her first glass, now empty, back on his tray.

"Should we mingle?" Doona asked after her first sip.

"I suppose we should," Bessie said reluctantly. "Would you rather talk to the young people or the older ones?"

"I've met Elizabeth," Doona replied. "Her friends all look nice enough. Let's start with them."

The pair crossed the short distance to where Elizabeth and her friends were gathered. As they drew close, Bessie caught Elizabeth's eye, and the girl was quick to display the impeccable manners her mother had taught her.

"Aunt Bessie, do come and meet all of my friends," she gushed. She took Bessie's hand and pulled her into the group. "And, wait, I'll remember, give me a second, it's Donna, no, Doona, right? Such a lovely and unusual name. I wish my parents had given me an unusual name, but I mustn't complain as Elizabeth is a beautiful name, right, Aunt Bessie?" She winked at Bessie, who smiled back.

"You have a good memory," Doona told the girl.

"I try," Elizabeth laughed. "Anyway, everyone, this is Aunt Bessie, who is a very dear friend to my mother, and her friend, Doona, who works for the local constabulary and is very polite to everyone, even when they've been brought into the station to answer questions about a bar fight."

Elizabeth's friends all laughed. Muttered greetings followed the laughter. Bessie felt as if everyone was suddenly staring at her and Doona, but Elizabeth was quick to introduce the others.

"Okay, so these are my friends," she told Bessie. "You met Bruce already," she said, nodding towards the man, who had changed into a dark suit.

"Good to see you again," he said, his speech sounding slightly slurred.

"This is Howard," Elizabeth said. She slid her arm possessively around the man who was standing next to her. Howard appeared to be about the same age as Elizabeth. He was at least six feet tall with dark brown hair and matching eyes. To Bessie he was almost too handsome, but she could certainly see why Elizabeth was attracted to the man. He was wearing jeans and a sweatshirt that didn't look particularly clean.

"Yeah, hi," he muttered, glancing at Bessie and Doona and then looking away.

"Howard and I went to uni together, but he was a year ahead," Elizabeth said. "He's working in the City now, making heaps of money."

Bessie knew that "the City" was shorthand for a job in London for one of the large investment banks that seemed to pay young men like Howard an awful lot of money for whatever it was that they did all day.

Howard shrugged and stepped away from Elizabeth. "I'm going to check out the food," he muttered before he walked away, heading towards a long table in the corner that staff was busy covering with all manner of deliciousness.

Elizabeth looked as if she wanted to follow the man, but after a moment she shook her head and then forced a fake-looking smile onto her face. "Where was I?" she asked. "This is Jeremy," she told Bessie. "I met him through Howard. They went to school together when they were children."

The young man she indicated smiled and bowed to Bessie and Doona. "It's a real pleasure," he said, offering his hand.

Bessie shook his hand while she took in his very dark brown hair and stunning blue eyes. He was probably six feet tall and slender in his tuxedo that appeared to have been made for him. He shook Doona's hand as well.

"I'm going to find a tray of drinks," he told the crowd. "Is everyone happy with more champagne or can I get anyone anything else?"

Everyone seemed happy with champagne, so Jeremy headed towards the bar after a quick, smiling bow.

"And that just leaves Sarah and Emma, who both went to uni with me," Elizabeth told Bessie, nodding towards the two women who'd remained behind.

Sarah was a slightly plump blonde woman, with green eyes that sparkled with life. She greeted Bessie and Doona as if they were old friends, giving them both hugs and complimenting everything from their shoes to their hairstyles.

Emma was also blonde, with blue eyes. Her blonde hair was perfectly straight and fell almost to her waist. She was quiet, especially when contrasted with Sarah. Almost painfully thin, she looked fragile to Bessie, who shook her hand gently.

"It was nice that so many of you could come over to celebrate the new year with Elizabeth," Bessie said after the introductions were out of the way.

"It was a party," Sarah replied. "I never say no to parties."

"Ain't that the truth," Elizabeth drawled.

"And I get to be close to Bruce," Sarah said in a confiding tone. "One of these days he'll get over Elizabeth and when he does, I want to be standing right there, to snatch him up."

Elizabeth and Emma both laughed. "I've told him a dozen times or more than he's not my type," Elizabeth said.

"But he doesn't listen," Emma added. "Because he's dazzled by your brilliance."

"I'm brilliant, too," Sarah said grumpily.

"And Bruce will realise that one day," Emma said, patting Sarah on the shoulder.

"In the meantime, champagne," Jeremy interrupted. He'd returned with a tray full of glasses of the bubbly drink and Elizabeth and her friends were quick to help themselves.

"Oh, I'm fine," Bessie said when he held the tray out to her. She waved her still half-full glass at him.

"Why not?" Doona muttered. She took a full glass and then quickly swallowed what was left in the one she'd taken earlier.

"That's the idea," Jeremy said cheerfully. He set the tray down on a nearby table and took a glass for himself. "Happy New Year," he said loudly before downing his drink in one gulp.

Bessie and Doona chatted easily with the group of young people for a few moments. Elizabeth seemed distracted, watching Howard as he helped himself to a plate full of food, but she stayed with Bessie and the others rather than follow him. Bessie felt relieved when a few of her friends began to trickle into the great room.

"Oh, there's John," she exclaimed as Inspector John Rockwell entered the room. "Doona and I must go and talk to him."

"He's gorgeous," Sarah said loudly.

"He's a police inspector," Elizabeth told her. "He's very nice when you're in a bit of bother, but he's also very keen on following the rules and that sort of thing. You'd hate it."

Sarah laughed. "Okay, I suppose he isn't for me," she agreed.

Bessie and Doona crossed the room to greet him. As Bessie gave him a hug, she thought about how right Sarah was about the man. He was gorgeous with his dark hair and green eyes. In his early forties, he worked hard to keep himself in shape. He and his wife were in the middle of a surprisingly friendly divorce, as his wife had recently been reunited with her first boyfriend, whom she'd never stopped loving. Bessie hid a grin as John gave Doona a perfunctory hug. Bessie had her suspicions that John and Doona might have feelings for one another, but neither was willing to discuss the issue at the moment.

"It's good to see you," Bessie told John. "You look very handsome in that suit," she added. While John wore a suit for work every day, she'd never seen this particular one, which was especially nice.

"Thank you," he replied. "You both look lovely."

A moment later Hugh Watterson and his girlfriend, Grace Christian, joined them. Hugh was in his mid-twenties, but he looked younger, even though he was over six feet tall. Bessie had known him since he'd been a small child and she still had trouble thinking of him as an adult. He'd seemed more mature lately, as he'd been courting Grace, a very pretty blonde primary schoolteacher a year or two younger than himself.

Bessie was not very happy with Hugh at the moment, though, as he'd been planning to propose to Grace at Christmas, and as far as Bessie knew, he still hadn't actually done it. As she hugged Grace, she tried to check the girl's left hand surreptitiously. Hugh shook his head from behind Grace's back, earning a frown from Bessie.

"Happy New Year to you both," Bessie said. "Let's hope the new year brings some exciting changes for you." She gave Hugh a pointed look. He flushed and turned away.

"Ah, I think I'll go and see what's on the buffet," he muttered.

Grace laughed. "We've only been here for thirty seconds and you're already hungry," she teased.

"Lunch was a long time ago," he replied.

"But we had a snack at your flat before we came here," Grace reminded him. She gave him an affectionate kiss on the cheek. "You go and get yourself something to eat," she said. "I'll stay here and chat with Bessie and Doona."

Hugh nodded and was gone before anyone else spoke. Bessie shook her head.

"He's always hungry, isn't he?" she remarked.

"He certainly seems to be," Grace replied with a smile. "And he can eat anything and everything and he never gains weight."

"Lucky him," Doona said.

"He spends a lot of time walking around Laxey on patrol," John pointed out. "Back in my early days on the Manchester force I did a lot of foot patrols and I could eat whatever I wanted, too. Now that I'm behind a desk most of the time, I have to be a lot more careful."

"You could do with putting on a few pounds," Bessie told him. "It wouldn't do you any harm." John had lost some weight recently as his marriage had fallen apart. Bessie was pleased that he'd regained enough that he no longer looked gaunt, but she thought he could gain a bit more.

"Inspector Rockwell, you look absolutely delicious tonight," Elizabeth cooed as she joined the group. "I must say it is much nicer to see you here than down at your station."

John smiled. "I'm glad I haven't seen you down there lately," he replied.

Elizabeth laughed. "I don't intend for you to see me there again," she told him. "But maybe, if I promise to be good, we could see each other socially?"

John blushed. He opened his mouth, but no words came out. Elizabeth laughed and moved closer to him. "This is a gorgeous jacket," she said, running her hand down John's chest. "It looks as if it were made just for you."

"I think I'll go get some food," Doona said loudly.

"That sounds good," John said quickly. He spun away from Elizabeth and grabbed Doona's arm. The pair crossed the room to where Hugh was still filling his plate.

Elizabeth shrugged as she watched him walk away. "Men don't usually run from me," she remarked.

"Lizzie? Where's the champagne?" a voice called loudly from the entrance to the great room.

Elizabeth sighed. "Oh, goody, Nigel's here," she muttered.

Bessie watched as the girl walked across the room to greet the new arrival. The man was tall and good-looking, but he had an unattractive scowl on his face as he waited for Elizabeth to reach him.

"He looks unpleasant," Grace remarked quietly.

"He does, although he's very handsome," Bessie replied.

"But he knows it and he uses it," Grace said.

"Indeed."

Elizabeth waved a waiter over and Nigel allowed himself a small smile as he helped himself to two glasses of champagne. He and Elizabeth had a short conversation and then Elizabeth turned to walk away. She had only gone two steps when someone else swept in through the door.

"I do hope you weren't flirting with my man," the new arrival said loudly. She was a beautiful redhead with a stunning figure that was showcased by her tiny white sequin-covered dress. In her ridiculously high heels, she was taller than Elizabeth as she glanced around the room and then sighed dramatically. "I suppose, now that we're here, it's too late to go to a proper party, isn't it?"

Bessie watched as Elizabeth turned around to greet the woman. "Gennifer, you look lovely," she said.

"Hardly worth the effort, though, was it?" the woman shot back. "I was expecting something a bit more exciting than this."

"But you look good for me," Nigel said. "It's worth it for my benefit, surely?"

Gennifer shrugged. "Champagne?" she asked.

Nigel handed her one of the glasses he was holding. Gennifer took a sip and frowned. "It's warm," she snapped.

Elizabeth waved over one of the waiters, who handed Gennifer a fresh drink. Bessie turned away from the pointless drama.

"Let's go and get some food before they do," she suggested to Grace.

"Yes, let's," Grace agreed quickly.

The pair joined their friends near the buffet table. Bessie quickly filled a plate with several of the different hors d'oeuvres that she knew she liked from having sampled them earlier.

"Who are those two?" Doona asked Bessie as they stood together nibbling on the delicious food.

"He's called Nigel Hutton, but that's all I know. The stunning redhead is Gennifer, with a G. I've forgotten her surname, but it's one of those posh hyphenated ones. Mary isn't fond of her, but she didn't say why," Bessie replied.

"I'm sure I can guess," Doona remarked.

They watched as the woman walked through the room, stopping to speak to the various other young people in Elizabeth's group. Bessie couldn't hear what Gennifer was saying, but she left everyone she spoke with looking unhappy. Nigel followed behind her, drinking steadily. Elizabeth kept a few paces behind the couple, having a few words with each person as Gennifer swept past them. Only a few moments later, Gennifer headed for the buffet table.

"Goodness, they've invited the whole island, haven't they?" she asked as she surveyed Bessie's group of friends. "Little old ladies, middle-aged women, and pretty little blonde girls who dress like old spinster ladies."

Bessie flushed and bit her tongue before she spoke too quickly. She could see tears forming in Grace's eyes at the cruel words. Grace was wearing a floral dress that was pretty but very modest, especially when compared to the tiny scraps of fabric that Elizabeth and her friends seemed to favour.

"Gennifer, don't be so tiresome," Elizabeth said in a weary voice. "These people are family friends."

"Your family does have peculiar taste," Gennifer replied. "Although, hello there," she said suddenly. She took a couple of steps towards

Hugh and then grinned. "You're rather tasty," she cooed at him, sliding an arm around his waist. "I'm Gennifer. Let's go sit down somewhere and get to know one another."

"I say, Gennifer, that's out of line," Nigel protested.

"Oh, hush," the girl told him. "I love making new friends. You know that."

Nigel shook his head. "I thought you wanted something from the buffet," he said.

"I did, and now I've found it," Gennifer replied. "What's your name?" she asked Hugh, staring into his eyes and licking her lips.

"Um, I'm Hugh," he stammered, turning bright red.

"Hugh, yes, it suits you," she purred. "Do you like my dress?"

She took a step back from him and turned very slowly, making sure that everyone got a very good look at her revealing outfit. Then she stepped back to Hugh's side and leaned against him. "What do you think?" she asked in a husky voice.

"I, that is, you, I mean..." Hugh stuttered.

Gennifer laughed throatily. "What do you do, Hugh?" she asked.

"I'm a police constable," Hugh replied after a deep breath.

"Really? I don't suppose you have any handcuffs with you? I've always fancied, oh, but that's a conversation for later, just between the two of us."

Bessie didn't think it was possible for Hugh to turn any redder or look more embarrassed. He glanced around, his eyes a bit desperate.

"This is Grace," Bessie said loudly. "Hugh's girlfriend."

Grace squared her shoulders. "It's nice to meet you," she said in a voice that was too loud.

Bessie could tell that Grace was close to tears, and she silently cheered Grace on as she watched Grace meet Gennifer's eyes.

"Hugh's girlfriend? How cute is that? But no ring on your finger? I suppose that says a lot about your relationship, doesn't it?" Gennifer teased.

Grace glanced at Hugh and then looked away.

"Come on, Gennifer, playtime is over," Nigel said crossly. "Leave the poor man alone and come and get some food."

"I think the poor man is about to have the best night of his life," Gennifer said, running her fingers through Hugh's hair. "Don't you?" she whispered into Hugh's ear.

"Stop now," Nigel said. "You know I hate it when you flirt with other men. Just stop it or I'll, well, I'll make you sorry."

"Are you going to break up with me?" Gennifer asked mockingly. "That would be a tragedy, wouldn't it? Oh, no, it wouldn't. Honestly, little Emma has been chasing after you for months. You should take her out. I'm sure she'd tire of you almost as quickly as I have."

"Gennifer, I mean it," Nigel shouted. "You're going too far this time."

"I think you need to calm down," John Rockwell said, taking a step towards the angry man. "Why don't you have something to eat in a quiet corner somewhere?"

"Don't you try to tell me what to do," Nigel yelled. "Gennifer is mine and I protect what's mine."

"Gennifer can make up her own mind about that," the girl said, laughing. "Right now Gennifer is thinking that Hugh is awfully attractive and that you are behaving very badly."

"What's all the excitement over here, then?" George asked as he joined the group. He looked around at all of the tense faces and then smiled brightly. "Now, now, this is a party, isn't it?"

Everyone was silent for a moment. Eventually, Bessie couldn't stand the awkwardness any longer.

"It is a party and we're all very grateful to you for inviting us," she said with artificial cheer.

George looked around again and then focussed on Gennifer, who was still clinging to Hugh. "Ah, Gennifer, my dear, I did want you to meet Robert. He's a business associate and I've been telling him about the little company I've been thinking about funding with your father. You must come and meet him."

Gennifer frowned. "I'm quite happy right here," she said, pouting.

"It won't take more than five minutes and then you can rejoin your friends," George promised. "But you know as well as I do how your father would feel."

Gennifer sighed and rolled her eyes. "Yes, I know. The things I do for that man." She took a step away from Hugh and then turned back towards him. Leaning in very close, she whispered something in his ear that caused him to redden even more. She giggled and Bessie was sure, from the shocked look on Hugh's face, that she'd just pinched his bottom.

"Come on, then," she told George. "But only five minutes. I don't want Hugh to get tired of waiting for me."

George offered his arm and escorted the woman away from the group.

Nigel watched their progress with narrowed eyes. "She's going to be sorry," he muttered to no one in particular. After a moment, he helped himself to another glass of champagne from the table behind him and stalked off after Gennifer.

"I'm so very sorry," Elizabeth said quickly. "Gennifer is, well, you've seen, I suppose. She and Nigel haven't been together for long and they seem to take weird pleasure in making each other angry. One or the other of them is always flirting with someone else." She didn't wait for anyone to reply before she hurried off behind Nigel.

"What an unpleasant couple," Bessie said, trying to lighten the tension that remained after Elizabeth's departure.

"They deserve each other," Doona suggested.

"Hugh didn't seem to mind the attention," Grace said softly.

"Of course I minded," Hugh told her. "I just didn't know what to do."

"You could have introduced me, rather than leaving it to Bessie," Grace said, clearly angry. "And you could have moved away from her, rather than just stand there and let her rub herself all over you."

"She wasn't exactly rubbing herself all over me," Hugh protested.

"Well that's what it looked like from here," Grace snapped. "And you didn't seem to mind at all."

"Ah, Grace, you know how I feel about you," Hugh said.

"No, I'm not sure that I do," Grace replied. "And I don't really want to talk about it right now."

She turned on her heel and walked away. There was a small area with chairs and couches near the windows and Grace made her way over there and sat down, her back to Hugh and the others.

"Should I go and try to talk to her?" Hugh asked Bessie.

"I don't know," Bessie replied.

While the group stood and watched, Bruce, Jeremy, Sarah, and Emma walked over and sat down with Grace. Within minutes the group was chatting easily together.

"Give her a little bit of time to calm down," Doona suggested. "Just make sure you're there to give her a kiss at midnight. And stay away from Gennifer."

"Believe me, I intend to," Hugh said with alacrity.

"It's Gennifer's intentions that I'd be worried about," John said seriously.

"Maybe I'll just go and hide in the loo until midnight," Hugh muttered.

"We can all keep an eye on Gennifer and try to help keep her away from you," Bessie said. "If you're sure that's what you want."

Hugh looked at Bessie and sighed. "She's gorgeous and all, but I love Grace with all my heart. The last thing I want to do is anything that might spoil things between me and Grace. I want to spend the rest of my life with her, you know that."

"I do, but Grace doesn't," Bessie pointed out.

"I'm an idiot," Hugh said. "I should have proposed at Christmas like I planned."

"Ask her at midnight," Doona suggested. "That would be awfully romantic."

"I didn't bring the ring with me," Hugh said miserably.

"Surely it's more important that Grace knows how you really feel," Bessie said.

Hugh shrugged. "We'll see," he said, looking down at his shoes.

People kept arriving, including many more of Bessie's friends. She was happy to see Liz and her husband, Bill, arrive. Bessie had first met Liz at a Manx language class and then worked with her at "Christmas at the Castle." She was a vivacious blonde with two small children and a third on the way. Tonight Liz was wearing a form-fitting dress and Bessie fancied that she could just see a hint of a bump developing.

She greeted the girl with a hug. "You look stunning," she said.

"I feel as if I look bumpy," Liz laughed. "But Bill said no one would notice."

"I noticed, but I already knew about the baby," Bessie said. "I'm sure if I hadn't known, I wouldn't have guessed."

"We're ready to start telling people anyway, so I suppose it doesn't matter either way," Liz said.

Bessie greeted the woman's handsome young husband with another hug. "Congratulations on the impending new addition," she told him.

"Thanks," he said with a grin. "We're very excited."

As Bessie chatted with the pair, she kept one eye on Gennifer, who was talking with several of George's business associates. Liz glanced around the room and then frowned at Bessie.

"Is that Gennifer Carter-Maxwell?" she hissed.

"Yes, she and Elizabeth, Mary's daughter, are friends," Bessie replied.

Liz looked at Bill, who flushed and looked at the ground.

"You didn't know she was going to be here, did you?" Liz demanded.

"Of course not," Bill replied quickly. "I haven't spoken to her in five years or more."

The woman in question interrupted the conversation.

"Bill Martin, it is so very lovely to see you again," Gennifer said silkily. She wrapped her arms around him and hugged him for an uncomfortably long time.

"I think that's quite enough," Liz snapped.

"Oh, Liza, isn't it? Are you and Bill still together? I never imagined you'd last this long," Gennifer said as she released the man.

"We're married with two children," Liz said steadily. "And we're very happy, thank you."

"Yawn," Gennifer replied. "And you used to be so much fun," she said to Bill. She whispered something into his ear and then winked at Liz. "Good luck," she said before she walked away.

Bessie watched as the woman sashayed away, this time heading towards Nigel. Whatever she said to him, his face reddened. A moment later Bessie watched as Gennifer swept out of the room. A glance at her watch told Bessie that she still had another hour to wait for midnight. As soon as they'd rung in the new year, Bessie was determined to head for home.

"It's quite wet and windy out there," Hugh told her a short time later when he joined her near the bar.

"Is it? It wasn't a bad walk over," Bessie said.

"Grace and I came in a taxi so that we could both have a few drinks, but you're welcome to ride home with us," he replied.

"I may have to take you up on that," Bessie said.

"That is, if Grace is speaking to me again," he added sadly.

Bessie turned and spotted Grace, still sitting with a small group of Elizabeth's friends. "Maybe you should go over and talk to her," Bessie suggested.

"I've tried, like ten times," Hugh replied. "But she won't even look at me. I finally went for a walk outside to calm down, but it's really awful out there."

"I'll have a word, shall I?"

"I don't know," Hugh said. "I don't want you dragged into the middle of all of this."

"Maybe you can talk in the taxi on the way home, once you've dropped me off," Bessie said.

"She's meant to be staying with me for a while," Hugh told Bessie. "The girls she had that flat with in Lonan all split up to go their separate ways, so I told her she could stay in my spare room to save having to drive back and forth from Douglas every day from her parents' house."

"She's still working in Laxey?" Bessie asked.

"Yes, she's going to be supply teaching there for the rest of the school year and I thought, well, I thought we were going to be engaged by now anyway when I asked her to stay with me," Hugh sighed deeply. "I've made a real mess of everything," he said gloomily.

"I'm sure you'll be able to make things up to her," Bessie said. "You just have to keep trying."

"I hope so," Hugh said. He asked the man behind the bar for a pint of lager. Drink in hand, he squared his shoulders. "I'm off; wish me luck," he told Bessie.

"Good luck," she said, hoping that her good wishes would help. She really liked both Hugh and Grace and she thought they were perfect for one another.

The minutes continued to tick along slowly. Bessie enjoyed the delicious food and drank a bit more champagne than maybe she should have. Mostly, she appreciated the chance to chat with some of her friends. Nearly everyone seemed to be having a good time, although she kept a worried eye on Grace and Hugh and also Liz and Bill, who seemed at odds with one another. Bessie couldn't work out if Elizabeth's friends were having fun or not. They all seemed to be drinking a great deal and every time she looked over at them it appeared that different pairs of men and women were snuggled up together.

With only a few minutes to go until midnight, everyone began to gather around a large television that was showing the celebrations in London city centre. In the corner of the screen, the last five minutes of the year were being counted down. Bessie found herself standing next to John and Doona as Mary and George passed around party poppers and those annoying party blowers that make too much noise.

Bruce and Howard seemed to be having a contest to see who could make more noise with his blower and Bessie found herself wishing she'd taken some headache tablets before she'd come out. Elizabeth seemed to have lost her shoes somewhere, and as Elizabeth whispered something to Emma, Bessie noticed the sparkling silver clip that was holding up Emma's hair.

"5 – 4 – 3 – 2 – 1, Happy New Year!" the crowd shouted as the countdown finished.

Bessie smiled as John and Doona hugged and then jumped apart

31

quickly. She hugged the handsome policeman and then gave her best friend a squeeze. Looking across the room, she watched as Grace turned her back on Hugh as he held out his arms. She frowned when she saw Liz giving Bill a perfunctory kiss on the cheek. Elizabeth and Howard were caught up in an embrace that Bessie found embarrassing to watch. Jeremy, Bruce, Sarah, and Emma had an awkward sort of group hug, with Sarah hanging on to Bruce a little bit longer than strictly necessary. As the noise level rose and then dropped again, Nigel came rushing into the room.

"Has anyone seen Gennifer lately?" he demanded in a loud voice.

CHAPTER 3

"She's probably gone to her room to sulk because she wasn't getting enough attention," Sarah called out.

"Which man is missing?" Bruce asked. "She'll be with him, wherever he is."

"Who else is missing?" Elizabeth giggled. She looked around the room and then shrugged. "I don't see anyone else missing except for daddy. She won't be with daddy, of course."

Bessie glanced around in surprise. Elizabeth was right; George Quayle wasn't in the great room. She caught Mary's eye and raised an eyebrow.

"George had to deal with a small matter," Mary said. "I believe he's still in the wine cellar."

"I'd like everyone to remain here," John said, taking charge. "Mary, could you show me where to find the wine cellar?"

"What's going on, then?" George demanded from the doorway.

"Ah, there you are," John replied. "It seems that no one knows where Gennifer has gone."

"I haven't seen her," George said quickly. "Not for at least an hour."

John nodded. "She left the party just after eleven," he agreed. "Mary, can you send someone to check her room, please?" he asked.

"This is silly," Elizabeth said. "I have to say, you're very sexy when you're playing policeman," she said to John. "But I'm sure Gennifer has just found herself a new plaything from among the staff and is off having some fun. I refuse to let her spoil the party."

"We can all split up and search the house," Mary suggested a moment later when one of the maids returned to report that Gennifer wasn't in her room. "Maybe she wandered into one of the wings and can't find her way back here."

"That's a good idea," John said. "Maybe a few people would like to volunteer to help with the search? Everyone else can get back to enjoying themselves."

Bessie, Hugh and Doona all quickly walked to where John was standing. Bruce and Emma joined them as well, as did a few of George's middle-aged businessmen friends that Bessie didn't know. Behind them, Elizabeth loudly demanded more champagne.

John frowned and then turned to Mary. "You know the house and I don't. What's the best way to split it up and search it?"

"There are half a dozen wings, each starting from a different part of the main house," Mary explained. "I can't imagine who designed the place; it's really something of a mess. Anyway, if you want to follow me, I can show you the entrance to each wing and someone can check all of the rooms there. Almost the entire house is empty now, so the search shouldn't take long. I'll search Elizabeth's wing and the rooms where George and I have been staying myself."

"I can help with that," Emma offered. "As I'm staying in Elizabeth's wing, I mean."

"Thank you," Mary smiled at the girl.

The little group made their way into the corridor. "This hallway has about ten empty guest rooms," Mary told them, gesturing down a dimly lit passage. "I don't think anyone has ever actually used these rooms. I can't imagine why they're here, but they are all furnished, at least lightly."

"When the Pierce family first bought the house, they used to have elaborate parties with dozens of guests from across," Bessie told her.

"I'm sure they used every room in the house in the early days. Over time, the parties got smaller and smaller."

"Well, we're going to turn them into suites for the other children and the grandchildren," Mary said. "But not until after we've finished our own suite and Elizabeth's wing."

"Bessie, why don't you and Doona check this wing," John suggested. "When you've checked all of the rooms, just wait here for us to come back and collect you."

Bessie was quick to agree. The group moved on with Mary talking about the next wing, which housed servant quarters, while Bessie and Doona started down the corridor.

"John gave us this section because he doesn't think we'll find anything," Doona complained.

"I do hope he's right," Bessie replied.

Bessie turned the handle and pushed open the first door they came to. She switched on the light and shrugged. The large bedroom looked as if it had never been slept in.

"Is there an en-suite?" Doona asked.

"Undoubtedly," Bessie said with a chuckle. It only took a moment to check that that too was empty.

They continued on, checking room after room. The rooms were all beautifully decorated and seemingly untouched.

"This is sad and almost creepy," Doona said after a few minutes. "So much wasted space."

"I'm sure it will all look and feel totally different once Mary is done with it," Bessie said. "And it will be nice for her children to be able to stay with them once in a while."

"Because they all live so far away in Douglas," Doona laughed.

"I'm surprised neither of the boys were at the party tonight," Bessie mused. "Perhaps they were busy with their own friends."

They'd reached the last door on the hall. "Here goes nothing," Doona said. She opened the door and switched on the light.

"Well, that's interesting," Bessie said as she looked around the room. Unlike the other rooms they'd inspected, the bed in this room appeared to have been recently disturbed.

"It looks as if someone has been sleeping in here," Doona said.

"Or at least using the bed," Bessie commented.

Doona held out her arm to stop Bessie from entering the room. "Someone might still be in here," she whispered.

"Hello?" Bessie shouted. "Is there anyone here?"

"You're going to get us both killed," Doona hissed.

"The room feels empty," Bessie told her. "I think someone just used it for a, um, romantic interlude or something."

"You could be right," Doona agreed. "But who?"

Bessie pushed Doona's arm away and crossed the room. She pointed to one of the pillows, where a long red hair was clearly visible. "I could guess," she said to Doona.

Doona sighed. "She has her own room," she said. "Why use this one?"

"Why not?" Bessie shrugged. "Anyway, it might not have been Gennifer. The bed might have been like this for months or even years. Mr. and Mrs. Pierce clearly weren't using this wing and the house has been on the market since last March. Maybe someone from the security team was having secret trysts here or something."

Doona checked the en-suite. "Someone ran water in there recently," she told Bessie. "The sink is still wet and so is the shower."

"So we've discovered something, if not the missing Gennifer," Bessie said.

"Now we just have to wait for John and the others to come back for us," Doona said as they exited the rumpled room.

"Where does this go?" Bessie asked, pointing to a door on the back wall of the corridor.

"I don't know, outside maybe," Doona said.

Bessie turned the lock and pulled the door open. Hugh was right, it was windy and rainy outside. She looked out, trying to orient herself. "We're right on the path that goes around the back of the house," she told Doona. "You don't suppose…"

Doona looked at Bessie and both women frowned. "Let's get John," Doona suggested.

"We should take a quick look," Bessie argued. "I'd hate to waste John's time."

"It's pouring," Doona pointed out.

"I'll just walk a short distance and see if I see anything."

"I'm coming with you," Doona said firmly.

The pair stepped out into the strong wind and driving rain. They shuffled forward slowly, following the path that meandered behind the mansion before arriving at the steep stairs to the beach. The feeling of dread in the pit of Bessie's stomach told her what to expect before she saw it.

"We need John," she said loudly, pointing towards the beach below them.

Doona spotted what Bessie had seen and sighed deeply. "It's going to be a long night," she muttered as she and Bessie turned back towards the house.

The pair stood in the corridor, dripping wet, while Doona dug her mobile phone out of her bag.

"Stupid, tiny fancy handbag," she muttered in frustration.

"Can't find your mobile?" Bessie asked.

"Oh, I've found it, but it's stuck. It's only a little bit smaller than the bag itself."

Doona finally wrestled the device from the bag, sending a comb, lipstick and at least a dozen coins flying through the air as she did so. She sighed and then punched in a number. Bessie gathered up coins as she listened to Doona telling John what they'd seen.

"He wants us to wait here," Doona told her when she'd finished the call. "He's calling for backup, in case we're right about what we saw on the beach."

"I hope they hurry," Bessie said. "They may still be able to help her."

Doona raised her eyebrows but said nothing. Bessie knew that her friend was thinking the same thing that she was: there was nothing that anyone could do for the broken figure they'd seen below them. But until she'd been told otherwise, Bessie was determined to remain positive. She'd survived a fall down the steps behind Thie yn Traie herself, and Gennifer was somewhat younger.

It felt like a very long time before John and the others joined Bessie and Doona. John's face was grim and he was talking into his mobile as he walked down the corridor. He disconnected when he reached them.

"Which room do you think was used?" he asked.

Bessie pointed to the nearest door. John opened it and stepped inside. He was only gone for a moment. When he emerged from the room, he pulled the door shut behind him again.

"Doona, you're on guard duty here," he barked. "No one is to go into that room until the crime scene team arrives."

"Yes, sir," she said, stepping over to stand in front of the door.

"I can do that," Hugh suggested. "Doona's just a civilian." He flushed. "No offense," he told Doona. "But it isn't really your job, that's all."

"I think it's best for Doona to handle it," John said. "I'm going to take a look outside. The nearest patrol officer should be in place at the bottom of the stairs by now."

"I'll come as well," Hugh said quickly.

"I think you'd better wait here with the others," John said firmly. "No point in all of us getting soaked, is there?"

Hugh opened his mouth to argue, but Bessie caught his eye. She shook her head. Clearly young Hugh hadn't yet realised that he might be a suspect in whatever had happened to Gennifer. The idea seemed obvious to Bessie, although she knew there was no way Hugh had done anything to harm the young woman. Still, John had to be very careful with the investigation.

John opened the door and sighed deeply. "Why do these things always happen when it's wet and windy?" he asked.

"Here," Mary said. "I had one of the staff bring your coat and an umbrella." She held out the objects, earning a warm smile from John.

"Thank you so much," he said.

"I've asked the kitchen staff to start preparing soup and sandwiches and lots and lots of coffee. If everything goes the way it looks as if it might, we're going to be overrun with police in a short while. I can't improve the weather, but at least I can provide hot food and drinks for everyone when they can come inside."

"That's very thoughtful of you," John told her. "I'm still hoping everything is going to be fine, though."

"Hope for the best, prepare for the worst," Mary said grimly.

John nodded and then, with his coat pulled tightly shut, he walked out into the rain, closing the door behind him. Bessie glanced at her watch and then looked around at the others.

"Bessie, are you okay?" Mary asked, her voice full of concern.

"I'm fine, just sad," Bessie replied. "Tonight was supposed to be a celebration and a new beginning. I hate the thought of the new year starting with such a tragic accident."

"If it was an accident," one of the men who was a stranger to Bessie muttered.

"What's that supposed to mean?" Bruce demanded.

"Nothing," the man said, colouring under Bruce's angry look. "That girl, Gennifer, right? She just seemed determined to make herself enemies tonight, that's all."

"It would probably be best if we didn't talk about all of this," Bessie said.

"What else is there to discuss?" the man snapped. "I hardly think this is the time for casual conversation."

Bessie was saved from replying when the door to the outside opened behind her. John walked in, rain dripping from his coat. He frowned and handed a badly mangled umbrella to Mary.

"Sorry, the wind took it," he said.

Mary handed it off to one of the household staff who was standing at the edge of the group. The girl hurried away, presumably to dispose of the broken umbrella.

"So, what's happening?" Hugh asked.

John looked at him and sighed. "You all need to go back to the great room for now. I'll stay here to keep the curious out of this room. As soon as more of my staff arrives, I'll be in to speak to you."

"So you've found Gennifer?" Mary asked.

"We've found Gennifer," John replied.

"Is she okay?" was Mary's next question.

"No, she isn't," John said shortly.

Bessie could tell that John didn't want to answer any more questions, even if Mary couldn't. She took Mary's arm and turned her away from the policeman. "John said we are all to wait in the great room," she said. "Let's get out of the way so he can do his job."

Back in the great room, the party was still going on. Mary stopped in the doorway and shook her head. "This simply won't do," she said to Bessie. She walked over to the band and spoke to one of the members. He motioned to the others and they all stopped playing.

"Mummmmm," Elizabeth wailed. "That was a great song."

"There's been an accident," Mary announced.

Elizabeth sighed dramatically. "Gennifer's had an accident? This is going to be just like that time when we went skiing and she managed to break her leg. We all ended up spending the entire week waiting on her hand and foot. Well, not this time. She can just fly her broken leg home and get her daddy's staff to look after her."

"It's rather more serious than that," Mary said quietly.

Elizabeth stared at her mother for a moment. "She's okay, isn't she?" she demanded. "I mean, she's a horrible bitch, but she's still my friend."

"I don't know," Mary replied, shaking her head.

"I'm sure she's okay," Elizabeth said firmly. "You're just looking for an excuse to end the party early."

"The police will be here in a few minutes," Mary announced to everyone. "We're all to remain in here until they arrive."

"The police?" one of the suited businessmen demanded. "I don't want to waste my evening talking to the police. Come on, Joan. We're going."

"I'm afraid I'm going to have to ask you to stay here," Hugh said in an authoritative tone. "I'm Constable Watterson with the Laxey Constabulary. Until we know exactly what happened to Miss, er, to the young lady in question, I'm afraid everyone needs to stay here."

"Don't be stupid," the man snapped. "Whatever happened to the girl, it's nothing to do with me. You were the one who followed her out when she left the room. I hope your position with the police doesn't mean you're above suspicion. If I were your senior officer, you'd be the first person I'd want to question."

"Actually, I was planning to save Mr. Watterson for last," a cool voice from the doorway announced. "There's no point in making you all wait while I question him, is there?"

Bessie felt a cold chill run through her as soon as she recognised the voice. She turned slowly, hoping she was mistaken. Inspector Anna Lambert stood in the doorway, surveying the room. If the inspector had been at a New Year's Eve party herself, she'd managed to find time to get home and change into yet another black suit that was strictly professional. The woman's grey hair was in a tight bun and her grey eyes were expressionless. Bessie felt herself flushing when their eyes met.

"Miss Cubbon, why am I not surprised to find you here?" the inspector asked, sounding amused. "Every time a dead body turns up, there you are. It's enough to make a senior policewoman suspicious."

Bessie bit her tongue and counted slowly to ten, and then twenty. She was just moving on towards thirty when Elizabeth seemed to suddenly realise what the inspector had said.

"Gennifer isn't dead," Elizabeth shouted. "She can't be dead. I don't know who you are, but you need to go away and let us have our party."

The policewoman nodded coolly. "I should have started by introducing myself," she said. "I'm Inspector Anna Lambert from the Laxey Constabulary. I'll be in charge of the investigation related to the unexplained death of one Gennifer Carter-Maxwell, whose body was found on the beach a short time ago. I will be questioning each and every one of you myself about everything that happened here tonight. Another of my colleagues will be questioning the band and the rest of the household staff. While you wait for your turn to speak with me, I'd appreciate it if you'd gather your thoughts and try to arrange them into a concise narrative. If you've been drinking, and I assume most of you have, I'd like to ask you to stop now so that you can provide me with a reasonably sober assessment of the evening. Does anyone have any questions?"

No one spoke. Elizabeth began to cry softly. Howard crossed to her and tried to put his arms around her, but she pushed him away. After a moment, Mary walked over and pulled Elizabeth close. The girl cried on her mother's shoulder for a short while before Anna spoke again.

"I must ask that you all refrain from speaking to one another," she said. "Please just remain in here quietly until it is your turn to meet with me. I'll be leaving several officers in here to keep you company and ensure that you comply with my request."

One of George's friends opened his mouth to speak, but Anna simply looked at him for a moment, causing him to press his lips together.

"Any questions?" Anna asked.

No one spoke. After a moment, while she'd seemingly studied the crowd, Anna spoke again. "One of my colleagues, who was a guest here tonight, has provided me with a list of many of your names. I'd like to start by talking to Mary Quayle."

Mary stiffened and then patted her daughter on the back. "I have to go, baby," she said to Elizabeth.

Elizabeth nodded and then turned and walked to the windows, taking a seat with her back to the room.

"Mrs. Quayle, the first thing I'll need from you is a complete guest list. If you have a written one somewhere in the house, I'd be grateful if you could get that for me now," Anna said.

Mary nodded and then left the room with Anna right behind her. As soon as they were gone, half a dozen uniformed constables entered and spread themselves around the room. Bessie glanced at Doona, who shook her head. Unable to speak and unhappy with the way the investigation had begun, Bessie settled herself into the nearest chair. With nothing else to do, she watched her fellow guests.

After a few uncomfortable minutes where no one seemed to know quite what to do, people began to make themselves comfortable. George and his friends moved towards one corner of the room, pulling up chairs and even a small sofa until they had enough seats for everyone in their group. As soon as they were settled, one of the young constables took up a position immediately behind them. George frowned at him, but he didn't appear to notice.

Elizabeth was still crying softly. Now Emma and Sarah joined her on her couch. After a moment, Howard crossed the room and attempted to sit next to Elizabeth. Bessie couldn't see Elizabeth's face, but she saw Howard redden from whatever look Elizabeth had given him. When he opened his mouth to speak, one of the police constables interrupted.

"I'm sorry, but we really have to enforce silence," he said sternly.

Howard gave him an angry look and then flopped down onto a chair. Elizabeth turned on the couch so that her back was to him. He sighed deeply, glancing at the constable as he did so.

Nigel had been standing in the centre of the room, looking confused. Now he walked over to the constable nearest to him. "Did she say Gennifer is dead?" he demanded angrily.

"I'm sorry, sir, but the no talking rule also applies to me," the man replied.

"Gennifer is my girlfriend," Nigel shouted. "If she's dead, I ought to be told."

"I'm sure Inspector Lambert will tell you what you need to know when you speak to her," the constable said.

"Where is she?" Nigel asked. "I want to see her."

"Sir, you need to sit down and wait for Inspector Lambert," the constable said.

"I want to see Gennifer," Nigel shouted. "I loved her. Don't you understand? I wanted to marry her. When I find out who hurt her, I'll, well, I'll kill them."

"I'm very sorry for your loss," the constable said. "Why don't you sit down over here and I'll see if I can't get the inspector to speak to you next." He led Nigel to a quiet corner. Nigel sat down, looking dazed.

"Would you like a hot drink?" the policeman asked.

"A hot drink? Are you serious? The woman I love is dead. I want answers. I want to know what happened to her." Nigel jumped back up. "Do you know who I am? My father could buy this pitiful little island ten times over. I need to ring him."

"Yes, sir, if you could just wait for the inspector," the constable replied.

"I won't," Nigel shouted. "I'm going to ring my father and my solicitor and..."

"And I think that's quite enough," Anna Lambert's icy voice cut through Nigel's tirade. "I was going to leave Ms. Carter-Maxwell's friends for later in the questioning, but if you're so desperate to speak to me, we can talk now."

Nigel looked over at her and then glanced around the room. Everyone was watching him. He flushed and then sat down abruptly. "I'll wait my turn," he muttered. "I may have had too much to drink."

"I'm inclined to believe that," Anna said sharply. "Anyone who does want their solicitor or advocate present during questioning is, of course, welcome to have them. If you'd like to make such arrangements, please ask one of my constables to assist you. I'm not sure how available any of them will be tonight, but you're welcome to wait in one of the holding cells at the Laxey station for them to arrive if you don't want to speak to me without them."

She spun on her heel and walked back out of the room, leaving Bessie with a grudging admiration for her. Most of the guests at the party were wealthy and no doubt used to special treatment. It appeared that Inspector Lambert had little patience with such ideas.

Doona slid into a seat opposite Bessie and sighed. Bessie tried to smile encouragingly, but she didn't feel as if she'd quite accomplished it. After another moment, Hugh took a seat next to Doona. Bessie looked at him, but his eyes were focussed on Grace, who was standing by herself near the windows. Bessie briefly considered joining the girl, but as they couldn't speak there seemed little point. Across the room, Liz had taken a seat near George and his friends. Her husband, Bill, sat down next to her and Bessie frowned as she saw Liz inch away from him.

Bessie watched as Jeremy and Bruce, the only two people still standing, glanced around the room and then at each other. Bruce pointed towards Nigel, and Jeremy shrugged. With all eyes on them, they crossed to where Nigel was sitting and sat on a couch across from him.

Time seemed to almost stand still as everyone sat in silence. Bessie found herself wondering what had happened to John Rockwell. He'd been guarding the door to the room that Bessie and Doona had discovered had been disturbed, but with the mansion almost over-flowing with police now, surely he'd been relieved from that position. Anna had mentioned getting a partial guest list from a colleague. Once John had provided that, had he been sent home or was he taking a part in the interviews?

Over the next hour, George's various friends and their wives were sent for, one after another, until George was the only one left in his corner of the room. Mary hadn't returned after her session with Anna, and Bessie could only hope that her friend was coping with everything that was happening.

Liz and Bill were the next to be questioned. Bessie gave her young friend an encouraging smile as the woman left the room. She hated seeing her under so much stress, especially during the early stages of pregnancy.

A short while later, Jeremy was called to be interviewed. Bessie shifted uncomfortably in her chair as she waited for each of Eliza-beth's friends to be questioned in turn.

"About bloody time," was Nigel's opinion when he was asked to join the inspector to give his statement.

Elizabeth was the last of the group to be called and Bessie was pleased to see that the girl seemed to have stopped crying by the time she left the room. George followed his daughter, leaving only Bessie, Doona, Hugh and Grace in the huge great room.

Grace was called next. As she walked past him, Hugh tried to catch her eye, but Grace stared straight ahead, looking sad and exhausted. Another twenty minutes passed before the constable at the door spoke.

"Miss Cubbon? Inspector Lambert would like to see you now."

CHAPTER 4

*B*essie got to her feet and stretched. Feeling as if every muscle in her body ached simply from sitting still for such a long time, Bessie found herself walking quite slowly towards the door. She gave Doona a forced smile. Hugh didn't look at her as she walked past. Bessie followed the young man down the corridor to a small room near the mansion's kitchen. Inside was a small wooden table with two chairs behind it and one in front. Anna Lambert and a uniformed constable were behind the table.

"Come in and sit down," the woman offered, waving a hand at the empty chair.

"If you don't mind terribly, I'd like to stand for a few minutes," Bessie replied. "I've gone very stiff from sitting still for so long."

Anna frowned and then sighed. "I feel as if we started off on the wrong foot," she said. "I know you and John Rockwell are good friends and I'd really like to work with you, not against you, in this investigation."

Bessie swallowed a sigh. She didn't believe one word the woman said, but this wasn't the time to challenge her. "Of course I'll do whatever I can to help with the investigation," she said. "Although beyond answering a few questions about tonight, I'm not sure what I can do," she added.

"Yes, John is always talking about how your background knowledge of the island is so very valuable, but it isn't going to be much help in this case, I can't imagine. I assume you didn't know the victim well?"

Bessie shook her head. "I met her tonight," she replied. "I didn't know her at all. I don't even think I spoke to her."

"But, of course, John thinks very highly of both your intuition and your observation skills. That's what I'd like to tap into now, if I may."

"As I said, I'll do whatever I can."

"Excellent," Anna smiled tightly. "Tell me about the party, then. I just want you to walk me through the evening, from the time you arrived until the time you found the body."

Bessie began with the phone call from Mary Quayle and her early arrival at Thie yn Traie. She told Anna everything that she could remember that she thought might be relevant.

"So, Gennifer was making a play for young Hugh?" Anna asked when Bessie was finished.

"I don't know if she was serious or just trying to cause trouble," Bessie replied. "She made a point of talking to every young man at the party."

"I take it Hugh's girlfriend was quite upset."

"Yes, at least she seemed to be. I didn't get a chance to talk to her about it."

"What time did Gennifer leave the party?"

"It was shortly after eleven," Bessie replied. "I was keeping an eye on her, trying to make sure she stayed away from Hugh, so I noticed when she left."

"And you checked the time?"

"I wanted to see how close it was to midnight," Bessie said. "I was rather hoping it was nearly time for the party to wind down."

"And what time did Hugh leave the party?"

"I don't know. I wasn't keeping track of him."

"Come now," Anna said. "You were trying to keep Hugh and

Gennifer apart. You took note of when Gennifer left, surely you noticed when Hugh left as well?"

"I wasn't paying attention to Hugh," Bessie replied defensively. "I knew he was trying to avoid the woman, so I wasn't worried about what else he was doing."

"But he told you later that he'd gone outside?" Anna checked.

"Yes, he said something about going out to get some fresh air, but that it was too wet and windy for him."

"Who else went outside after eleven?"

"I haven't the foggiest idea," Bessie said. "People were in and out of the great room all evening for all sorts of reasons."

"Such as?"

"Well, for a start, the loos were across the hall," Bessie said, feeling annoyed.

"Did you stay in the great room all evening? Or at least until the search for Gennifer began?"

"I went to the loo at least once or twice," Bessie told her. "But otherwise, I stayed in the great room. That was where the party was and it would have been rude to wander around the house."

"But others weren't so shy about exploring Thie yn Traie," Anna suggested.

"Some of the other guests were staying here, of course," Bessie pointed out. "They had every right to be wandering around the house."

"What about George Quayle's associates? Did you see any of them talking with Gennifer?"

Bessie thought back. "George took Gennifer over specifically to speak to one of them, as I said. She spent a good deal of time talking with them all, as I recall."

"And was she flirting with them like she had with young Hugh?"

"Not as much," Bessie said. "The man George wanted her to meet was one of her father's business associates. She seemed to behave better with them than she did with her own friends."

"If you consider flirting bad behaviour," Anna said lightly.

Bessie pressed her lips together and didn't reply. Flirting was one thing, but Gennifer had gone too far with Hugh.

Anna had many more questions, and Bessie dutifully supplied answers, explaining again how she and Doona had come to discover the disturbed guest room and the body.

"One last question," Anna said eventually. "Is there anyone that you are absolutely certain had nothing to do with Gennifer's demise? That would be anyone that you are sure never left the great room after Gennifer did."

Bessie thought hard and then shook her head. "As I said, everyone was in and out and I wasn't paying attention to anyone specific. It was a party and I was having fun chatting with my friends. Besides, I was in and out myself."

"And you can't give me an estimate on how long Hugh was away from the party?"

"As I said, I didn't even notice that he'd gone," Bessie replied.

"That's a shame," Anna said, making a note in her notebook.

"I don't suppose it was just an unfortunate accident?" Bessie had to ask.

"We can't be sure of anything until the coroner has completed his examination of the body," Anna told her. "But I'd stake my reputation on it being murder."

"That's awful," Bessie said.

Anna nodded. "I'm going to have one of my men take you home," she said. "I know the island runs on rain and gossip, but I'm going to ask you not to talk about what happened here tonight, at least for a day or two. I'm hoping to wrap things up rather quickly in this investigation."

"I hope you do," Bessie said.

"I hope you still feel that way once I've made an arrest," Anna told her.

Bessie let the young constable lead her out of the mansion, her mind racing. From Anna's last words, she could only assume that the woman suspected someone that Bessie considered a friend. As her mind raced, she followed the policeman to his car and climbed inside.

49

"She couldn't possibly suspect Hugh," Bessie exclaimed as the thought crossed her mind.

The young constable who was slowly pulling the car out of the car park glanced at her in surprise. "I think he's her chief suspect," he said quietly. "But you didn't get that from me."

Bessie shook her head. "Hugh wouldn't hurt a fly," she said angrily.

"No, he wouldn't," the young man agreed.

Bessie sat, silently fuming, as they drove the very short distance to her cottage. "Is that your car?" the constable asked her as he pulled into the parking area next to the cottage.

"No, I don't drive," Bessie answered, looking over at the dark sedan. She was certain that she recognised it, but her tired brain couldn't seem to focus.

"You wait here," the man instructed her. "I'll just check it out."

As he climbed out of the car, the driver's side door opened on the sedan. Bessie was relieved when its interior light went on and revealed John Rockwell emerging from the car.

"Oh, Inspector Rockwell, I didn't realise that was your car," the young man exclaimed.

"I wanted to check on Bessie," John said. "Thank you for bringing her home."

"Just following orders, sir," he said smartly.

John opened Bessie's door and helped her from the car. "You look tired," he told her as they walked to the cottage door.

"I'm totally done in and ready to sleep for a week," she replied.

"I won't stay long, then," Rockwell said. "I'll just check the cottage before I go."

Bessie opened the door and switched on a light. She stood in the kitchen, wondering if she should make coffee, while she listened to John walking around the upstairs. When he walked back into the kitchen, she forced herself to smile.

"I can make coffee," she suggested.

"I was going to go and let you sleep," he reminded her.

"But you didn't wait outside my cottage for goodness knows how long just so you could check it was secure," Bessie said. "You must have wanted to talk to me about something."

Rockwell sighed. "Something, indeed," he said.

"Sit down and I'll start a pot of coffee," Bessie instructed him. "There's no way I'll stay awake otherwise."

John nodded and fell heavily into one of the kitchen chairs. Bessie frowned as she looked over at him. He looked exhausted. She dug around in the cupboard for biscuits, passing him the first packet she came to.

"No plates?" he asked, surprised.

Bessie took a deep breath. Even though she was exhausted, he was right. There were certain standards that needed to be upheld. She handed him a large plate to put the biscuits on and put two smaller plates on the table for each of them to use. It wasn't long before the cottage was filled with the smell of coffee brewing.

John took a deep breath. "Just the smell helps," he said.

Bessie chuckled and breathed in. "You're right," she agreed. "Not as much as drinking it will, though."

It wasn't until she'd poured the drinks and they'd both had their first cautious sips that John started the conversation.

"As I was a guest at the party, I'm just as much a suspect as everyone else," he told Bessie. "Anna will be responsible for the investigation."

Bessie frowned. "I don't like Anna and I don't think she's a competent investigator," she argued.

"I'm being reassigned to Castletown while the investigation is taking place."

"Castletown?" Bessie echoed. "That's a very long drive for you every day."

"Yes, I may just take a short leave of absence rather than take up the posting," John replied. "Inspector Armstrong has his own way of doing things in Castletown and I'm not sure I'd fit in well down there. The Chief Constable has given me the weekend to make a decision as to what I want to do, but he's suggested that an unpaid leave of absence would be one of my better options."

"Unpaid?" Bessie asked. "But that isn't fair. It isn't your fault you were at a party where someone got murdered. It was murder, then?"

"Yes, it was murder," John replied. "Although I don't know exactly why they're so certain about that."

Bessie shook her head. "What about Doona and Hugh? They were both there as well."

"Doona is being moved to Douglas until the case is solved," John told her. "They could use an extra pair of hands down there anyway. Pete will take good care of her."

"And Hugh?"

John frowned. "I believe that Hugh is going to be given unpaid leave," he said.

"Anna thinks he killed Gennifer, doesn't she?" Bessie asked.

"I can't imagine that she would seriously think that," John replied. "But he has to be considered a suspect. He had, well, interactions with the victim, after all."

"She threw herself at him," Bessie said. "That's hardly a motive for murder."

"She caused a disagreement between him and his partner," John replied. "And he was out of the room for a considerable amount of time during the relevant time period."

"Hugh wouldn't hurt a fly," Bessie said stoutly.

"I'd agree with that assessment," John replied. "But Anna doesn't know him as well as we do, and she has to consider the evidence."

"Everyone was in and out of the great room all night," Bessie said. "Anyone could have pushed Gennifer over the cliff."

"It seems likely that someone arranged to meet her in that empty guest room," John said. "Anna is hoping whoever was there left behind some trace."

"Well, she needs to stop looking at Hugh and start investigating all of Elizabeth's friends," Bessie said. "They've all known her long enough to have real motives for wanting her dead."

"I'm sure she's going to investigate everyone thoroughly," John said. "But in the meantime, I was hoping you wouldn't be too tired to take me through your day."

Bessie bit back a sigh. When caught up in investigations, John always wanted her to walk him through her entire day, sometimes minute by minute, when he questioned her.

"I know you're tired," he added. "But I'd like to do it while it's still fresh in your mind. I'm not asking in any official capacity, though. You've already given a statement to Anna. You don't have to indulge me."

Bessie smiled at him. "I have a lot more faith in your abilities to solve this murder than in Anna's," she told him. "Let me top up my coffee and then I'll bore you with exactly how my day went."

John was a great deal more thorough than Anna had been, starting with Bessie's internal alarm at six that morning and moving slowly through her rather boring morning and afternoon. John was yawning as she told him about lunch and the book she was reading when Mary rang. He looked more alert once she told of her arrival at Thie yn Traie.

"So Mary didn't like Gennifer," John said thoughtfully a great while later, when Bessie had finally finished.

"She wasn't especially likable," Bessie replied. "Please don't tell me that Mary is a suspect."

John shook his head. "She's about the only person I can say isn't a suspect," he told her. "She never left the great room after Gennifer did."

"She didn't?"

"No," John replied. "I didn't either, but I doubt anyone noticed. Anyway, I was keeping a close eye on everyone and I'm certain that Mary didn't leave. She was talking with some of George's associates and then she moved over to chat with Liz, who was upset about something. As it grew closer to midnight, she started rounding everyone up to watch the telly broadcast of the countdown."

Bessie shut her eyes and thought back. She could picture Mary moving around the room, chatting with everyone and keeping everything running smoothly. John was probably correct. Mary was too good of a hostess to leave the party.

"I wish you could rule out Hugh," Bessie said.

"I can, based on what I know of him as a person," John said. "But he did leave the great room, and he was gone for at least twenty minutes."

"And when he came back, his hair and clothes were wet," Bessie added. "He spoke to me when he came back in, to tell me that the weather was bad. There's no way he could have talked about the weather with me like he did if he'd just killed a woman."

"I agree, but Anna will be dealing with facts, not feelings."

"What about Doona?" Bessie changed the subject before she could feel too bad for poor Hugh.

"She left the room at least once," John replied. "We were talking, and she excused herself to go to the loo. She was gone about ten minutes, which seems a long time."

"There was a queue for the loo," Bessie told him. "I had to wait several minutes myself when I went."

"Hardly surprising, considering how many guests there were," John told her.

"The woman in the queue behind me ended up going off in search of an alternative. I would imagine she wasn't the only person wandering around the place."

"No, that's part of the problem, of course. No one would have stopped any guests from going just about anywhere. It's a huge house and besides dozen of guests, there were at least twenty staff working at the party."

"And any of them could have had a disagreement with Gennifer," Bessie suggested.

John shrugged. "Mary hadn't heard about any problems, but that doesn't mean there weren't any."

"What a mess," Bessie sighed.

"Yes, in some ways I'm not sorry that I don't have to try to sort it out."

"You don't mean that. And I have a great deal more confidence in your abilities than I do in Inspector Lambert's."

"The Chief Constable will be keeping a close eye on things," John told her. "Maybe someone has already confessed and we're wasting our time."

Bessie laughed. "Why do I doubt that?" she asked.

"Anything is possible. I'm sorry. I feel as if I'm wasting your time. I have no idea what's going on in the investigation. We should both get some sleep and see what tomorrow brings."

"I'm worried about Hugh," Bessie told John.

"Try not to worry too much," John said. "It's very early in the investigation. As I'm certain that Hugh didn't do it, I'm sure he'll be fine in the end."

"I'm not sure Grace will ever speak to him again," Bessie said.

"That's another matter altogether," John replied. "I did think she was awfully hard on him, even though he did handle the whole thing badly."

"I suspect that the remark about her not having a ring on her finger hurt a lot. I'm sure she's been expecting Hugh to propose for a while now."

John sighed. "I need to go home and get some sleep," he said. "Luckily tomorrow is a bank holiday and then it's the weekend. Maybe Anna will have everything sorted by Monday and I can just go back to work as normal."

"You mean today is a bank holiday," Bessie corrected him. "It's nearly time for me to get up."

John looked at the clock. "I'm sorry. I shouldn't have bothered you tonight."

"We both needed to talk about things, at least a little bit," Bessie replied. "I shall sleep better knowing that you don't think Hugh did it either."

John nodded and got up from the table. He needed to use both hands to push himself up and steady himself.

"Maybe you should just sleep in my spare room," Bessie suggested.

"I'm only a short distance from home. I appreciate the offer, but I'd much rather sleep in my own bed."

"I can ring for a taxi."

"I'm fine," John insisted. "At this hour of the morning, the roads will be deserted anyway."

Bessie walked him to the door. When she opened it, the cold wind nearly took her breath away.

"Well, that's woken me up for sure," John said as he struggled to button his coat.

Bessie watched as he climbed into his car and slowly drove away. Back in the kitchen she piled the used plates and cups in the sink. The washing-up could wait until she'd had some sleep. After a quick check that both doors were securely locked, Bessie climbed the stairs and got ready for bed.

Bessie glanced at her clock as she snuggled under the duvet. In only a few hours, her internal alarm would probably try to wake her. She was certain there was no way it would succeed, however.

When Bessie next opened her eyes, it was nearly ten o'clock. She sat up in bed and stared at her clock. She couldn't remember the last time she'd slept that late, but it must have been when she'd been ill. After a shower, she got dressed automatically, paying little attention to the clothes she pulled from her wardrobe. In the kitchen, she set a fresh pot of coffee brewing and slid bread into the toaster. While she waited for it to pop, she did the washing-up from the night before. She was still so tired that the events of the previous evening felt almost unreal to her.

It wasn't until after her first cup of coffee that she looked at her answering machine. Of course the message light was flashing frantically. Bessie thought about leaving the ringer on her phone switched off, as she did during the night, because she knew the phone would probably be ringing all day. Sighing, she turned the ringer on and pressed play on the machine. Nearly all of the messages were from friends around the island who'd heard about Gennifer's sudden death.

It seemed from the tone of the messages that most of them seemed to think her death had been a tragic accident. Bessie felt a tiny twinge of hope that they were correct and that she'd misunderstood what Anna had said on that subject. The last call was from police headquarters.

"Mrs. Cubbon, this is Carol at the Laxey Constabulary. Inspector Lambert has some more questions for you and will be sending a car to collect you at one o'clock this afternoon to bring you to the station to meet with her. Please ring me back if you have any questions."

Bessie had several questions, but she didn't think ringing back the station would help. She frowned at the answering machine. Her phone rang before she'd decided what to do.

"Bessie, it's Doona. I was just ringing to see how you are."

"I'm fine," Bessie said automatically. "Very tired, of course. How are you?"

"The same," Doona replied. "I'm off work until Monday, but then I've been reassigned to Douglas until Gennifer's murder is solved."

"It was murder, then?" Bessie asked.

"Apparently," Doona said. "I'm not being told anything officially, but from what my sources have said, it was murder."

Bessie didn't doubt Doona's sources as they would be her coworkers at the Laxey police station.

"Of course," Doona continued, "no one is saying much of anything, especially to me, as I was there and must be considered a suspect."

"John said he's being sent to Castletown," Bessie said.

"Yes, I gather he is, if he doesn't just take a leave of absence."

"And Hugh is being suspended."

"As I understand it, yes," Doona said. "Which suggests that he's really a suspect."

"Which is nonsense," Bessie said firmly.

"Of course it is," Doona agreed quickly.

"I've been summoned to see Anna this afternoon," Bessie said. "I shall have a word with her about poor Hugh."

"I'm not sure that's a great idea. If I were you, I'd just answer her questions and not say anything else about anything at all."

"I'm not afraid of Anna Lambert."

"I am," Doona admitted. "Although I have to work with her; you don't."

"And you don't while you're in Douglas," Bessie pointed out.

"True, every cloud has a silver lining," Doona agreed.

"I don't suppose your sources have given you any useful information?"

"No one from the station is meant to be speaking with me at all," Doona replied. "I ran into a nameless source at the bakery this morning. He gave me a quick hug and said he was sorry to see me tied up in another murder investigation. That's all I got."

"Well, if it looks as if Anna really is going after poor Hugh, we might have to try tapping your sources," Bessie said.

"I'm sure John won't let that happen," Doona told her. "John knows Hugh isn't capable of murder. I'm sure he'll do everything he can to help."

"I intend to do everything I can to help, as well," Bessie replied. "Starting with ringing a few friends and asking some questions."

"Bessie, you made Anna cross when you got involved in her last case," Doona said. "You really don't want her to think you're poking your nose into this one. Especially not when you're a suspect."

"I'm not a suspect," Bessie scoffed. "What possible motive could I have had for killing Gennifer?"

"You have about as much motive as I do, but every guest at the party is a suspect, whether they have a motive or not."

"Hopefully, Anna is smart enough to realise who the real suspects are, though."

"Who would you consider real suspects, then?"

Bessie thought for a moment. "I suppose Elizabeth's friends are the only ones who might have had a motive," she said eventually.

"Why don't I come over tonight?" Doona suggested. "I'll see if John and Hugh are free as well."

"That sounds good," Bessie agreed. "I'm going to ring Mary and see if I can find out more about Elizabeth's friends."

"Just be careful," Doona said. "You don't want Anna angry at you."

"I care a good deal more about Hugh than I do about Anna," Bessie retorted.

They agreed that Doona would come around six and bring Chinese food with her. "I'll make something for pudding," Bessie said.

"More Christmas cookies would be fine with me," Doona told her. "It's still the Christmas season, isn't it?"

Bessie laughed. "Maybe I'll make chocolate chip cookies, then. They're good all year-round, not just at Christmas, anyway."

"Perfect," Doona said happily.

Bessie put the phone down and got up to check that she had what she needed for the cookies. She'd only taken a few steps towards the cupboard where she kept her baking supplies when the phone rang again. The little voice in her head suggested she ignore it, but she picked it up, hoping it might be someone she wanted to speak with. It was.

"Bessie, are you okay?" Mary's voice was tense.

"I'm fine, really, just a little bit sad to see a young life cut short," Bessie replied.

"Yes, it's very sad," Mary agreed. "Gennifer's parents are flying over this afternoon. I've no idea what I can say to them. I feel so responsible."

"That's silly. You are in no way responsible for Gennifer's death," Bessie said firmly. "Just be your usual kind self and I'm sure you'll be fine."

"It's just so awful," Mary said. "I can't imagine losing a child. They'll be devastated. And even worse, she was murdered."

"Do you know her parents well?" Bessie asked.

"I don't know them at all. George has had business dealings with Gennifer's father, but only tangentially, through other friends. Elizabeth went to school with Gennifer, but they weren't really friends. Gennifer's family is old money, you see. She was only at the party because she's been seeing Nigel and he wanted to come."

"Are they going to stay with you at Thie yn Traie?"

"Oh, goodness, no," Mary exclaimed. "They're only coming over for a few hours. They didn't want to stay the night on the island. From what Mrs. Carter-Maxwell said, there was nothing suitable in terms of hotel accommodations, anyway. I gather they have very high standards."

"So why are they coming?" Bessie had to ask.

"She said something about walking in her daughter's last footsteps or something. Apparently Inspector Lambert would like to speak to them, as well. She's coming to Thie yn Traie to talk to them at two."

"Is she? I'm meant to be meeting with her at one. I hope that means my conversation with her will be a short one."

"Mrs. Carter-Maxwell told me that she's told the inspector that she can have twenty minutes of their time, but no more. Apparently, the inspector has agreed."

"I wish I could tell her the same thing," Bessie said. "I've never really cared about having a lot of money, but sometimes it does seem as if it has its advantages."

"It has its disadvantages as well," Mary told her. "Anyway, the reason I rang is to ask you for a favour, and I'm ever so sorry to do that after just asking for one yesterday that, well, didn't exactly turn out for the best."

"What can I do for you?" Bessie asked.

"I was wondering if you'd like to come to tea at three? I'm having a proper tea for the Carter-Maxwells and I really don't want to face them on my own."

"Of course I'll come," Bessie said quickly.

"Elizabeth and her friends will all be here, of course, but I've no doubt George will find some excuse not to come and I will feel rather alone with just the children for support."

"I understand," Bessie said soothingly. "It's fine. I shall have to try to think of nice things to say about their daughter before I arrive."

"Yes, that's part of the problem," Mary said. "I found her difficult to like, especially because she caused so many problems within the group. Elizabeth has had friends here on numerous occasions and this is the first time there has been any difficulty."

"She was beautiful," Bessie said, almost to herself.

"On the outside, anyway," Mary replied.

Bessie found herself thinking about Gennifer as she made herself a light lunch. Beyond her looks, there seemed little that Bessie could think of to compliment the girl. She was still trying to work out what she could say to the bereaved parents when someone knocked on her door.

The young constable who'd arrived to collect Bessie for her interview with Anna Lambert was one that Bessie had only a nodding acquaintance with. She tried to start a conversation on the journey to the station, but he gave only monosyllabic answers to her queries about the weather and the traffic. She didn't bother asking him anything about the case. No doubt he'd been told he wasn't to speak to her.

He pulled up in front of the station with two minutes to spare. "I have to go out on patrol now, so you can just jump out here."

"I haven't jumped anywhere in years," Bessie muttered as she climbed out of the car.

He pulled away as soon as she'd pushed the door shut behind her. Bessie squared her shoulders and took a deep breath. Just answer the questions, she told herself sternly as she crossed the pavement and pushed open the station's door.

CHAPTER 5

*T*he young, dark-haired woman sitting in Doona's chair behind the reception desk was a stranger to Bessie.

"I'm Elizabeth Cubbon. Inspector Lambert wanted to see me," Bessie told her.

"Ah, yes, Mrs. Cubbon. Take a seat and I'll let the inspector know you're here."

"It's Miss Cubbon, actually," Bessie couldn't resist saying.

"It's what?" the girl asked.

"You called me Mrs. Cubbon, and I'm actually Miss Cubbon," Bessie explained patiently.

"Oh, sure, whatever," the girl shrugged and snapped her gum. Bessie walked over and sat down in the tiny reception space while the girl pressed a button on her phone.

"Miss Cubbon is here for you," she said, putting loud emphasis on the first word. "She'll be out in a bit," the girl told Bessie as she put the phone down.

Bessie smiled and flipped through the magazines that were stacked on a small side table. They were all several years old and mostly seemed to be about home decorating. She shook her head and then settled back in her seat to wait. After a moment she felt her eyes beginning to close as her very late night caught up with her. She shifted in her seat. It simply wouldn't do to fall asleep here.

"Ah, Miss Cubbon, thank you for coming in," Anna Lambert was suddenly standing at Bessie's elbow.

Bessie stood up and forced herself to smile. "Always happy to do what I can to help out in a murder investigation," she said, putting as much energy into her words as she could muster.

"Indeed," Anna murmured. "Come back to my office, please. I only have a few questions."

Bessie followed the woman through the side door and down the short corridor. Anna stopped in front of an open door. "Here we are," she said, gesturing for Bessie to enter the office.

Bessie walked in and looked around. Anna had been with the Laxey station for some months now, so Bessie was surprised to see that the room looked almost unoccupied. A beat-up metal desk sat in the very centre of the space. Behind it was a large desk chair. The chair in front of the desk was wooden and looked uncomfortable. A small metal filing cabinet was the only other piece of furniture in the room. There were a few sheets of paper on the desk, along with a computer and a phone, but there wasn't a single personal item in the room.

"Please have a seat," Anna said. She waited until Bessie was seated before she walked behind the desk and sat herself.

"This is nothing like John's office," Bessie said, almost without thinking. She knew John had a similar space a few doors away. He kept his space tidy, but he had photographs of his children on his desk and artwork on his walls.

"No, I prefer to keep my work space completely uncluttered," Anna told her in a cool voice.

"Every inch of my cottage is cluttered," Bessie said with a rueful grin. "I've lived there too long and acquired too many things for it to be anything else."

"Perhaps you should have a good clear-out," Anna suggested.

"Maybe one day," Bessie replied.

"I wish we had more time for small talk," Anna told her. "But I have other appointments this afternoon. I'd just like to ask you about Hugh and his girlfriend. What can you tell me about their relationship?"

Bessie's first instinct was to refuse to tell the woman anything. She couldn't imagine that Hugh and Grace's romance was any of Anna's business. "I'm not sure what you want to know," she prevaricated.

"Are they serious about one another or just casual?" Anna asked.

"I believe they're serious," Bessie replied. "I'm pretty sure Hugh is planning to propose to Grace in the near future."

"Really? Too bad they had that big fight last night, then," Anna said.

"It was a minor disagreement," Bessie said, hoping she was right. "Gennifer more or less threw herself at Hugh and he was too polite and embarrassed to deal with it the way Grace thought he should, that's all."

"Was Grace very angry?" Anna asked.

"She was pretty upset. I'm not sure angry is the right word, more sad."

"At whom would she have been most angry, Hugh or Gennifer?"

Bessie shook her head. "She wasn't angry. She was hurt that Hugh didn't, I don't know, chase Gennifer away maybe, that's all."

"How much of her upset did she direct at Hugh, and how much was aimed at Gennifer?"

The reworded question didn't fool Bessie. Surely Anna wasn't suggesting that Grace had murdered Gennifer? "I've no idea," Bessie said. "I would imagine she was mostly upset with Hugh, as she didn't even know Gennifer."

"But she might have blamed Gennifer for coming between them."

"She might have," Bessie agreed, tired of the conversation. "You should really ask her how she felt."

"I have done," Anna replied. "But I have to consider that she might have reasons to lie to me."

"You can't think she had anything to do with Gennifer's murder," Bessie blurted out.

Anna raised an eyebrow. "At this early point in the investigation, everyone is a suspect."

"I'm more likely to have killed Gennifer than Grace is," Bessie found herself saying.

Anna sat back in her chair. "Are you now? Why is that, then? What did you have against the woman?"

"Nothing at all," Bessie said, feeling frustrated. "I just meant that there's no way Grace did anything, that's all."

"Grace was upset that Gennifer was trying to seduce the man she loves. It seems a fairly straightforward motive."

"Maybe for some people, but Grace Christian is a primary school-teacher and one of the sweetest people I know," Bessie said defensively.

"When you've been doing this job as long as I have, you learn that anyone can commit murder, if suitably provoked," Anna said condescendingly. "For what it's worth, I don't think Grace killed Gennifer, although I haven't totally eliminated her from consideration."

"Then why are we having this conversation?" Bessie challenged, feeling both brave and foolish.

"I need to work out who had a motive," Anna told her. "While Grace's seems a bit thin, Hugh's is considerably stronger."

"Hugh didn't have anything to do with Gennifer's death," Bessie said dismissively. "You need to take a good look at Elizabeth's friends. One of them will have had a motive that's much better than a tiny quarrel between two people in love."

"Okay, then, what can you tell me about Elizabeth's friends?" Anna asked.

Bessie shook her head. "I don't really know anything about them," she said.

"Which is why I've focussed my questions to you on the people you do know," Anna replied. She sighed. "I know you have a special relationship with John Rockwell and that he seems to think you're an asset to his investigations, but I would greatly appreciate your not trying to tell me how to do my job. I was CID in Derby for ten years before I came here. I know how to conduct a murder investigation and I'll get the job done much more quickly without you interfering in it."

Bessie flushed under Anna's angry stare. "I'm sorry, but I worry about my friends," she said eventually.

"You should only be worried about Hugh if you think he killed Gennifer," Anna told her. "Innocent men have nothing to fear from me."

Bessie thought about Niall Clague, a man who'd been guilty of nothing but a clouded memory. In her opinion, Anna had hounded the poor man to death, but Bessie didn't dare accuse her of it. "Was there anything else?" she asked after a moment.

"I think that's enough for today," Anna told her. "If I didn't have another appointment I'd ask you more about Hugh and Grace, but I don't know that you'd be very cooperative anyway."

Bessie stood up. She didn't bother to defend herself, as Anna was quite right. The last thing she wanted to do right now was cooperate with the disagreeable woman.

"I hope I don't have to see you again in regard to this investigation," Anna told Bessie as she escorted her back into the reception area. "I'm expecting to have it wrapped up quite quickly and I'm sure you know better than to get involved." She turned and walked back towards her office before Bessie had worked out a suitable reply.

"Is someone meant to be taking me home?" Bessie asked the girl behind the desk.

She wrinkled her nose. "Oooh, I don't know," she said. "I'll just ring the inspector and ask, shall I?"

"Don't bother," Bessie said quickly. "I'll get a taxi."

"Right then, thanks for coming in," the girl replied.

Bessie turned and headed out of the station. There was a taxi rank a few doors away, and if that was empty she could pop into the nearby pub and ring for a car from there. She didn't want to spend another minute at the station. As luck would have it, there was a single car idling at the taxi rank. Bessie climbed in and gave the driver her address.

"That isn't too far," the man said cheerfully. "I don't suppose you have any biscuits in the cupboard? You could make me a cuppa and I could forget to charge you for the short journey."

Bessie laughed as she recognised the man. "Dale Sommers? What are you doing back on the island?"

"Ah, we all come back eventually," the man told her. "I've been bouncing back and forth between here and Blackpool for the last few years, but mum's health isn't great, so me and the wife decided it was time to move back for good. I'm retired anyway, but the taxi is a good excuse to get out of the house and make a bit of spare cash. Mostly, though, it gets me out of the house. Mum and the wife get along like a house on fire and they're always nagging me to do things. I'd rather drive a car full of drunk lads to Port Erin than listen to those two when they get going."

"You don't mean it," she said as they pulled up to her cottage.

"Nah, they're both wonderful and I love them dearly, but it's nice to get out a couple days a week with the taxi anyway."

"Come in for that tea, then," Bessie suggested. "Although I won't be having any as I've been invited to tea later this afternoon."

"Do you need a ride for that, then?" the man asked as he walked Bessie to her door.

Bessie looked at the cloudy skies and shrugged. "It's only a short distance down the beach, but I might do, if it's raining. I'd hate to ruin my special occasion clothes."

"Going to Thie yn Traie for tea?" Dale asked. "It was those lads there that I was thinking of earlier."

"They were drunk and you took them to Port Erin?" Bessie asked, surprised.

"Actually, I collected a bunch of them at Ronaldsway," Dale told her. "They were well drunk when they got off their plane and they were, um, not enjoyable company on the trip to Thie yn Traie."

"I don't suppose you got their names?"

Dale frowned. "I heard there was some trouble up at the mansion last night," he said. "I don't want to be talking about things I shouldn't."

"One of the young women who was staying there was killed," Bessie told him. "The police need to know everything they can about her friends. Maybe you can help."

"Oh, I don't want to bother the police," Dale said hastily. "I was just talking, like, telling you about the life of a taxi driver, that's all."

Bessie made the man some tea and put some biscuits on a plate. "So tell me about the life of a taxi driver," she said encouragingly. "Tell me about collecting that group from the airport. How many people did you collect?"

"I had four in my cab, and my mate, he had another three in his. Mrs. Quayle booked us, you see. She likes to use local companies. She's a real lady, is Mrs. Quayle."

Bessie smiled at the assessment of her friend. "Was anyone particularly badly behaved?" she asked.

Dale shrugged. "All of them," he said. "I took the guys and my mate took the ladies. It seemed best to split them up because they were all fighting pretty badly."

"Were they now?"

"Oh, aye," Dale said. "One of the women was really unhappy about being on the island and she wasn't shy about blaming her boyfriend for dragging her here."

"Did she have red hair?" Bessie asked.

"Yeah, I didn't catch her name, but she was really pretty. She was by far the prettiest of the girls."

"That was Gennifer," Bessie told him. "She's the girl who died last night."

Dale put his cup down and frowned. "That's really sad," he said. "She was something special with all that red hair and those long legs. She was pretty awful to her boyfriend, though. She seemed as if she was used to getting her way, and it was clear that coming to the island was Nigel's idea."

"Yes, someone else told me that as well," Bessie said. "What about the others? What were they like?"

"I didn't pay much attention to the girls; as I said, they went in the other car. To be honest, next to that redhead, they pretty much faded into the background. I felt sorry for Nigel. I only got his name because she kept talking so loudly about how Nigel had ruined her weekend."

"And the other men?"

Dale shrugged. "They seemed like typical spoiled rich kids, really. One of them was nicer than the others, but mostly they all seemed cut from the same sort of tall, dark, handsome and rude cloth."

"Did you overhear what they were talking about on the journey to Thie yn Traie?" Bessie asked.

"At first the others were all teasing Nigel about his girlfriend." Dale flushed. "Some of the conversation was pretty rude. I won't repeat it."

"That's fine," Bessie assured him.

"Mostly they were talking about, well, which girls they were planning to, um, well, sleep with while they were here. Someone told Nigel to give up on his girlfriend and just, um, well, be intimate with Emma, whichever one she is."

"Do you know why they suggested Emma?"

"The one guy, he was shorter than the others, he said something about Emma being in love with Nigel for years and everyone laughed," Dale shook his head. "I wasn't really paying that much attention, you know. I was just driving. They were just typical fares, drunk, rude and cheap."

"You should stop in at the police station and tell them about all of this," Bessie told the man. "They're trying to find out all they can about the dead woman and her friends. Your friend should make a statement as well."

"I don't want to be bothering the police," Dale said firmly. "Anyway, I shouldn't be repeating what I heard in my taxi. It's like with a solicitor, privileged communication or whatever."

Bessie frowned, but she wasn't surprised. In her experience, very few people were eager to talk to the police.

"I hope you don't mind if I repeat what you've told me to a friend of mine," she said instead. "He's with the police, but he's not part of this investigation. He was actually one of the guests at the party. I told him I'd share anything interesting that I heard with him."

Dale shrugged. "I suppose it doesn't matter," he said. He swallowed the last of his tea. "Now, what time do you need to be at Thie yn Traie?"

"Oh, goodness, in about twenty minutes," Bessie exclaimed. She'd been so interested in their conversation that she'd nearly forgotten about tea with Mary. "I need to change into something more appropriate."

"You run up and change," Dale said. "I'll wash up the dishes, just like I did when I was a teenager. You really did train us well."

Bessie grinned and then headed up the stairs. As she changed into a grey dress and pulled her black jacket on over it, she thought about what Dale had said. She'd always welcomed her teenaged guests, letting them spend the night with her when they were struggling to get along with their parents. But she had strict rules. She often felt that her rules were part of the attraction. As so many parents tried to be friends with their children and raise them in an environment with hardly any structure, the regulations at Bessie's must have made it feel like a safe place.

Everyone who stayed knew exactly what Bessie expected. If she served tea and biscuits, it was the guest's job to take care of the washing-up. Bessie smiled as she patted some powder on her nose. No doubt a great many coddled young men and women in Laxey had done their first lot of washing-up in Bessie's tiny cottage.

Back downstairs, Dale was just drying the last cup. He put it in the cupboard and then turned to Bessie. "I'll drive you over. It's raining too heavily for you to walk, no matter how much you'd like to."

Bessie glanced out the window. The man was right; the rain was coming down in sheets. She pulled on her waterproof coat and her Wellington boots, tucking her low black heels into a small bag. She'd just have to change once she'd arrived at Mary's mansion.

"What about an umbrella?" Dale asked as Bessie opened her door.

"Too windy," was Bessie's verdict.

Dale helped Bessie into his car before getting in himself. By that time he was soaked through.

"You need to go home and change out of your wet things," Bessie told him.

"I think I'll give myself the rest of the day off," he said cheerfully. "Any excuse, you know."

Bessie chuckled. The drive was a short one. Dale insisted on parking and walking Bessie to the mansion's front door. Bessie rang the bell and then waited under a small overhang to be admitted.

"You get back to the car and get home," she told Dale. "There isn't room for both of us under here and there's no need for you to get any wetter."

Dale took a step towards his car before Bessie spoke again.

"But wait, I haven't paid you," she said.

"It's on me," the man replied. "After all the times you welcomed me into your home when I was a spoiled, self-absorbed teen, a few rides is the least I can do."

Bessie would have argued, but just then the door behind her opened.

"Ah, Miss Cubbon, do come in," Bruce said, stepping backwards and bowing.

Dale used the interruption as his chance to get away. When Bessie turned back to him, he was already in the car, starting the engine. With a sigh, Bessie walked into Thie yn Traie.

"Mary told us you were coming for tea," Bruce said. "I do hope you'll be able to lighten the mood in there."

"I can't imagine how awful this is for Mr. and Mrs. Carter-Maxwell," Bessie replied. "I'm not sure anything I can say will help."

Bruce shrugged. "At least, with you here, I've someone else to talk to," he said. He offered Bessie his arm and the pair made their way into the house.

"You look tired," Bessie told the young man.

"We didn't get to bed until quite late last night," Bruce said. "And then I couldn't sleep. I couldn't get Gennifer out of my head. I feel as if I might never sleep properly again."

"Perhaps you should see a doctor," Bessie said. "They can give you something to help for a few days, until the shock has worn off."

"I'm fine," Bruce said, shaking his head. "Someone has to stay sane around here."

Bessie wondered what he meant, but didn't get the chance to ask as they arrived at the great room. A large group of people were gathered in one of the seating areas, and Bruce and Bessie headed for them. They were only halfway across the room when Mary jumped up to meet them.

"Ah, Bessie, there you are," she said, sounding relieved. "Come and meet Gennifer's parents."

Mary took her other arm and Bessie found herself being almost dragged across the room. "Mr. and Mrs. Carter-Maxwell, this is Miss Elizabeth Cubbon. She's our nearest neighbour and a dear friend."

Bessie smiled at the couple who were sitting together on one of the couches. Mr. Carter-Maxwell had a full head of grey hair and he looked like a banker or a solicitor. Bessie would have placed him in his early sixties, if she'd had to guess his age. His wife wasn't much younger, which surprised Bessie. It appeared that the woman was doing her best to fight the aging process, though. Her face had an artificially tight appearance that suggested cosmetic surgery. They were both dressed in black, the clothes obviously expensive.

"You must call me James," the man said, nodding his head at Bessie. She'd been about to offer her hand, but the nod stopped her.

"And I'm Harriet," his wife added, giving Bessie a chilly smile.

"I'm so very sorry for your loss," Bessie said.

"Do sit down," Mary said. "They'll be bringing tea in shortly."

Bessie took the nearest empty chair and found herself sitting between Emma and Howard. Elizabeth and the rest of her friends were scattered in chairs and on couches that made up something like a circle. No one was looking at anyone else.

"Gennifer was a beautiful girl," Bessie said once she was settled. "I was never blessed with children, and I can't imagine how difficult this is for you. I'm very sorry."

"Thank you," Harriet said after an awkward silence. She looked at her husband for a moment and then back at Bessie. "It is difficult, of course."

"I must go and see how the staff is getting on," Mary said.

After more uncomfortable silence, Bessie felt she had to speak. "I didn't get a chance to get to know Gennifer, so I know nothing about your family. Do you have other children?"

Again, Harriet looked at her husband before she spoke. He was staring straight ahead and didn't meet her eyes.

"Our sons, Charles and Andrew, are older than Gennifer, and we have a second daughter, Millicent, who is two years younger," the woman finally replied.

"I'm sure they're a comfort to you," Bessie murmured, feeling as if everything she was saying was wrong.

"Of course," the woman agreed.

Bessie looked around at the others, but they all appeared busy inspecting the carpet under their chairs, the view out the window or their fingernails. Bessie was just about to try again when Mary came back in, followed by two maids with large tea trolleys.

"Here we are, then," Mary said.

For a few minutes everyone was busy getting drinks and filling small plates with finger sandwiches, scones and tiny cakes. When everyone settled back into their seats with their hands full, Bessie could only hope some of the tension had been relieved.

"When will the rain stop?" Howard asked suddenly. "It feels as if it has done nothing but rain since we arrived."

Mary and Bessie exchanged looks. "It does rain a great deal here in the winter," Bessie told him.

"And in the summer," Elizabeth chimed in. "It's a small island surrounded by sea. If it isn't raining, it's just stopped raining or just about to rain."

"It isn't that bad," Mary said.

"It really is," Elizabeth retorted. "And don't get me started on the fog."

"And now we're stuck here," Nigel complained. "The police won't let us go anywhere until they work out what happened to Gennifer."

"From what the woman they sent to talk to us said, that shouldn't take long," James Carter-Maxwell said. "She seemed to think she knows what happened. She just needs to find enough evidence to make an arrest."

"Really?" Bessie said. "I didn't realise the inspector was that far along in the investigation."

"She seems to think a young police constable was involved," Harriet said. "Young people today." She shook her head.

Bessie quickly swallowed half of her cup of tea to keep herself from speaking. As much as she wanted to defend Hugh, there was no point in upsetting the grieving parents. More than anything, she was angry at Anna Lambert, but there was nothing she could do about her.

"Well, I hope they get it sorted quickly," Howard said. "I don't mind spending the weekend here, but I have to be at work on Monday morning."

"We all do," Sarah said. "And some of us can't go running to mummy and daddy if we lose our jobs, as well."

"Oh, please," Elizabeth groaned. "I know it was difficult when your parents turned you out and told you that you had to do something with your life, but they've bankrolled everything you've done since. You know if your little shop went under tomorrow, they'd bail you out again. Anyway, you hardly ever work there. The last three times I've visited, you weren't anywhere near the place."

"I do a lot of the administrative tasks from my home office," Sarah said defensively. "You wouldn't believe how much paperwork is involved in owning a shop like mine. We import goods from all over the world and ship things on as well. I need to be home Monday to go over our orders for this new year. And I haven't asked my parents for money for ages. They're really making me do it all by myself now."

Elizabeth rolled her eyes but didn't reply.

"We're all eager to get home," Jeremy said, placating. "But we all want the police to work out what happened to Gennifer, as well. Let's just hope they can manage that before Monday."

Another uncomfortable silence fell now and Bessie found herself looking at the clock on the wall. Time seemed to be standing still as she tried to think of something to say.

"I wish all of you could have visited the island in the spring or summer," Mary said. "It's so beautiful when the weather is warmer and drier."

"Maybe we should have another party in the spring," Elizabeth suggested.

Mary frowned at her daughter. "I don't think that would be appropriate," she said softly, glancing at Gennifer's parents.

Elizabeth flushed. "I didn't, that is, I wasn't, I'm, oh, never mind. I think I need to go and lie down." She rushed out of the room before anyone spoke.

"I am sorry," Mary said, her cheeks turning pink. "She's very upset about losing her friend, but that's no excuse for her behaviour."

"It doesn't really matter," Harriet said.

"What time is our flight?" James demanded suddenly.

"Six," Harriet told him.

"Maybe we should get back to the airport, then," he suggested.

Bessie glanced at the clock. She couldn't imagine why the pair needed to be at the airport nearly three hours early, but she wouldn't be sorry to see them go.

"I'll have someone drive you down," Mary said. "You can leave whenever you're ready, of course, but you have time for a bit more to eat, if you'd like."

"I have no appetite," Harriet said in a monotone.

"I'm not much for fussy bits and pieces," James said. "But we appreciate the hospitality, of course."

"It's the very least I could do under the circumstances," Mary replied.

"It was kind of you to come and pay your respects," James said to Bessie as he and his wife stood up.

Bessie rose to her feet. "I'm glad I had a chance to do that," she told the man. "Again, I'm terribly sorry for your loss."

Harriet gave Bessie a tight smile and then she turned and walked away. Mary followed quickly, with James on her heels. As soon as the trio was out of the room, Bessie sank back in her chair and blew out a long breath.

"That was awful," Emma said.

"I have more sympathy for Gennifer now," Jeremy told the others. "I can't imagine she had a very happy childhood."

"She did, actually," Nigel said. "Her father was never home and her mother was always busy with charity things, so she was pretty much raised by a succession of nannies, most of whom she loved. I never heard her complain about her childhood, actually."

"They aren't any different to my parents," Howard said with a shrug.

Bessie nibbled on a cake, listening intently. She was all but certain that Gennifer had been killed by one of the people in this room. Now she just had to work out which one did it. The conversation turned to idle chatter about the weather and UK politics. Bessie remained silent, taking it all in and forming her own impressions about the young people. It wasn't long before Mary rejoined them.

"They're gone," she said, relief evident in her tone. "I'm not sure why they came, but I am pretty sure they were disappointed in what they found here."

"They wanted to be where Gennifer spent her last hours," Bruce said. "Morbid as that is."

"As I said, I can't imagine how difficult this must be for them," Bessie said.

"Thankfully, neither can I," Mary said. "If anything happened to any of my children, I know I'd be inconsolable for weeks or months." She poured herself another cup of tea, her hands shaking slightly.

Bessie joined her at the tea trolley and got her own second cup. While she was selecting a few more treats, she patted Mary on the back. "If you need to get away at all, you know where I am," she said, soothingly.

"Does that offer extend to all of us?" Sarah asked. She'd come up behind Bessie and was filling a plate.

"Of course," Bessie said, surprised by the question. "I'm just down the beach, past the row of holiday cottages. You're all welcome to come over any time and visit. I should warn you, though. I can manage tea and a few biscuits, but nothing like this beautiful feast."

"Maybe, if it ever stops raining, we'll all take a stroll down to your cottage," Bruce said.

"As there's nothing else to do on this rock," Howard drawled.

"There are a number of fascinating historical sites," Bessie told him. "Douglas has an excellent museum, and there's a wonderful new one in Peel as well."

"Yawn," Howard said. "Where is the closest decent pub?"

"There are a couple of pubs in Laxey," Bessie replied. "As I don't frequent them, I couldn't tell you any more than that they're there, but as I understand it, they both do a pretty good trade."

"That's my evening sorted, then," Howard said with a satisfied smile.

Mary frowned, but didn't speak. After a few minutes, Elizabeth walked back into the great room. She'd clearly been crying.

"Have they gone?" she asked.

"Yes," Mary replied.

"Thank goodness," Elizabeth sighed. "I couldn't take another minute with them. They just seemed to suck all of the life out of the room."

"That's an unfortunate metaphor," Bruce laughed.

Elizabeth shook her head. "I suppose I should be more grateful for the parents I have," she said, glancing at Mary. "It could be worse."

Bessie watched as Mary pressed her lips firmly together.

"We're all going down to the pub later," Howard told Elizabeth. "You'll get us a driver, won't you?"

"Sure," Elizabeth shrugged. "Why don't we just go now? There's no reason to stay here. We can get fish and chips or something in the village."

Bessie wasn't sure she'd ever seen that particular group of young people move so quickly. Within seconds, they had all left the room, leaving cups and half-full plates balanced on the arms of chairs and stacked in piles on the floor.

"Bye, mum," Elizabeth shouted as she disappeared. No one else bothered to acknowledge Mary or Bessie.

"I'm sorry about their manners," Mary said with a sigh as the eager footsteps faded away.

"They seem very young for their age," Bessie replied.

"They've all been spoiled with too much money," Mary told her. She began to pick up cups and plates and stack them neatly on one of the tea trolleys. Bessie was quick to join in the effort.

"You shouldn't help. You're my guest," Mary protested.

"I don't mind," Bessie told her. "I can't just sit here and watch you work. That isn't the way I was raised."

Within minutes they had the room tidied and the trolleys ready to go back to the kitchen

"I'll have someone come and deal with them," Mary said. "Let me get someone to take you home."

"I can walk," Bessie protested.

Mary glanced out the window. "It's still pouring," she pointed out. "Anyway, we have extra staff around because of the party last night. It will be good to put at least one person to work."

Bessie was going to argue, but Mary was right. The rain was still falling heavily and she really didn't want to walk home in that.

Within minutes, she was following a young man through the house to the garages.

"I do like having garages when it's raining," Mary said as she led Bessie to one of the cars.

"Thank you for inviting me," Bessie said.

"Oh, you're welcome. I know it was ghastly, and I'm ever so grateful that you came. It would have been much more dreadful without you."

Bessie shook her head. "I don't think I was much help at all," she protested.

"You were wonderful and I owe you a huge favour," Mary said. "But now I'm going to take some headache tablets and go to bed. I've had a migraine all day and it's just getting worse."

Bessie gave her a hug. "I'm not far away if you need to talk," she reminded her friend.

"Maybe tomorrow," Mary said. "When my head clears."

Bessie climbed into the large and comfortable car and settled back on the leather seat. The driver pulled out into the rain and drove slowly towards Bessie's cottage. Bessie felt exhausted by everything that happened over the last forty-eight hours, but she still had guests coming for dinner. It was time for another pot of coffee, she thought as she watched the windscreen wipers sliding back and forth. It was almost hypnotic and Bessie felt herself being lulled to sleep as the car purred along.

CHAPTER 6

*S*omeone needed some water or maybe a throat lozenge, Bessie thought as loud coughing penetrated her tired brain. When the coughing didn't stop, she forced her eyes open.

"We're at your cottage, Miss Cubbon," the man behind the wheel said.

Bessie felt herself blushing bright red. The drive couldn't have taken more than five minutes, but she'd fallen into quite a deep sleep.

"Oh, my goodness," she exclaimed. "I'm ever so sorry. I didn't get very much sleep last night, you see, and it's been such a busy day."

"It's no problem," the man assured her. "No harm done and no one need know."

Bessie thanked him for the ride and climbed out of the car as quickly as she could. Before she had gone more than a step or two, the man was at her side, holding an umbrella over her head. Of course, Bessie then struggled to find her keys, which insisted on hiding at the very bottom of her bag. Then she couldn't get the right key to fit into the lock properly. Mary's driver was well and truly soaked by the time Bessie pushed open her cottage door.

"Thank you again," she said, unable to meet the man's eyes.

"My pleasure," the man replied.

Bessie pushed the door shut behind her before she began to laugh. His pleasure indeed, she thought. A glance at the clock told her that she had nearly two hours before her friends were due to arrive. She could almost hear her pillow calling to her. A short nap might be just the thing to perk her up. But then, it also might cause havoc with her body clock and leave her unable to sleep that evening. Being tired didn't help make Bessie more decisive. She wavered for a moment and then remembered that she'd promised to provide pudding. Cookies took a long time to bake. She'd better get started.

When John finally knocked on her door just after six, Bessie was feeling much better. Fuelled by an entire pot of coffee and a great many chocolate chip cookies, she felt almost like her normal self. She greeted the man with a hug.

"I'm just about to start another pot of coffee," she said as he settled in at her kitchen table. "Unless you'd rather have tea?"

"I think maybe tea would be a better choice," John replied. "I've drunk an awful lot of coffee today, trying to stay awake."

Bessie's hand hesitated over the coffee pot. John was right. If she kept drinking coffee, she'd never get to sleep later. With a sigh, she filled the kettle and switched it on.

"How are you doing?" John asked.

"I'm just tired," Bessie replied. "It's been a strange sort of day, as well."

"How so?"

"It's just been busier than normal. I usually spend New Year's Day on my own, being self-indulgent as it's the first day of the year. This year I've been dashing about."

The kettle boiled just as someone knocked on Bessie's door. John got up to answer the door while Bessie concentrated on tea.

"I didn't realise I was so hungry," Bessie exclaimed as Doona carried in a large box filled with takeaway containers. "But it smells wonderful."

"I brought enough for us and for Hugh, but I'm not sure if he's coming or not," Doona replied. "I've left about ten messages on his mobile and the answering machine in his flat, but he hasn't rung me back."

"I hope he's okay," Bessie said, suddenly concerned about the young man.

"If he doesn't turn up here, I'll go and track him down after we've eaten," John said. "I'm sure he's very upset about everything that happened last night."

"I don't suppose anyone has spoken to Grace?" Bessie asked.

Both John and Doona shook their heads.

"Maybe I'll give her a ring tomorrow," Bessie said. "I'm sure she could use a sympathetic ear."

"If she doesn't think you've sided with Hugh over their quarrel," Doona said.

Bessie sighed. "I hope she knows I haven't taken sides, and that all I want is for both of them to be happy."

"I'm sure she does, really," John said. "But she might be feeling too upset to see it that way at the moment."

Doona spread out the boxes of food and everyone filled a plate. They ate silently for several minutes, with Bessie feeling too tired to make small talk. She decided to save her energy for the more serious conversation that she knew would come after the meal.

"That was delicious," John said as he pushed his empty plate away.

"I made cookies for pudding," Bessie said.

"That's why you're my best friend," Doona told her.

Bessie laughed. When the plates were cleared and the rest of the food was packed away into Bessie's refrigerator, she put a plate of cookies in the centre of the table and refreshed everyone's tea.

"I suppose we should talk about the murder," John said.

"Even though we don't want to," Doona said.

"I want to," Bessie interjected. "It's horrible and tragic and I want to see it solved quickly."

"So let's talk about possible motives," John suggested. "I'm going to start by saying that I think we should assume that all of Elizabeth's friends had some sort of motive."

"Based on Gennifer's personality," Doona said.

"Let's just say Gennifer seemed like she might be a difficult person to like," John said.

"But surely that isn't a motive for murder," Bessie objected.

"Not in itself," John agreed. "But we don't have any background information on those young people. I think, for the sake of argument, that we have to take it as given that they each had a motive."

"Are we including Elizabeth in that list?" Doona asked.

Bessie opened her mouth to object. She didn't know Elizabeth well, but she knew her better than the others. She couldn't imagine the girl killing anyone, even the disagreeable Gennifer. Before she could speak, John held up a hand.

"I think we have to include her at this early stage," he said. "I know I would if I were the investigating officer."

Bessie frowned, but she nodded her agreement.

"What about George's business colleagues?" Doona asked. "Are we assuming motives for them as well?"

"What do you think?" John asked. "I'd rather not make the suspect list overly long at this point, but I also don't want to cross off anyone who might be a possibility."

Bessie was surprised to hear John asking for opinions. "You're the expert here," she pointed out.

"On this case, I'm as much a suspect as you and Doona," he replied. "I'd like our efforts to be as collaborative as possible."

"I didn't see a lot of interaction between Gennifer and George's guests," Doona said. "George took her off to talk to someone, though. I don't suppose either of you know who he was?"

"George called him Robert, but that was all he said," John replied.

"I can ask Mary about him," Bessie suggested.

John nodded. "I'm afraid you're going to have to ask a lot of questions this time around," he said. "I can't talk to any of the suspects myself, not unless I bump into them at ShopFast or something."

"But I can be a nosy old lady, just like I always am," Bessie said with a laugh.

"You'll need to do it very carefully," John cautioned. "Anna isn't going to be happy if she thinks you're interfering in her investigation."

"I don't like that woman," Bessie said.

"I don't think she's particularly fond of you, either," Doona said wryly.

"Officially, I'm telling you to stay out of the investigation," John said in a serious voice. "It might be best if you stayed away from Thie yn Traie and limited your conversations with Mary to the telephone, or at least a neutral meeting place."

"I had tea at Thie yn Traie today," Bessie told him.

"Did you now?" John asked, sighing deeply.

"Mary invited me," Bessie said, feeling defensive. "Gennifer's parents came over and she didn't want to have to entertain them on her own."

"What were they like?" Doona demanded.

"I can't rightly say," Bessie told her. "They barely spoke. I suppose they were just keeping up appearances, you know, stiff upper lip and all that."

"Surely it's acceptable to be upset when your child is murdered?" Doona asked.

"Maybe not in their social circle," Bessie said. "It isn't one I'm very familiar with. Anyway, they weren't there for long. They were in a rush to get back to the airport in plenty of time."

"Did you see anyone else at Thie yn Traie?" John asked.

"Just about everyone," Bessie replied. "Elizabeth and all of her friends had tea with us."

"And what did they all have to say?" Doona wondered.

Bessie told her friends everything that had happened at tea. "They're all miserable and snapping at one another," she concluded. "Maybe one or two of them will come by and visit me and I'll be able to find out more."

"As they're all suspects, I don't like the idea of them visiting you," John said with a frown.

Bessie sighed. "You don't want me to visit Thie yn Traie and you don't want anyone to visit me here. How are we going to solve Gennifer's murder if I can't talk to people?"

"It's Anna's job to solve the murder," John said quietly.

"But she's too busy trying to pin it on Hugh to succeed," Bessie said. "I told you she told Mr. and Mrs. Carter-Maxwell that Hugh was the chief suspect."

"I just don't want you putting yourself in any danger," John said.

"I'll be fine," Bessie replied. "Anyway, a little danger, if it will save Hugh, is worth it."

John shook his head, but he didn't argue any further.

"Where are we then?" Doona asked. "We started with motive. I agree with Bessie that Elizabeth's friends are the most likely to have had one, although we can't rule out George's business associates. Is there anyone else we haven't considered?"

"What about the staff?" John asked. "Did they all come from Mary's Douglas home or did she hire them especially for last night?"

"I don't know," Bessie told him. "But I can certainly find out."

"What possible motive would any of the staff have had?" Doona questioned.

"Depending on where they came from, they might have known the girl elsewhere, or maybe she was just so impossibly demanding that someone snapped and gave her a good push," Bessie said, speculatively.

"It seems unlikely, but it needs to be checked," John said.

"Oh, speaking of staff, I met a taxi driver today that had some interesting things to say about the guests at Thie yn Traie," Bessie said. She told John and Doona what Dale had said about his passengers.

"He should talk to Anna," John said when Bessie was finished.

"I told him that, but he doesn't much like the police," Bessie said. "I can't say as I blame him for that, at least where Anna is concerned."

"So Gennifer didn't like the island," Doona said thoughtfully.

"I don't think any of them are very fond of it, at least not now," Bessie replied.

"So why was she here?" Doona asked.

"She came with Nigel," Bessie said.

"But why? I mean, when we saw them at the party, she didn't really seem like she was so in love with the man that she'd follow him anywhere, did she?" Doona queried.

Bessie thought for a moment. "She didn't even seem to like him. He was following her around, but mostly she was ignoring him."

"When he started making threats, she laughed and asked if he was going to break up with her," John reminded them. "I'd like to know why didn't she break up with him."

"I need to talk to Elizabeth," Bessie said. "And probably the others as well, although I'd be happy at this point with just Elizabeth."

"Just be discreet," John said. "If Anna thinks you're interfering, things could get difficult. And I'd hate to think what would happen if she thinks Doona and I are getting involved."

Bessie sighed. "I'm almost sorry you were invited to the party now," she told John. "At least, if you hadn't been a guest, you could be in charge of the investigation."

"Yes, well, we can't change that," John said. "And it's getting late. Let's quickly talk about means and opportunity. I want to get out and start looking for Hugh before too much longer."

Bessie exchanged a worried look with Doona. Where was Hugh?

"From what I can remember, everyone had the means to do it," Bessie said. "I mean, everyone was in and out of the great room all night long. I suppose they just had to find Gennifer, persuade her to step outside, and then give her a push."

"There might be more to it than that," John said. "But I'm still trying to get some clarification from my, um, sources."

Doona chuckled. "Maybe I should try my sources," she suggested. "The constables at the station love working for you, but they're all a little bit afraid of you as well. They won't want to tell you anything that they know they shouldn't, just in case you're testing them. I'd like to think they'll talk to me, though. I make them tea and buy the biscuits for the staff room, after all."

John nodded. "I've been hearing rumours, but I can't seem to pin anyone down. Maybe you can find out more." He sighed. "It's so frustrating, being on the outside."

"Especially when none of us have any confidence in Anna Lambert," Bessie said.

"That isn't fair," John told her. "I think she's a solid investigator.

She just doesn't know the island or the people very well. We know Hugh didn't do it, but if I look at it from her perspective, I can see why he's her top suspect."

"It seems like means and opportunity are much the same in this case," Bessie mused, not wanting to argue more about the inspector she disliked. "Everyone had plenty of opportunity to leave the great room and no one was stopping people from wandering around the entire house."

"Mary Quayle didn't leave the room between the time Gennifer walked out and when we starting searching for her," John said. "She's the only person I can say that for with certainty."

"If you're sure about that, you mustn't have left, either," Bessie said.

"I didn't, but Anna only has my word on that. Mary wasn't paying attention to who was coming and going. She was supervising the staff, making sure the guests were all mingling, and trying to enjoy the night," he replied.

"I wasn't keeping track of George's group of business associates," Bessie said. "Some of them might be in the clear, but I can't be certain."

"Actually, they aren't and I am certain," John said.

"George took them all out to show them something," Doona said. "I remember one of the wives complaining about it as George insisted on dragging them all away."

"I must have missed that," Bessie said.

"I didn't," John replied. "I'm not sure where they all went, but not long after Gennifer left, he gathered them all up, including their wives, and they all disappeared. They weren't gone long, but I'm pretty sure they were gone long enough to push someone off a cliff."

"But it was raining heavily," Bessie protested. "Surely people would have noticed if someone came back to the party dripping wet?"

John shrugged. "If the killer had a raincoat or an umbrella, he or she might have stayed dry enough. I'd love to time it and see how quickly it could have been done. I'm sure that's something that Anna will be doing."

"I certainly hope so," Bessie said. "Hugh's already admitted he was out in the rain, of course, and he was gone for quite a long time, really. I wonder if he saw Gennifer or anything interesting while he was walking around."

"That's just one of the things I intend to ask him when I see him," John told her. "I have quite a list," he added dryly.

"And now I have one for Mary," Bessie said. "I need to ask her where George took all of his friends, for one thing."

"And you need to find out where the staff from the party came from," John reminded her.

"I think I should be taking notes," Bessie said. She found a pencil and some scrap paper in a drawer and jotted down the two items. "What else do I need to talk to Mary about?" she asked the other two.

"You were going to ask Elizabeth why Gennifer came with Nigel," Doona said.

"Yes, but maybe I'll ask Mary first," Bessie said thoughtfully. "Or maybe I'll ask Mary to have Elizabeth stop over and visit me."

John made a noise that signaled his displeasure with that idea.

"Or maybe I'll invite Elizabeth to meet me somewhere for lunch," Bessie said, hoping that idea might meet with John's approval.

"That would probably be better," John told her.

Bessie shook her head. "As if we didn't have enough obstacles in this investigation," she muttered.

John reached over and patted her hand. "I don't want anything to happen to you," he said softly. "You've become rather important to me over the last year."

"Has it been a year?" Bessie asked in surprise.

"Well, almost," he replied. "You found your first body in March, last year."

Bessie nodded slowly. "So much has happened," she said. "In some ways it feels as if it was just yesterday, but in other ways it seems as if it was a long time ago."

"It's been a very strange year," Doona said. "We were all shocked when Danny Pierce turned out to have been murdered, but now murder seems all too common on our little island."

"It's still rare," John said firmly. "And the island is still one of the safest places in the world. We've just had a run of, well, unusual events. Keep in mind as well, in many cases the murderer, the victim, or both, have been from across."

"Aside from the jam ladies," Bessie muttered.

Doona rubbed Bessie's arm. Bessie knew that Doona understood how much that particular case still upset her.

"And again this time, the victim is from across and it seems likely the murderer is as well," John continued. "I'm sure Anna is checking to see if anyone on the island knew Gennifer, but that seems unlikely."

"Bill Martin," Bessie gasped. "I'd forgotten about him."

"What about him?" John asked.

"He and Liz both knew Gennifer. She came over and, well, spoke to him. Liz was very upset," Bessie said.

"I noticed that Liz was upset," Doona said. "But I wasn't sure why."

"Apparently Bill went out with Gennifer for a while, some years ago," Bessie said.

"I wonder if Anna knows that," John said.

"I'm sure Liz and Bill told her when she interviewed them," Bessie replied.

"I certainly hope they did," John said. "I saw that they appeared to be fighting, and I also noticed that they both left the room and didn't return for longer than most."

"Together or separately?" Bessie asked.

"Separately," John said.

Bessie frowned. "I'm sure there's a simple explanation," she said. "They're both such lovely young people, they couldn't possibly have had anything to do with what happened to Gennifer."

"I thought Liz and Bill had been together forever," Doona said. "Aside from when she went out with Mack Dickinson, very briefly. Isn't that what she told us?"

"It is. Maybe his relationship with Gennifer took place before he met Liz, when he was much younger," Bessie said. "Anyway, I shall have to ring Liz and ask her all about it." She didn't have to look at John to know that he was frowning.

"I think that's about all we can do tonight," he said after a moment.

"I'd really like to get out there and start looking for Hugh. Any ideas where he might be?"

"Let me ring a few people and see what I can find out," Bessie suggested.

She started by ringing Hugh's flat, but no one picked up. "He's either turned his answering machine off or it's full of messages," she said after she'd disconnected.

"I left at least half a dozen message," Doona said. "So it may well be full up."

Bessie tried his mobile next, but got the same result.

"I left a bunch of messages on his mobile as well," Doona said, a touch sheepishly. "I might have filled up his voice mail."

"Let me try his parents' house, then," Bessie said.

"Ah, good evening, Harriet. It's Bessie Cubbon. I'm just trying to track down young Hugh. He isn't there by any chance, is he?"

"No, Bessie, he isn't," the woman's voice came back down the wire. "I haven't seen him since Christmas. He was going to Grace's for dinner today. They're probably still down in Douglas, having a meal and celebrating 1999."

"She didn't sound as if she knew about the murder or that Hugh and Grace have been fighting," Bessie told her friends after she'd wrapped up the call. "She suggested that he's down in Douglas with Grace and her family."

"That seems unlikely," John said.

"It does, but I'll ring them anyway," Bessie said.

No one answered at the Christian family home, however. "Does anyone have a mobile number for Grace?" Bessie asked when she'd given up on a response.

"I do," Doona said. "She's Hugh's emergency contact at work. I keep all those numbers in my phone in case of, well, emergency. I didn't feel right ringing her now, though, under the circumstances."

Bessie nodded. "But finding Hugh is important," she said. "Would you rather ring her yourself?"

Doona shook her head. "You ring," she said. "I don't want her to think there's anything official in our search for Hugh."

Bessie dialed the number that Doona gave her. While she listened to it ringing, she found she was holding her breath.

"Hello?"

"Grace? It's Bessie Cubbon."

"Oh, Aunt Bessie," Grace said. Bessie could tell from just those few syllables that the girl was crying.

"I wanted to see how you were doing," she said.

"I'm, well, I'm holding up," the girl replied, sniffing loudly.

"Maybe you should come and have tea with me tomorrow," Bessie suggested. "You sound as if you could use a change of scenery."

"I, that is, maybe," Grace said. "I just don't know what to do, you see. I had dinner with my parents today, but that was awful because they wanted to know what was going on with Hugh and I couldn't explain. Every time I tried, I burst into tears." As soon as the words were out of her mouth, Bessie could hear her beginning to sob.

"Now, now," she said soothingly. "You definitely need to see a friendly face. Why don't you meet me at the tea shop in Ramsey around two tomorrow and we'll have tea and cakes and see if I can't cheer you up."

"That's very kind of you," Grace said after several shaky breaths. "I'm not sure I'm ready to go out in public, but perhaps that would be better than coming to your cottage and simply sobbing."

"Ring me if you change your mind," Bessie said. "Otherwise, I'll see you there."

"Thank you, Aunt Bessie," Grace said.

"Oh, before I forget," Bessie added, trying to sound offhand. "I've been ringing Hugh's flat and he isn't answering. I don't suppose you know if he's at home or not?"

"But that's just it," Grace replied. "He agreed to let me stay with him because the lease on the flat I was sharing ran out today, the first of January. I'm at Hugh's, but he isn't here and I have no idea where he is." She began to cry again, leaving Bessie frowning down the line at her.

"Now really, Grace," she said sternly. "Crying won't help the situation. We all need to work together to help Hugh."

"I'm not sure I want to help him," Grace said between sobs. "I'm still so cross with him that I can't even think straight."

"Yes, well, we'll talk it all through tomorrow," Bessie said soothingly. "I'll ask the manager if we can have the little room in the back so we won't be disturbed."

"That's probably a good idea. I can't imagine I'll be able to talk about Hugh without crying."

"Yes, well, we'll have to see how we get on, won't we?" Bessie replied. "I'll see you at two."

She disconnected and sighed deeply. "She's at Hugh's flat. He'd agreed to let her stay when the lease ran out on the flat she was sharing in Lonan, so she's there, but he isn't."

"I don't suppose there's anyone else you can think of to ring?" John asked.

Bessie shook her head. "I'm afraid she was my last resort. Doona, was Hugh especially friendly with any of the other constables?"

"Not really," Doona said. "Especially not since he's been with Grace."

"Where did he used to spend his time, before he met Grace?" John asked.

"I have no idea," Bessie replied. "I know he met Grace in Douglas, but I don't know if he had a regular place he went down there or if it was just a chance meeting."

John frowned and got to his feet. "I'm going to start by just driving around Laxey, then. Maybe I'll spot his car. If either of you can think of any likely places for me to look, please let me know immediately."

Bessie and Doona both nodded. Bessie walked John to the door, trying to tell herself not to worry. Hugh was upset, but he wasn't about to do anything stupid, she assured herself. She opened the door and then gasped. Hugh was standing on the step outside, still in his suit from the previous evening, looking as if he hadn't slept since she'd last seen him.

CHAPTER 7

"*H*ugh," Bessie gasped. "Where have you been? Are you okay? You look exhausted. Come in out of the cold."

John stepped backwards to let Hugh in. Bessie grabbed his arm and gently pulled him into the kitchen.

"I wasn't sure, that is, I don't think," Hugh sighed and took a deep breath. "I feel as if I'm not really welcome anywhere," he said, his voice shaky.

"But Doona rang you a dozen times to invite you to come tonight," Bessie said. "I'm not sure what else we could have done."

"Oh, I haven't really been checking my phone," he said apologetically. "That is, I haven't been back to my flat, and the battery in my mobile died hours ago."

"Well, you're pale and you look exhausted. Come and sit down and I'll make you some tea," Bessie told him.

John took Hugh's coat from him and then removed his own. They both sat down with Doona while Bessie refilled the kettle.

"We had Chinese for tea," Bessie said. "I can warm up whatever you'd like. Or I can just warm it all up," she added, laughing.

"I'm not really hungry," Hugh muttered, staring at his hands, which were folded on the table in front of him.

Bessie stopped what she was doing and stared at the man. In all the years she'd known Hugh, she'd never known him to not be hungry.

Doona caught her eye and Bessie could see how concerned her friend was for the man. This would never do.

"I'll just make you some toast, then," Bessie said. "A few slices of toast with honey will be just the thing with your tea."

"You mustn't fuss over me," Hugh said. "I'm sure I can't eat."

Bessie ignored him and slid some bread into her toaster. While she bustled around the kitchen, finding the honey and a jar of strawberry jam, Doona rubbed Hugh's back. After a few minutes, Bessie set tea and toast in front of Hugh and then sat down next to him.

"There now," she said soothingly. "You'll be able to manage at least that much and it will make you feel much better."

Hugh didn't speak as he sipped the tea and nibbled listlessly on the toast. He didn't bother to add jam or honey, and Bessie wasn't feeling any less concerned about her young friend when he finally finished the first piece.

"I know you're upset about everything that happened at Thie yn Traie," she said. "But you have to keep your strength up."

"Inspector Lambert thinks I killed that girl," Hugh said morosely.

"What gives you that idea?" John asked.

"Da, er, one of the, er, someone rang me up and told me," Hugh eventually spit out. "But I won't say who."

John nodded. "Whatever Inspector Lambert thinks, we all know you didn't do it," he said. "Don't waste your time worrying about what she thinks."

Hugh shrugged. "I suppose I don't mind going to prison," he said miserably. "It isn't as if Grace is ever going to speak to me again."

"Now don't be silly," Bessie said sharply. "Grace might still be a little bit angry, but she's also worried about you. She loves you and she'll come around eventually. I'm having tea with her tomorrow and I intend to straighten her out on a few things."

"I should have proposed at Christmas," Hugh said. "Now I'm afraid I've ruined everything."

"It will all come right in the end," Bessie said firmly. "You just need to give it a bit of time. And while you're waiting, you can help us work out who killed Gennifer."

"I wish I knew," Hugh replied. "It could have been anyone. She was a horrible woman."

Bessie felt slightly better as Hugh spread a bit of jam on his second piece of toast. "I'll just heat up a bit of sweet and sour chicken," she suggested. "I know that's one of your favourites."

Hugh shrugged. "I'm not really hungry," he repeated.

"But it will just go to waste in my refrigerator," Bessie said. "You're doing me a favour if you can manage to eat some of it."

"I suppose I can try," Hugh conceded.

"We were just talking about motive, means and opportunity," Doona told the man while Bessie got to work. "We've concluded that everyone had the means and opportunity. Pushing someone off a cliff isn't that difficult."

"She was stabbed first," Hugh said.

"Where did you hear that?" John demanded.

"I can't tell you that, sir," Hugh replied. "I don't want to get anyone in trouble."

John nodded. "That's fair enough," he said. "As much as I don't like the idea of my constables talking about active investigations with suspects, I do appreciate that they are looking after one of their own."

"She was stabbed?" Doona echoed now.

Hugh nodded. "It was one of the knives from the kitchen there, so that's no help in identifying anyone, though."

"And no fingerprints?" Bessie asked.

"No," Hugh said.

"It was cold. It wouldn't have been surprising if whoever it was put gloves on when they went outside," John said thoughtfully.

"Gennifer wasn't wearing gloves when they found her, was she?" Doona asked. "From what I could see from where we were, she was just wearing the dress she'd worn to the party. She didn't have a coat on, either."

"I don't know anything about that," Hugh said. "D, er, my source didn't say anything about the, er, body."

"So when did you leave the party and how long were you gone?" John asked.

"I left at about ten past eleven," Hugh said. "And I was gone for maybe twenty or twenty-five minutes. I wasn't in any hurry to get back."

"Where did you go?" was John's next question.

"I wandered around for a bit and then I thought I wanted to go outside and get some fresh air. Actually, I thought about just walking home. It would have been a long walk, but it might have been worth it."

"But you didn't," Doona commented.

"No, it was really cold, wet, and windy outside. I didn't even stay out there for very long. I went out the door by the garages and walked a short distance and then turned around and went back inside. I hadn't thought to grab my coat or anything," Hugh said.

"Who did you see while you were walking around the house?" John asked next.

"Just about everyone," Hugh said with a shrug. He held up a hand as John opened his mouth. "I know it's important and that I might have seen something relevant, but I wasn't really paying attention. I felt awful about Grace and I was trying to work out how I could make it up to her, and I was, well, I was trying to avoid Gennifer. I wasn't interested in anyone else."

"Did you see Gennifer?" John asked.

"No, but that's because I avoided where she'd be," Hugh said.

"How did you know where she'd be?" Bessie demanded.

Hugh flushed. "I, that is, er, um." He took a deep breath, his face bright red. "At the party earlier, when she walked away with George, before she left she whispered in my ear. She told me to meet her at half eleven by the front door and she'd, well, um, anyway, she told me to meet her."

"So you left a few minutes before this arranged meeting and deliberately didn't go towards the front door?" John checked that he'd understood.

"Exactly," Hugh said. "I went towards the back of the house and the garages and stayed as far from the front door as I could."

"And you didn't see Gennifer at all," Doona repeated.

"No, and I didn't pay much attention to who else was wandering around. Inspector Lambert wanted me to go through every minute of the time and tell her exactly who I saw, but I simply couldn't do it. I was watching for Gennifer or Grace. The Queen could have stumbled past me and I wouldn't have noticed."

"And then you went back to the party and talked to me," Bessie said. "And we all waited for midnight."

"And then Nigel announced that Gennifer was missing and I helped with the search. I have to say, I was really hoping I wouldn't find her," Hugh said. "She terrified me. I mean, I'm sorry she's dead, but I'm not sorry I won't have to see her again."

"And where have you been since the party?" John asked.

Hugh shrugged. "I told Grace she could stay at my flat, and I didn't think she'd want to see me. I can't talk to her now; not until someone is arrested for the murder. I'm too afraid that she might think I did it."

"Grace knows you better than that," Bessie said softly.

"I don't know. She was so upset about what went on at the party; who knows what she thinks?"

"I'm going to see her tomorrow," Bessie reminded him. "I'll talk to her and find out what she's thinking. Whatever it is, I'm sure she knows you didn't kill Gennifer. She's just confused and upset."

"She isn't the only one," Hugh said.

Bessie put a steaming plate of food in front of the man and handed him a fork. "Eat. You'll feel better."

Hugh gave Bessie a weak smile and took a tentative bite. Once he'd eaten a few more, Bessie sat back down next to him.

"So where did you sleep last night?" she asked gently.

"I didn't really, I mean, I stopped in a car park in Ramsey for a little while and dozed off, but mostly I just drove around and thought. I drove down to Port Erin and walked on the beach today. It was dry down there, even if it was cold."

Bessie shook her head. "You need food first and then sleep, lots of it."

"I can't go back to my flat," Hugh protested. "And I don't want to worry my parents by showing up like this."

Bessie knew that Hugh had a somewhat difficult relationship with his parents anyway. "You'll stay here, of course," she said firmly. "You can sleep in the spare room or on the couch, whichever you prefer."

"I can't impose on you like that," Hugh said. "Not when I'm the chief suspect in a murder investigation."

"It's no imposition," Bessie said, trying to convince herself as much as Hugh. "This way we'll be able to keep track of you. Besides, maybe you'll be able to remember more about what happened while you were walking around once you've had some sleep."

Hugh shrugged. "I don't think sleep will help with that, but if you're really sure, I'd be hugely grateful for a place to stay."

"Of course I'm sure," Bessie said stoutly. "And when I see Grace tomorrow I'll ask her if you can drop by the flat and collect some of your things. You'll want clean clothes and the like, I imagine."

Hugh nodded. "But I don't want to see Grace. Not until everything is worked out."

"You're too stubborn for your own good," Bessie told him. "Grace will be on your side once she stops being so upset."

"I wish I could believe that," Hugh said.

Bessie was sure she could see tears in the young man's eyes. She reached over and patted his back. "It will all work out in the end," she told him. "Just wait and see."

"If I get Grace back, I'm going to propose right away," Hugh said. "And I'm going to insist that we get married as soon as it can be arranged. I'm not risking losing her again."

"Yes, well, let's focus on working out what happened to Gennifer before we worry about all of that," Bessie said.

John spent several more minutes asking Hugh questions, but the young man wasn't able to help any more than he already had.

"I think I'd like to go up to the guest room and get some sleep," he said when John had finally sat back in his chair with a sigh. "Would it be a problem if I had a quick shower first? I didn't get one today and I feel as if I'm awfully smelly. I'd hate to get into bed like this."

Bessie nodded. "By all means," she said hastily, "have a shower."

"While you're doing that, I'll run home and find some old pyjamas and maybe some jeans and T-shirts that should fit you," John said. "I did a clear-out when I was moving, but I put everything into rubbish bags and never managed to get them to a charity shop. You're welcome to the lot."

"That's very kind of you," Hugh said, tears springing into his eyes.

"You haven't seen what's there yet," John said with a laugh. "None of it's stylish and all of it has been well worn, but at least you won't have to put that suit back on."

Hugh stood up and headed for the stairs. "Thank you all for this," he said. "Especially you, Aunt Bessie."

The trio at the table watched and listened as he climbed the stairs. After several minutes of banging noises, they heard the shower turn on.

"I'd better go and get those clothes," John said.

Bessie let him out. While she was doing that, Doona got to work on the washing-up, sighing as she scraped at least half of Hugh's dinner into the bin.

"We'd better get to work on this murder," Bessie said as she watched. "Otherwise young Hugh will starve to death."

Doona left a short time later, and John didn't even come in when he returned with the three bags of clothes for Hugh. "I wish I could invite Hugh to stay with me," he told Bessie. "But it would be awkward under the circumstances."

Bessie understood completely. Hugh was under investigation for murder, and John was his supervisor and a police inspector. Having Hugh as a houseguest would probably get him into trouble with the Chief Constable and it would certainly get people talking.

The bags weren't heavy, although they were somewhat awkward to carry. It took Bessie three trips to get them all up the stairs. She could still hear the shower running, but as she tapped on the door, it stopped.

"I've left the things from John in the guest bedroom," Bessie called through the door. "Get yourself to bed and I'll see you in the morning."

"Good night," Hugh called back. "And thank you again."

"Now that's enough of that," Bessie said.

Back downstairs, she checked that the kitchen had been thoroughly tidied and then settled into the sitting room with a book. There was little point in trying to get herself to bed until Hugh was out of the way. It was difficult for her to concentrate on the story she'd chosen as Hugh made an incredible racket above her head, but she did her best.

"You've lived alone for too long," she said softly as she finally gave up on the book and settled back in her chair. She'd amuse herself by trying to work out what the man could possibly be doing that was so noisy, she decided. As tired as she was, however, after only a few moments she drifted off to sleep. She woke some time later, stiff from the awkward position she'd been sitting in. After looking around guiltily to make sure no one had noticed her impromptu nap, Bessie quickly headed up the stairs. She was ready for bed within minutes and asleep as soon as her head touched the pillow.

It felt like only a few minutes had passed when Bessie looked at the clock and groaned softly. It was only half five, but there was little chance of her falling back to sleep now. Hugh's loud snoring had woken her up and no matter how much she tried to ignore it, she couldn't. She sighed and pushed back the duvet. With so much to get done today, an early start wasn't a bad thing, even though she was still quite tired. All too aware of her sleeping guest, Bessie showered as quickly and quietly as she could and then headed down to get some breakfast.

After a moment of indecision, she set a pot of coffee to brew before she reached for the bread. Another bout of uncertainty had her shaking her head at herself. She was normally a very decisive person, at least about breakfast. But now that the idea was in her mind, she couldn't stop thinking about pancakes. Besides, she told herself, maybe a treat like that would encourage Hugh to eat something. Of course, if she was going to make pancakes, she'd have to wait until Hugh was up and about. As it wasn't much past six, that could be some time, she realised. With a sigh, she grabbed an apple from the fruit bowl and waited for her coffee. After she'd finished her first cup, she felt warmer and slightly more awake, although no less hungry. The apple wasn't doing much for her, either, but she finished it dutifully.

A morning walk held little appeal, as it was grey and wet outside, but Bessie forced herself into her Wellington boots and waterproofs. She didn't have to walk far, but she knew her routine was part of what kept her healthy and fit, even at her age. Walking quickly, she took several deep breaths of the fresh sea air. There was little wind for a change and after she'd reached the holiday cottages, she decided to press on a little bit further. She walked as far as the stairs to Thie yn Traie, frowning as she spotted the yellow police tape that still roped off a large section of the beach just beyond the steps. This visual reminder of Gennifer's murder had her feeling sad and turning for home.

Hugh was still snoring loudly after she'd finished drying off. She didn't want to wake him, not after he'd missed getting any sleep the previous night, but she really wanted her pancakes. She was pacing around the kitchen, trying to decide what to do, when the phone rang. Grateful for the interruption, she snatched it up.

"Bessie? It's Mary," the voice on the other end said. "I knew you'd be up. You always are."

"Indeed," Bessie replied, happy to hear from the woman who was first on the list of calls she needed to make. "What can I do for you?"

"I don't know," Mary said, sounding a bit desperate. "I'm just so worried about everything. I can't sleep, wondering what happened to poor Gennifer. I'm afraid that one of Elizabeth's friends had something to do with the girl's death, and Elizabeth is still staying at Thie yn Traie with them. I'm just beside myself and I can't work out what to do next."

"Why don't we get together and talk," Bessie suggested. "Are you not still staying at Thie yn Traie?"

"No, George wanted to get back to Douglas right away," Mary told her. "Elizabeth and her friends are there, as they've been told they can't leave the island, but I think I already said that."

"What are you doing for lunch?" Bessie asked. "I have to meet a friend for tea this afternoon, but we could meet for lunch before that, if you'd like."

"Give me a minute," Mary said. "I just need to make sure that George didn't make plans without telling me."

While she was gone, Bessie was happy to hear the upstairs shower turn on. Once she'd finished with Mary, she could start on the long-awaited pancakes.

"He's having lunch in Port St. Mary with some people who want to build a new industrial complex down there," Mary told her when she returned. "So lunch would be wonderful."

They agreed to go to one of Bessie's favourite places. "I hope half eleven isn't too early," Bessie said apologetically. "But I'm meeting someone for tea at two and I can't be late."

"It's fine," Mary assured her. "I'd agree to just about anything to see you. I'll collect you at eleven-fifteen so that we have plenty of time."

Bessie disconnected and immediately began working on breakfast. She decided to add bacon and toast to the menu. The pancake batter was resting when Hugh came down, looking almost like his old self, in spite of the borrowed and slightly tattered jeans and faded T-shirt he was wearing.

"I smell bacon and coffee," he said, greeting Bessie with a huge hug. "I'm almost hungry, as well."

"I hope you slept well," Bessie said as she started cooking pancakes.

"I did," Hugh said. "And I am feeling a lot better for it. I was feeling quite sorry for myself and rather hopeless last night, but now I'm determined to help John work out what really happened to Gennifer, before Anna Lambert locks me up."

"Anna's not going to be locking anyone up," Bessie said soothingly. "Not with John, Doona, and me on the case. We'll soon have the killer behind the bars and you'll be on your way to planning your wedding."

"I hope so," Hugh said fervently.

Bessie slid a stack of pancakes onto a plate and added bacon. Handing the plate to Hugh, she passed him a full toast rack. "Sit down and eat," she urged him. "I'll just make myself a few pancakes and then I'll join you."

Hugh poured a generous helping of maple syrup over his breakfast and dug in. Bessie was relieved to see him eating with something like enthusiasm. By the time she joined him, his plate and the toast rack were both nearly empty.

"I'm suspended without pay," Hugh told Bessie between bites. "I don't even know what to do with myself today."

"John thought you might be at loose ends," she told the man. "He brought over a huge pile of old case files for you to go through. They're all what he called cold cases, some of the very earliest ones he could find. He's been going through them at home himself, but he thought you might like to take a look. He suggested that you might write up your ideas about each case as you go along and then you and he can compare notes."

"Really?" Hugh asked. "I really hit the jackpot when he was reassigned to Laxey. Of course, he's spoiling me for any other boss, ever."

Bessie nodded. The way that John treated his staff always impressed her. "I have to go into Ramsey for a few hours this afternoon. I can bring you back anything you need."

"I think I'm okay for now," Hugh said with a shrug. "John included a few toiletries in the bags he brought for me. What I really want to do is get back into my flat for an hour, but I won't do it if it might upset Grace."

"I'll be talking to her later. I'm sure we'll be able to work something out."

"If not, John's given me more than enough to survive on for a few days," Hugh said. "I was worried that he might not stand by me, with Inspector Lambert seeming so convinced I did it, but he's been great about everything."

"Let me make you some more pancakes," Bessie suggested as she cleared Hugh's empty plate.

He looked at it in surprise and then shook his head. "That's okay. They were delicious, but I'm quite full up."

"Well, there's leftover batter, so I'll just put it in the refrigerator and we can have pancakes again tomorrow. That is, unless you get hungry for them between now and then."

Hugh helped Bessie with the washing-up, and then he settled in with his case files while Bessie read a book. At eleven, she went upstairs to get ready for her afternoon out.

"There's plenty of food in the refrigerator for lunch," she told Hugh. "I'll cook something for our evening meal when I get back."

"Um, hm," Hugh muttered, barely glancing up from the file he was reading.

Bessie smiled to herself as she went into the kitchen to wait for Mary. John's old case files seemed to be just what Hugh needed.

Mary was right on time, but Bessie was surprised to see a driver climb out of the car when it arrived. She was out of the house and locking up behind herself before he reached her.

"Right this way, madam," he said with a small bow.

He held open a door at the back of the car and Bessie climbed in. Mary grinned at her. "I hope you don't mind," she said. "I usually drive myself, but I'm still a bit too tired to want to have to concentrate that hard. Anyway, parking isn't easy in Ramsey, especially on a Saturday. This way I don't have to worry about that."

As Bessie didn't drive, she never gave parking a single thought. "Of course I don't mind," she told her friend. "I'm just grateful to you for collecting me so I didn't have to get a taxi."

Mary kept the conversation light on the short drive, presumably for the benefit of the young man behind the wheel. "I'll ring you when I need collecting," she told him as he helped them both from the car.

"Very good," he replied.

"I'm starving," Mary told Bessie as they made their way into the nearly empty restaurant. "I don't remember eating after our tea yesterday and I know I didn't have any breakfast this morning. I felt too unwell to eat, but now I'm hungry enough to eat just about anything."

Bessie requested a quiet corner, which the hostess was easily able to find. "It will get busier later," she warned them as she seated them. "I'll try to keep people out of the corner, but once we get full up everywhere else, I won't have a choice."

"That's fine," Bessie assured her. "And we're very grateful for that."

Mary tried to press a note into the girl's hand, but she shook her head. "I'd do the same for anyone who asked nicely," she said. "Anyway, Aunt Bessie's a regular here."

Mary laughed. "I should have known. Everyone knows you."

Bessie shrugged. "When you've lived your whole life in one place, you do get to meet quite a few people," she said.

They placed their orders before Bessie got down to business. "I'm afraid Inspector Lambert is quite suspicious of young Hugh Watterson," she told Mary. "Of course, we all know he would never have hurt Gennifer, but the inspector isn't convinced. Obviously, I'm doing everything I can to help the poor man."

"I don't know him as well as you do," Mary replied. "But I know him well enough to know that he didn't kill Gennifer. If there's anything I can do to help, please just ask."

"I do have some questions for you," Bessie said.

"Ask away," Mary replied easily. "I'll tell you whatever I can."

"John Rockwell was wondering where you found the staff for the party," Bessie began with the easiest of her queries.

"Most of them came from our house in Douglas," Mary said. "We used an agency in Peel to supply most of the waiters and waitresses and a few other helpers around the place."

Mary dug around in her handbag for a moment and then pulled out a business card. "This is the agency we used," she told Bessie. "They're very good and I've never had a problem with anyone they've sent whenever I've used them."

Bessie tucked the card into her bag as their waitress delivered their drinks. After a sip, Bessie moved on to her next question. "At one point in the evening, George invited all of his guests and their wives to go with him somewhere. Do you know where they went?"

Mary sighed. "He wanted to show off the wine cellar," she said.

"Only a few of them cared at all, and none of the wives were interested, but the house came with an extensive wine cellar that's stocked with some very valuable bottles."

"I'm surprised Mr. Pierce didn't take the wine with him," Bessie said.

"He said he didn't want anything from the house here," Mary told her. "They left food in the pantry and clothes in the wardrobes." She shook her head. "It's all very sad."

"But where is the wine cellar?" Bessie asked, knowing she'd not ever seen anything in the house that looked like an entrance to a cellar.

"The door is near the garage wing," Mary told her. "It was only a short walk for everyone and it only took a few moments for all of the guests to pretend to be impressed."

Bessie smiled. "I'm sure some of them were genuinely impressed," she said.

"Maybe," Mary shrugged. "Anyway, one of the wives tripped on her skirt and managed to knock a couple of bottles onto the floor. Of course they shattered. None of them were valuable, but George stayed behind to clear them up while everyone else went back to the party. That's why he missed midnight."

"George cleared them up?" Bessie asked, unable to picture the man doing a job like that himself.

Mary laughed. "I should have said George stayed behind to supervise someone else as they cleaned up the mess," she clarified.

Bessie nodded. Before she could speak again, the food was delivered and she and Mary concentrated on enjoying their lunch. Mary told Bessie about her grandchildren and Bessie insisted on seeing the latest photographs as they ate. When the waitress had cleared their empty plates, Bessie moved the conversation back to the murder.

"John told me that you never left the room after Gennifer did," Bessie said. "But he also thinks you were the only person who didn't, aside from himself."

"He's probably right," Mary said. "People were everywhere in the house. I found empty glasses in half a dozen rooms the morning after.

Everyone simply made themselves at home, especially Elizabeth's friends, as they are staying at the house."

"I'd really like to learn more about them," Bessie said.

"You think one of them killed Gennifer."

Bessie hesitated and then nodded. "I can't imagine anyone else having a motive," she said.

"That's what I've been thinking as well," Mary replied. "I don't really know any of them well. Elizabeth has never invited any of them to the island before. You should talk to her."

"I'd like to, but I'm not really meant to be visiting Thie yn Traie at the moment, not during an active murder investigation."

"Why don't you have dinner with her?" Mary suggested. "I'll arrange it for tonight if you'd like."

Bessie thought for a minute. Both lunch and tea out were extravagant; having dinner out as well seemed too much. But she was too eager to talk to Elizabeth to pass up the opportunity. "If she's free, I'd be very grateful," she told Mary.

Mary made a quick phone call. Bessie tried not to overhear, but it did seem as if the woman was having some trouble persuading her daughter. Eventually, Mary ended the call. "It's all arranged. I thought, since you're already in Ramsey, that the little pub next to the bookshop would do, but if you'd rather go somewhere else, just say so."

"The pub is fine," Bessie said. They had good food and quiet tables in a small room at the back. Bessie would make sure she was early enough to secure one of them.

"I'd better get back to Douglas before George gets himself into any trouble," Mary said, rising to her feet. "We're trying to get the house ready to go on the market, and he's just in the way, mostly."

Bessie chuckled as she stood up to give the woman a hug. "Thank you for everything," she said. "I hope Elizabeth is as helpful as you were."

Mary shrugged. "I'll ring her later and make sure she understands how important it is that she help you. I can't promise that will make any difference, though."

As Mary walked away, Bessie glanced at her watch and frowned. It was only a few minutes to two and the other restaurant was some distance away. She drained her drink and waved to the waitress. "I need to pay for my lunch," she told the girl.

"Oh, the other lady took care of it," the girl told her. "She paid for both of you and left an incredibly generous tip as well. I hope you bring her back again soon."

Bessie sighed. She hadn't intended for Mary to pay for lunch. It was too late to argue now, so Bessie simply thanked the waitress and headed out. If she walked quickly enough, she might not be too late for her meeting with Grace.

CHAPTER 8

*G*race was sitting along the back wall of the restaurant, staring at the menu, when Bessie walked in. She hurried over to the girl, and when Grace looked up, pulled her out of her seat into a hug. Tears were streaming down Grace's face as she pulled back from Bessie and sat back down.

"You look as if you haven't slept in days," Bessie said, her voice full of concern.

"I feel as if I haven't as well," Grace replied softly. She wiped her eyes and swallowed hard. After a moment, she managed to force a small smile onto her face. "It's nice to see you, Aunt Bessie," she said.

"It's nice to see you, too," Bessie replied. "We have so much to discuss, but first, let's order tea and something sweet."

"I'm not very hungry," Grace told her. "Maybe just tea for me."

"Nonsense," Bessie said. "If you don't know what you want, have the chocolate gateau. Chocolate can't fix everything, but it can definitely make things better."

Grace's smile looked more genuine now. "Maybe," she said.

When the waiter appeared, Bessie ordered tea and chocolate gateau for both of them and Grace didn't object. Once he'd delivered their drinks, Bessie settled back in her chair and studied the girl.

"This is taking a huge toll on you, isn't it?" she asked gently.

"It's stupid, really," Grace said, frowning down at her cup of tea. "I got jealous of that woman, and now she's dead and I feel guilty for thinking such horrible things about her. I don't know where Hugh is and even if I did, I don't think I want to talk to him. It's all just a horrible mess. I have to go back to work on Monday and I don't know if I'll be able to stop crying long enough to teach a lesson." Fresh tears were flowing down her face when she finished speaking.

Bessie patted her hand and then handed her a tissue from the pack in the handbag. "First of all, we were all thinking horrible things about Gennifer. They say you mustn't speak ill of the dead, but she simply wasn't a nice person and I won't say she was. Secondly, I do know where Hugh is and if it's any comfort to you, he doesn't want to see you until the murderer is found. He thinks you think he killed Gennifer."

"He's such an idiot," Grace said, affection in her voice. "Of course I know he didn't kill her. I'm just not convinced that he wasn't attracted to her."

"She was beautiful and she threw herself at him. He may have handled that badly, but I suspect it was a new experience for him," Bessie said. "But he loves you and you should never doubt that."

"Then why hasn't he asked me to marry him?" Grace demanded. "I thought he was waiting for Christmas, but here we are on the second of January and I still don't have a ring on my finger, just like Gennifer said."

"He's terrified that you'll say no," Bessie told her.

"He really is an idiot," Grace repeated herself, all traces of affection gone from her voice.

Bessie laughed. "He's a young man with very little real experience with women," she explained. "He's fallen head over heels in love with you and he's at least as terrified as he is happy. He will get around to proposing, you just have to give him a little bit of time."

Grace shrugged. "I've been giving him time," she complained. "I'm not sure what I want to do now."

Bessie was silent as the waiter delivered their huge slices of cake.

She worked her way through the warm chocolate sponge, the rich and creamy icing and the contrasting vanilla ice cream slowly, letting Grace do the same.

"That was delicious," Grace said after she'd eaten the last bite of her serving.

"I'm glad you enjoyed it," Bessie said. "It seems to have improved your colour as well."

Grace chuckled. "You were right. It's improved my mood, too. The world doesn't look quite so bleak now as it did an hour ago."

"The police are working on solving Gennifer's murder, but at the moment it seems as if Hugh is their chief suspect," Bessie said.

"That's crazy," Grace said, shaking her head. "He's a police constable. He would never kill anyone."

"John and Doona and I are trying to help Hugh, but they've both been reassigned to other stations during the investigation because they're both suspects," Bessie continued.

"Even crazier," Grace replied. "Does that mean that Inspector Lambert is running the investigation? I didn't like her one bit."

"She is," Bessie confirmed. "Why didn't you like her?"

"She asked all sorts of questions about my relationship with Hugh that made me uncomfortable. Now that I think back, it does seem like she suspected Hugh of the murder. I didn't see it that way at the time, but now that you've said that, it makes more sense."

"Can you tell me anything that you think might help John with his unofficial investigation?" Bessie asked.

"Like what?"

"Everyone was in and out of the great room during the evening. Do you remember seeing anyone with Gennifer when you went out of the room?"

"I only went to the nearest loo and back," Grace said. "I didn't see anyone except one couple I didn't know. I think they were Mr. Quayle's friends. They were arguing about bottles of wine."

Bessie nodded. "What did you think of Elizabeth's friends?" she asked, remembering that some of them had joined Grace when she'd moved away from Hugh.

"I didn't really talk to them enough to form an impression," Grace said. "They all came over and sat with me, but they really just talked amongst themselves. One of them, Jeremy, was very kind and tried to make conversation with me, but I was too upset to be properly sociable."

"Do you think he was interested in you, or just being nice?" Bessie had to ask.

Grace blushed. "I couldn't possibly say," she exclaimed. "I'm fairly certain I'm not his type, though, considering the type of women he was at the party with."

"If you had to say who you thought killed Gennifer, who would it be?" Bessie asked.

Grace looked shocked. "I couldn't possibly, I mean, that's a job for the police, surely. I can't imagine anyone killing anyone. Are they really sure it wasn't an accident?"

"They're sure," Bessie said. "And I'd be grateful if you could think about that question for a bit. An answer might be helpful."

Grace nodded, but she didn't look convinced. "Is Hugh staying with you, then?" she asked tentatively.

"He is, although he'd like to stop at the flat to get some of his things."

"Oh, of course," Grace said quickly. "I didn't even think about that. The poor man only has the clothes he was wearing at the party. I really should just move back to Douglas. Then Hugh could have his flat back."

"But you would have to drive back and forth every day for work," Bessie said.

"Yes, and I'd hate that," Grace said with a sigh. "But it's Hugh's flat, not mine."

"I think you should stay there for now. As long as Hugh is staying with me, I can keep an eye on him," Bessie explained. "I don't think he should be on his own right now, and he doesn't want to stay with you."

"No, that would be awkward," Grace agreed. "But I have some shopping to do, so maybe you could ring him and let him know that the flat will be empty until, I don't know, maybe five? He could go over and get what he needs."

"I'll do that," Bessie agreed. "John has lent him some clothes, but I'm sure he'll feel better with his own things."

Grace insisted on paying the bill when the waiter brought it over. "You've made me feel ever so much better," she told Bessie. "Paying for your cake seems like a very small way to repay you."

"Please ring me if you think of anything that might help with the investigation," Bessie told her as they hugged again. "Or ring if you just want someone to talk to."

"I will," Grace promised. "And I'll think about who might have killed Gennifer, but I don't know if I'll get anywhere."

When she'd gone, Bessie pulled out her mobile and rang Hugh.

"Grace has gone to get some shopping and won't be back at your flat until five. She's happy for you to go and collect some of your things while she's out," she told the man when he answered.

"That's great," Hugh said. "Is she okay? Did she ask about me? Is she still really angry?"

"I'll tell you all about our conversation tonight," Bessie told him. "But she's fine and she's worried about you."

"Oh, thank goodness," Hugh exclaimed.

"I'm having dinner in Ramsey, so I won't be home until later. Please eat up all of the Chinese food in the refrigerator while I'm gone. I hope you had some for lunch."

"Oh, lunch, I forgot," Hugh replied. "I've been caught up in these cold cases and I never even thought about it. I'll have something in a little while."

"Make sure that you do," Bessie said sternly. "You need to keep your energy level up."

"Yes, Aunt Bessie," Hugh said dutifully.

Bessie chuckled and ended the call before she could lecture the man any further. She hoped he and Grace were both feeling better; she certainly felt more optimistic about their future together now that she'd spoken to Grace.

With a few hours to fill before her dinner with Elizabeth, Bessie decided to take a short walk. She headed out of the town centre, keeping to the pavement and heading towards the sea. It was cold but dry and she enjoyed wandering through the streets, admiring the various houses. She couldn't help but wonder what some of them were like inside. Maybe, if she ever needed to work, she should become an estate agent. They were allowed inside other people's houses all the time. It seemed the perfect job for someone as nosy as Bessie.

Time seemed to get away from Bessie as she walked. With a start, she realised that she'd gone some distance from the town centre and it was nearly time to meet Elizabeth. She was often in Ramsey to shop, but she couldn't remember the last time she'd simply walked through its streets. She'd have to do more of that when the weather improved, she decided.

Back in the familiar part of town, she hurried to the pub and asked for a table in the back. She'd only followed the host a few steps when she heard Elizabeth's voice behind her.

"There you are, Bessie," she called. "I was afraid I was late."

Bessie turned around to greet the girl and was dismayed to find that Elizabeth was surrounded by her friends.

"Oh, don't worry," Elizabeth said quickly, clearly correctly reading the expression on Bessie's face. "They've come along to have dinner themselves, but they'll sit out here and leave us alone so we can talk about whatever mum thinks is so important."

Bessie smiled. "I hope they don't mind, but I really do need to talk to you," she said.

"We don't mind," Howard said. "We just had to get out of that house for a while. And Elizabeth said the food here was good. We'll just have our dinner and then you both can join us for a few pints after you've eaten."

Bessie laughed. "I don't know about that, but thank you for the invitation."

"I've never seen such a dreary pub," Nigel said with a sigh. "Why am I not surprised?"

"Stop it, Nigel," Elizabeth scolded. "Have something to eat and try to enjoy yourself."

Nigel opened his mouth to respond and then shook his head and looked down at his shoes. After a moment, Howard spoke again. "Anyway, we'll need a table for six after you've seated them," he told the young man who was still waiting for Bessie to follow him.

"Yes, sir," the man replied.

"Oh, goodness," Bessie exclaimed. "Sorry to hold everything up."

She and Elizabeth followed him through a narrow doorway and into a tiny room. There were only four tables, seating no more than ten diners in total. He showed them to a table for two at the very back and left them with menus.

"It's too dark to read this in here," Elizabeth hissed as she looked at her menu.

"If you can't read it, I don't have a chance," Bessie said. "But I'm going to have the steak and kidney pie, so it doesn't really matter."

"If that's good, maybe I'll just have that as well," Elizabeth said. "It's certainly easier than getting eye strain trying to see what else is on offer."

With food and drinks ordered, Bessie tried to work out how to politely ask what she wanted to know. Elizabeth watched her for a moment and then laughed.

"I'm going to guess that you have a load of questions for me about my friends and you're trying to decide how to ask," she said. "You must think they're the best suspects for Gennifer's murder."

"Would you agree?" Bessie asked.

Elizabeth shrugged. "I don't know any of them all that well," she said. "I went to uni with them, but I wasn't there very long. I mean, Howard and I have been a couple for a few months, but we aren't serious or anything. Most of the others are his friends and he invited them across for the party."

"Would you mind telling me about each of them?"

"I suppose not," Elizabeth said. "As much as I know, anyway. Where would you like me to start?"

"Oh, anywhere," Bessie said. "I'd like to talk about Gennifer as well, but let's leave her for last."

"Okay, well, let's see, let's start with Bruce. He's a dear sweet man. I'm sure he has a little bit of a thing for me, but he's so not my type that it doesn't need mentioning. His father owns a chain of grocery shops and he'll inherit millions eventually, but that won't improve his looks, will it?"

"I don't know," Bessie commented. "I think a lot of women would find millions of pounds incredibly attractive, no matter to whom they were attached."

Elizabeth giggled. "Yes, well, I'm not that type. Anyway, he works for his father, when he feels like working, which isn't often. Is that enough?"

"How did he feel about Gennifer?"

"I suppose he might have felt slighted, as she was always hanging all over one man or another but never gave him a second look, but if he did, he never mentioned it."

"That doesn't seem much of a motive for murder," Bessie murmured.

"No, but I suppose it could have been. Anyway, let's move on to Jeremy, who is the sweetest guy I know. He's smart and he's kind and he's funny and he's gorgeous. He has a great job and he makes loads of money, and he's due to inherit a fortune one day as well."

"But you aren't interested in him," Bessie added.

Elizabeth wrinkled her nose. "Maybe in another ten years, when I'm ready to get married and have kids, he'll be what I want. But he's just too nice for now."

"And did Gennifer agree with your opinion of him?"

"Gennifer used to try to get him into bed, but he always politely refused. She gave up some time back, although I'm sure she'd have jumped at the chance if he'd given it to her. There is something incredibly sexy about the man, but I don't know what it is."

Bessie nodded. "What about Howard?" she asked.

"Oh, he's meant to be my boyfriend, but it isn't anything serious.

We have fun together when we see each other, but I'm sure he's seeing other women when he's in London."

"And that doesn't bother you?"

"Not really," Elizabeth shrugged. "We're both too young to be tied down. I'll worry about a serious relationship when I'm thirty."

"Was he seeing Gennifer, do you think?"

"Oh, no, they went out before we even met. He knew better than to go back to her. She treated him horribly."

"Really? How sad," Bessie murmured.

"Oh, not so badly that he'd kill her or anything," Elizabeth said quickly. "I wasn't suggesting anything like that. But I don't think Howard would have invited Nigel if he'd known that Nigel was going to drag Gennifer over with him."

"I see," Bessie said. "What does Howard do?"

"Oh, he works in banking," Elizabeth replied. "He's the second son, so he won't inherit as much as some of the others, but he's good at his job and he gets paid well."

"So tell me about Nigel," Bessie suggested.

"He's from old money, although I don't think there's really all that much of it anymore. Even so, he seems to think he's a good deal better than the rest of us. I don't know him very well, but Howard said something about how he'd never seen him so hung up on a girl before."

"Meaning Gennifer?"

"Yeah, he'd really fallen for her, I think, and she just loved torturing him with it," Elizabeth said.

"He seemed really angry at the party," Bessie remarked. "He made a number of threats to her."

"He didn't mean anything, though. He would never have hurt her, as crazy as he was about her."

Bessie didn't argue; she'd wait and bring the conversation back around to Nigel again later. "So tell me about the girls," she said.

"Sarah is good fun, but she's not very bright. She's been mooning after Bruce for years, I gather, but he isn't interested, probably because she's simply too available. She lives in London, primarily off of a trust fund, although she does have her own little shop that must pay some of her bills, I suppose."

"And Emma?"

"I've barely spoken to her," Elizabeth said. "She's very quiet and seems to almost fade into the background everywhere we go. I've seen her staring at Nigel with a weird sort of intensity, like maybe she has a thing for him, but she may just have been lost in thought and looking in his direction, for all I know. The guys all tease her about it, though, and they give Nigel a hard time about her, too."

"Can you think of any motive either of them might have for killing Gennifer?"

"If I'm right about Emma, then she might have wanted to get rid of her rival, but I can't see Nigel paying her any attention anyway. As for Sarah, I can't imagine. If she did do it, she'd have probably confessed by now anyway. She's very fond of talking about everything she does, good or bad."

"Why did Gennifer come to the party?" Bessie asked next. "I've heard she didn't like the island very much."

"Nigel invited her and she was having too much fun making his life miserable to not come. Well, that would be my guess, anyway," the girl replied. "I'm sure she didn't want to stay in London while her social circle was all here, anyway. I don't think she had many friends."

Bessie nodded. "So, if you had to pick out the murderer, who would it be?" she asked.

Their food arrived then, giving Elizabeth time to think. She took several bites before she replied to Bessie.

"Maybe one of the staff knew Gennifer from somewhere," she suggested.

"I'm sure the police are looking into that, but it doesn't seem very likely to me. If one of your friends did it, which one?"

"They aren't really my friends," Elizabeth argued. "And I'm sure I don't know them well enough to answer that."

Bessie wanted to push the issue, but she didn't want to upset the girl. On the whole, Elizabeth had been very cooperative, even if Bessie didn't think anything she'd been told was at all helpful.

"Do you really think one of them killed Gennifer?" Elizabeth asked a moment later, her voice slightly shaky.

"I think it's one possibility, for sure," Bessie replied.

"I thought the police had it almost all wrapped up."

"Maybe they do, but the last I heard, they were investigating Hugh Watterson, which is just silly."

Elizabeth nodded. "He's actually very nice, for a policeman. He's ever so polite and helpful when I get myself into trouble."

"And he couldn't possibly be a murderer, whatever the police believe," Bessie said.

"It's scary to think that there might be a murderer staying at Thie yn Traie with me, though."

"That's one of the reasons I'm trying to help John Rockwell work out what really happened that night," Bessie told her. "The sooner the killer is caught, the better."

"You should talk to everyone," Elizabeth said. "You're good at asking questions. I'm sure you could get the killer to confess if you asked them the right question."

"I'm not the police, I'm just nosy," Bessie replied.

"Let's finish up. Maybe you can talk to everyone tonight, since they're all here."

The pair finished their dinner and opted not to have pudding. One slice of cake a day was enough for Bessie, or so she tried to tell herself as Elizabeth waved away the sweets menu.

"I can't eat anything like that," she told Bessie. "Howard would disappear fast if I got fat."

"Then perhaps he doesn't truly appreciate you," Bessie suggested.

"Of course he doesn't," Elizabeth laughed. "We're just having fun."

"We're going out front to join my friends," Elizabeth told the waiter when he came back to check on them. "Just add all of this to the bill out there."

"Oh, you must let me pay my share," Bessie said.

"Don't worry about it," Elizabeth said airily. "I'm sure Nigel will end up paying for everything. He likes to make grand gestures like that and he can certainly afford to."

Bessie wanted to protest further, but again she didn't want to upset the girl. Sighing deeply, she followed her out of the room at the back and into the main building. While they'd been eating, the pub had been getting full. The noise level had increased dramatically, and it took Bessie several minutes to spot the group she was looking for in the rambunctious crowd.

"There they are," Elizabeth said in Bessie's ear. She took Bessie's arm and led her across the room to a small table where her friends were gathered. Bessie took one look at them and decided she would be wasting her time trying to speak to them that evening. While she and Elizabeth had been eating, they'd clearly been busy drinking. None of them looked as if they'd be able to manage to string a complete sentence together, let alone answer the sorts of questions Bessie wanted to ask. Clearly Elizabeth drew the same conclusion.

She shook her head and then pulled Bessie out of the building altogether. "They're all drunk. You won't learn anything tonight. What if I send them to you tomorrow, one at a time? I'll feel like Watson to your Holmes or something. Can we do that?"

Bessie nodded. "I'll be up any time after six," she said. "If you can find an excuse to send them to me, I'd be happy to talk to all of them."

"Oh, I'll think of something," Elizabeth said confidently. "Maybe you can wrap the whole case up tomorrow and they'll all be able to leave on Monday. I'm rather looking forward to getting rid of them."

"The last few days have been difficult for everyone. Hopefully it will all be over soon."

Elizabeth nodded. "You're welcome to come back and have a drink with us, if you'd like."

"No, I think I'd rather get home. I've been out all day, which isn't like me."

"Let me send you home in my car," Elizabeth said, pulling out her mobile. "We won't need it for hours yet and there's no point in you taking a taxi when my driver is just sitting around."

She made the call over Bessie's protests and then waited with Bessie until the car arrived. Before Bessie climbed in, they hugged. "Thank you for trying to work out what happened to Gennifer," she whispered in Bessie's ear. "I thought things were pretty bad when dad was in that trouble a few months ago, but this is worse. I shall have to get quite drunk if I'm going to sleep tonight."

Bessie thought about warning her not to, as there was a very real possibility that there was a murderer staying at Thie yn Traie, but she didn't want the poor girl any more worried than she already was. "Take care of yourself," she said instead.

"Oh, I will," Elizabeth assured her. "I'll start sending you people when we all get up tomorrow. Don't expect it to be early."

In the car on the way home, Bessie wondered if she should have offered to let Elizabeth stay with her. But she couldn't have left her guests on their own, and Bessie certainly couldn't accommodate them all. Besides, she was just trying to protect Elizabeth from the killer, and at this point Bessie didn't have any idea whom to suspect.

As they pulled into the small car park next to her cottage, Bessie was momentarily startled to see lights on inside her home. She'd nearly forgotten that Hugh was staying with her. Shaking her head, she thanked the driver and let herself in. As soon as she opened the door, she could hear Hugh snoring. A glance at the clock told her that it was only eight, so Hugh must have gone to bed very early.

She took a moment to tidy the kitchen, which was in much better shape than she'd expected it to be. Clearly Hugh had learned to keep Bessie's home neat when he'd visited as a youngster. She checked the refrigerator and was relieved to see that several of the food boxes were now missing. She'd have to go shopping soon if Hugh was going to be staying for long. Even if his normal extra-hearty appetite didn't return, she still needed to feed them both.

In the small sitting room, she discovered why she'd been able to hear the snoring so clearly. Hugh was sitting at the tiny writing desk in the corner with the pile of case files. One file was open and his head was resting on the papers inside. He was fast asleep and snoring away. There was no way she could just leave him there in that uncomfortable position, Bessie decided. After a moment's indecision, she headed back into the kitchen and opened the cottage door. After a moment, she slammed it shut, the wind making it even louder than she'd intended. The sound cut right through one of Hugh's louder noises, and Bessie grinned as she listened to him jumping out of his chair.

"Goodness," she said loudly as she walked into the sitting room. "I hope I didn't startle you too badly. The wind took the door right out of my hands."

"No, no, I was just, um, reading files," Hugh replied. "Did you have a good night?"

"I did, but I'm exhausted," Bessie told him. "If you don't mind, I'm going to have a very early night. We can talk tomorrow about everything I learned today."

Hugh nodded. "I might as well go up as well," he said. "I'll get ready for bed and then read for a while until I'm tired. That way I won't disturb you later."

Bessie smiled, as she'd been hoping for just that. The pair went upstairs. On the landing, Hugh touched her arm.

"Grace is okay, isn't she?" he asked, tears in his eyes.

"She's fine, and everything is going to work out in the end," Bessie assured him.

CHAPTER 9

$\mathcal{W}$hen Bessie opened her eyes at six the next morning, she was surprised that she'd managed to sleep at all. The noise coming from the guest bedroom was shockingly loud. She showered and dressed and then headed out for a long walk, hoping Hugh might wake up while she was gone. When she reached the police tape behind Thie yn Traie, she stopped and turned around. The skies were darkening and it seemed as if rain was likely. It would be good to get home. She'd only gone a few hundred paces when she heard a voice behind her.

"It's Betsey, isn't it?" someone called.

Bessie turned around and smiled at Sarah, who was slowly climbing down the stairs behind the mansion above them.

"Good morning," Bessie said. "I didn't think anyone would be awake at Thie yn Traie yet."

"No one is, except me and some of the staff. I haven't slept properly since, well, since the night of the party," she replied.

Bessie thought the girl looked surprisingly well-rested for someone who wasn't sleeping, but she kept the thought to herself. "It must have been a terrible shock to you all, losing your friend like that," she said instead.

"Oh, yes, horrible." Sarah shivered. "I actually felt better when I thought Nigel had done it, because he doesn't have any reason to kill me, but now I'm ever so worried."

"Why?"

"Oh, because Nigel has an alibi."

"He does?" Bessie asked.

"I'm sorry. I'm just all over the place today," the girl said. "Last night, when we were all drinking away our worries, Emma let it slip that she and Nigel were together from the time Gennifer left the great room until just before midnight when they came back to the party. That means Nigel couldn't have killed Gennifer, and now I don't know who did it."

"You mustn't worry yourself," Bessie said soothingly. "Were you and Gennifer particularly good friends?"

Sarah laughed. "Not hardly. Gennifer barely knew I was alive. I'm not nearly attractive enough to be friends with her, no matter how much money my father has. The only reason she ever spoke to me was because she liked to shop in my boutique. But she wouldn't be seen with me socially if she could avoid it."

"So how did you end up here for New Year's Eve?" Bessie wondered.

"Bruce invited me. I didn't realise that it was a huge party." The girl turned bright red. "Bruce asked if I wanted to go away for the weekend. I thought, that is, I didn't know." She stopped and looked down at the ground. "Everyone thought it was so very funny, the shocked look on my face when I met Bruce at the airport and they were all there, too."

Bessie felt a flood of sympathy for the poor girl and a flash of anger at Bruce. "That was cruel of Bruce," she said.

"He didn't mean to be cruel," Sarah defended him. "He just worded the invitation badly."

Bessie bit her tongue rather than argue further. After a moment the girl sighed. "You may be right," she admitted. "He may have been deliberately cruel. I've been in love with him for so many years that I don't see his faults as I should."

"There are plenty of other men out there," Bessie said. "Forget about Bruce and work on finding someone who will love you back."

"Easier said than done," Sarah told her. "Besides, Emma has given me new hope. She's been chasing after Nigel forever and she finally got him to pay some attention to her, in spite of Gennifer."

"Or maybe *to* spite Gennifer," Bessie suggested.

Sarah nodded. "I don't think Emma will care either way. Nigel is being much nicer to her now than he's ever been. Gennifer's death has been good news for her, anyway."

"Who else benefits from it?"

"The entire world," Sarah said bitterly. "She was a nasty woman and I don't think anyone will miss her. I did think Nigel might, but he's obviously already moved on."

"I'm sure her parents will miss her," Bessie said.

"Maybe, but they didn't seem too upset. They just looked like they were doing what they thought they should do."

"So if Nigel didn't kill her, who did?" was Bessie's next question.

Sarah's eyes went wide. "That's just it," she gasped. "I can't begin to imagine. It must have been an accident or something. She must have just slipped and fallen, or maybe she had a fight with one of the staff and ran out the door and off the cliff without realising it was there."

Bessie nodded. She wasn't about to tell the girl about the knife. "I hope you're right," she said.

"The police seem to think that young policeman killed her, but he didn't look like a killer to me. He looked really nice."

"He is really nice, and I promise you he didn't have anything to do with Gennifer's death."

Sarah shivered. "It's really cold down here and I think it's going to rain."

"You should get back up to the house and get warm," Bessie said. "And I must get back to my cottage."

"I wish I could go home," Sarah told her. "I don't like it here one little bit."

"Hopefully, the police will sort everything out quickly and you can be on your way," Bessie replied. She watched as the girl made her way carefully up the stairs, back towards the mansion above them. As she walked back to her own cottage, Bessie couldn't help but wonder what Sarah had wanted. Maybe she just needed someone to talk to, Bessie thought. She could only hope all of Sarah's friends felt the same way when Elizabeth sent them to speak with her.

Back at Bessie's cottage, Treoghe Bwaane, Hugh was making pancakes with the leftover batter from the previous day.

"I was just about to come looking for you," he told Bessie. "You were gone for a long time."

"I bumped into Sarah Davies, Elizabeth's friend, and we had a short chat," Bessie explained. While they ate pancakes and bacon for the second day in a row, Bessie told Hugh all about the people she'd spoken with the previous day.

"Do you think you'll learn anything from Elizabeth's friends?" he asked when she'd finished.

"It's worth trying," Bessie said. "I've already learned one thing anyway. It seems as if Nigel has an alibi."

She repeated her conversation with Sarah for the man.

"That's a shame," he said when she'd finished. "I was really hoping he did it."

"Sarah told me that Emma is in love with Nigel. It wouldn't surprise me if she was willing to lie for him," Bessie said. "I'm not crossing him off my list yet, anyway."

They tackled the washing-up together, and then Hugh said he wanted to spend more time on his case files. "I'll just stay out of your way," he told Bessie. "And when you do get company, I'll make sure I'm dead quiet."

As soon as he was settled in the sitting room with his papers, Bessie made a phone call she didn't want to make.

"Liz, it's Bessie Cubbon. I was just ringing to see how you're doing."

"Oh, Bessie, I'm, well, I'm mostly fine, although I'm not really sleeping. My doctor is keeping a close eye on me and the baby, though, and so far he isn't too worried. I'm sure I'll sleep better once the police work out who killed Gennifer."

"We all will," Bessie told her. "And that's the other reason I was ringing. I was hoping you might be able to help with the investigation. The police seem to think Hugh was involved, which is nonsense, of course. I don't suppose you know of any possible motive anyone might have had?"

"I suppose I had a better motive than most," Liz replied.

Bessie was surprised at the other woman's honesty. "But of course you didn't do it," she said.

"No, of course not, but I was almost angry enough to consider it," Liz said. "She and Bill went out for a while and she'd just dumped him when Bill and I met. For the longest time I was convinced that I was just his rebound girlfriend and that he'd soon tire of me and move on. That's why I had that flirtation with Mack Dickinson." Liz sighed deeply.

"I'm sure this is all very difficult," Bessie said.

"It's definitely that," Liz agreed. "When Bill told me that Gennifer had asked him to meet her by the front door at half eleven so they could celebrate the new year privately, I was ready to push her off the nearest cliff, I can tell you."

"She did what?" Bessie gasped.

"She asked him to meet her by the front door," Liz repeated herself.

"But Bill wouldn't do that."

"Of course not," Liz replied. "I went instead, intending to have it out with her, but she never came."

"How long did you wait for her?"

"Oh, quite a while," Liz said. "After ten minutes or so, Bill joined me and we waited together until nearly midnight. Then we went in to join in the celebration, although I didn't feel much like celebrating, I can tell you."

"I do hope you and Bill have made up now," Bessie said.

"More or less," Liz said with another sigh.

Bessie considered a dozen replies before she decided to keep it simple. "I'm sorry," she said.

"We'll work through it," Liz told her. "A lot of it is my own insecurity, especially now I'm pregnant and feel fat and frumpy. If they'd get the murderer locked up, I think we could move on more quickly."

"Please ring me if you think of anything I can do to help," Bessie told her. "Or if you just need to talk."

"Thank you, Aunt Bessie," Liz said. "I may just take you up on that."

Bessie put the phone down feeling sad. Gennifer was dead, but she was still making Liz and Bill and Grace and Hugh miserable. She got up and paced around the kitchen for a short while, finally deciding to bake something just to have something to do. A quick look through her recipe books had her digging around in the cupboards for the ingredients for snickerdoodles, an interesting sounding cookie that she'd found in one of her American cookbooks. She was mixing up the dough when someone knocked on her door.

"Howard, this is a lovely surprise," Bessie said when she found the man on her doorstep.

"Ah, yes, well, Elizabeth asked me to drop by. She found this coat in one of the spare rooms and wasn't sure if it might be yours?" He held up a large black coat that would have swamped Bessie's petite frame.

Bessie looked at it for a moment and then slowly shook her head. "It's not mine," she said.

"No, I didn't reckon it was," Howard replied.

"But as long as you're here, do come in for some tea," Bessie said. "I was just mixing up some cookies, American-style. If you can stay for a while, you can try them when they come out of the oven."

"I may as well," he shrugged. "There's nothing to rush back for at Thie yn Traie."

"Oh, dear, that doesn't sound good," Bessie said. She filled the kettle and switched it on. "You must be anxious for the police to work out what happened to Gennifer so you can all go home."

"You're right about that," he said. "We're all driving each other crazy, and some people seem to think there's a murderer loose in the house as well."

"You don't?"

"I think that young policeman did it," Howard said confidently.

"That's what the police have been suggesting and it makes sense to me. Gennifer was trying to get between him and his girlfriend and he decided it was easier to get rid of Gennifer than ignore her. I can sort of see his point. She was difficult to ignore when she wanted you."

"Elizabeth mentioned that you and Gennifer used to be a couple," Bessie said. The kettle boiled and Bessie made the tea, waiting for Howard to reply.

"It wasn't anything serious," Howard said, waving a hand. "Although I wouldn't have minded if it had been. Gennifer wasn't exactly the settling down type, though, was she?"

"I only met her very briefly, but she didn't seem like that sort to me, no."

Howard laughed. "Nigel was crazy to think he could tame her," he said. "Up until last night I thought he'd killed her, you know."

"But now you don't?"

"He was with Emma, which is weird, but she's the one who admitted it, not him."

Bessie nodded. "How long have you known Nigel?"

"Just about forever," Howard laughed again. "We went to school together from the time we were four or five until uni. He's one of my oldest friends."

"And you still thought he'd killed Gennifer?"

"Yeah, sure. Not like all planned out and everything, just spur of the moment, in the middle of a fight. Those two were always fighting. I can see Gennifer suggesting a romantic walk along the cliff and then her saying something that upset him. It wouldn't have taken much to push her off. She was wearing those really high heels. It couldn't have been hard to get her off balance."

Bessie found herself staring at the man. His description almost made it sound like he'd been there. What he'd missed out was the knife, but maybe that was deliberate, to throw her off. "You've given this a lot of thought," she said eventually, turning back to her cookie dough. She rolled the dough into balls and then rolled the balls in a mixture of cinnamon and sugar. When her baking tray was full, she slid it into the hot oven.

"I have given it a lot of thought," the man agreed. "There's nothing else to do at Thie yn Traie but think, or drink. I've done quite a lot of both."

"There's a large library," Bessie pointed out.

"I'm not much of a reader," the man replied.

Bessie knew she shouldn't hold that against the man, but she did anyway. The conversation switched to more general topics for a few minutes while the cookies baked. As she lifted hot cookies onto a plate, Bessie planned her next question carefully.

"So, tell me about your friends," she said as she put the plate of cookies on the table in front of Howard. "They all seem like very nice young people."

"Aside from Gennifer, you mean," Howard smirked. He took a few cookies and put them on his plate. "They're hot," he exclaimed.

"They should cool very quickly," Bessie assured him.

"I don't know what I can tell you. We talked about Nigel. Jeremy is everyone's friend, but he never gets close to anyone. Bruce is short and ugly and he has ridiculously high standards when it comes to who he's willing to get involved with. That's why he's single. Sarah is dumb and spoiled and she really thinks that one day she might have a chance with Bruce, which is really dumb. That just leaves Emma, who is about as bland as a person can be. I was surprised Nigel went for her, but she has been incredibly persistent and she's really pretty, in her own fragile flower sort of way."

"What about Elizabeth?" Bessie had to ask.

"She's lots of fun, but doesn't take anything seriously. Now that she's moved here for good, I doubt I'll see much more of her. It isn't like I'll be flying back and forth regularly, and she's said she doesn't like London any more."

Bessie nodded and bit into a cookie. She was surprised how much she liked it. Howard followed her example.

"These are really good," he said after he'd eaten two.

"I'm glad you like them," Bessie said. She slid a second tray into the oven. "Maybe some of your friends would like to stop over and try them," she said.

"Maybe," he said with a shrug. "But I need to get back to the house. I'm sure Elizabeth has a whole list of people she wants me to talk to about this coat."

Bessie let the man out and locked the door behind him. She hadn't even turned around when she heard Hugh coming into the kitchen.

"What are you baking?" he asked. "The whole house smells of cinnamon. I was drooling over my papers, but I didn't dare come in and interrupt your conversation."

"They're snickerdoodles, and before you ask, I don't know why they're called that," Bessie replied. "Try one."

Hugh didn't have to be told twice. "They're really good," he said around a mouthful of cookie.

"Don't talk with your mouth full," Bessie said tartly.

"Sorry," Hugh said, flushing.

As he helped himself to another snickerdoodle, someone knocked on Bessie's door.

"You'd better get back in the sitting room," she told him.

Hugh sighed. "Just when I'm getting my appetite back," he groaned.

Bessie waited until she couldn't hear his movements before she opened the door. Bruce Durrant grinned at her.

"I'm reliably informed that you have something called snickerdos and are willing to share them," he said brightly.

"Actually, they're called snickerdoodles, but I am more than willing to share," Bessie said. "Come in and have some tea as well."

Bruce sat down and looked around Bessie's small and crowded kitchen. "How long have you lived here?" he asked.

"My entire adult life," Bessie told him. "I bought the cottage when I was eighteen, although it was only two rooms then. I've extended it twice since."

"It suits you," Bruce said. "Even if it is a bit claustrophobic in here."

The kettle boiled quickly as it was still warm from earlier. Bessie prepared two cups of tea and then sat down opposite the man.

"Have a cookie," she encouraged him.

"Just the one," he said. "Because I told Howard I would."

He nibbled his way through it with a thoughtful look on his face. "It was good," he said when he'd finished. "But one is quite enough."

"So what brings you here?" Bessie asked.

"I had nothing else to do," Bruce replied with a shrug. "And Howard said you had cookies. Believe it or not, that was the most exciting thing I'd heard in days."

"And you don't even like cookies," Bessie added.

Bruce smiled. "No, but they were a good excuse to get out of the house and to talk to you."

"What shall we talk about, then?" Bessie asked.

"Murder," Bruce said dramatically.

Bessie picked up her tea and took a slow sip, leaving Bruce to speak again.

"I've heard that you don't believe that the young police constable killed Gennifer," he said after a long moment.

"I know he didn't," Bessie replied.

"I find that worrying. If he didn't do it, who did?"

"I'm sure you must have some ideas in that area," Bessie countered.

"I did wonder about Nigel, but he was busy elsewhere. Maybe Howard finally decided to get back at Gennifer for the way she'd treated him." He frowned. "But I'm not serious. None of us would have hurt Gennifer, no matter how disagreeable she was."

"Someone killed her," Bessie pointed out.

"Maybe she had a fight with one of the cooks or maids or something. She was always quarrelling with someone. Pushing her off the cliff might have just been an impulsive thing. Maybe they didn't think it would kill her. I had no idea it was high enough to kill someone, myself."

"Of course, they had to get her outside first," Bessie said. "That suggests some sort of planning."

"Maybe she arranged a rendezvous with one of Elizabeth's father's friends," Bruce suggested. "But then it all went wrong."

"Badly wrong," Bessie said.

"But seriously, if you don't suspect that constable, who do you suspect?" Bruce demanded.

"I don't know anyone well enough to suspect them," Bessie protested. "What can you tell me about your friends?"

Bruce laughed. "That's very clever," he said. "Ask me about them and see who seems like the best fit. Then you can work with your friend in the police to stitch them up and get the young constable off the hook."

"Is that what you think I'm doing?" Bessie asked angrily. "Because if it is, I have nothing further to say to you."

"Don't get all upset," Bruce replied. "I don't blame you for wanting to protect your friend. And luckily for you, I don't feel the same way about my friends. Let me tell you all about them all. Where shall I start?"

An hour later Bessie felt as if she needed a hot bath. Bruce had shared a great deal of very personal information about every one of the guests at Thie yn Traie. Bessie now knew a great deal more than she wanted to know, but none of it seemed relevant to Gennifer's murder.

"So there you are," Bruce said, sitting back with a satisfied smile on this face. "Everything I know about everyone. Has it helped you work out who to pin the murder on?"

Bessie shook her head. "Finding the killer is a job for the police," she said. "I'm just a curious bystander."

"Indeed, me too," Bruce said. "And on that note, I suppose I should head back to Thie yn Traie and send down the next victim, or should I say guest?"

Bessie flushed. "If any of the others would like to visit, I'd be happy to see them," she said. "But not for any of the reasons you seem to think."

"Yes, dear," he replied patronisingly. He strode to the door and then turned back to Bessie. "Thank you for the cookies and the chance to unload. It's been a diversion, if nothing else."

Bessie waited until he'd let himself out before she walked over and locked the door behind him.

"What a thoroughly unpleasant man," she said to herself as she did so.

"He was here for ages," Hugh complained from behind her. "All I could think about was those cookies. He'd better not have eaten them all."

Bessie had to laugh. "No worries," she assured him. "He was too busy being mean and vindictive about his friends to eat anything."

"Did he say anything especially interesting?" Hugh asked as he piled cookies onto a plate.

"Mostly it was just gossip," Bessie said with a sigh. "He seemed especially interested in telling me which of the friends had slept with one another."

"I'll bet he hasn't slept with any of them," Hugh said.

"No, he hasn't," Bessie replied. "But Sarah is very taken with him, the poor girl."

"She's cute and she seemed nice, too. He should feel lucky she's interested."

"But he thinks he's much better than she is," Bessie said. "He was very scathing about her looks and he doesn't think she's very bright, either. Mind you, he was pretty cruel about all of them. He doesn't much like anyone other than himself, as far as I could see."

"So why did he even come across for the party? Why spend time with people he doesn't like?"

"Ah, it seems young Elizabeth Quayle is the attraction," Bessie told the man. "She was the only one he said anything nice about. And he grew quite enthusiastic about her for a few moments, before I reckon he realised he was giving himself away. Then he started criticizing her for still living with her parents, but I could tell his heart wasn't in it."

"I wonder if Elizabeth knows?"

Bessie shrugged. "She mentioned it in passing, but she doesn't seem to take it seriously. I'm not going to bring it up with her again unless it becomes relevant in the murder case," she said.

She'd been so fascinated and appalled by her conversation with Bruce that she'd neglected her cookies. Now she gave the remaining batter a good stir and began to get another tray ready for the oven. She glanced over at Hugh and saw that he'd nearly cleared the plate in front of him.

"As glad as I am to see your appetite back, I think you've had quite enough cookies for now," she said firmly. "It's time for some lunch now."

"If you're busy with the cookies, I can make us both something," Hugh offered. "If it isn't anything too complicated, that is."

Bessie laughed. "I'm happy with anything, especially when I don't have to prepare it myself."

Hugh was inspecting the cupboards for ideas when the phone rang.

"Bessie, it's Doona. John and I will be over around six with pizza, if that's okay with you."

"Of course, that's fine," Bessie assured her. "I've been baking cookies, so we can have those for pudding. I think they'll be especially nice with vanilla ice cream, and I just happen to have some in my freezer."

"I'll look forward to that," Doona replied.

"I've been talking to some of Elizabeth's friends, but I don't feel as if I'm making any progress," Bessie added.

"I've been chatting with a few of my sources locally and I know John has been doing some digging of his own. When we put our heads together, I'm sure we'll come up with something," Doona said.

"I certainly hope so," Bessie replied.

"John and Doona are bringing pizza later," she told Hugh after she'd put down the phone. "Let's keep lunch fairly light."

"Soup and sandwiches?" Hugh asked.

"Perfect."

Hugh bustled around the kitchen, heating soup and making sandwiches while Bessie worked on getting the last two trays of cookies baked. Hugh had everything ready as Bessie slid the last tray out of the oven.

"This looks wonderful," Bessie exclaimed, hoping she didn't sound as surprised as she felt.

"It's just tomato soup from a tin," Hugh told her. "But I added a few herbs and spices and grated some cheese into it."

Bessie took a cautious bite. "It's delicious," she told the young man.

"I toasted the sandwich bread. I hope that's okay," Hugh said. "I like it better that way. The bread doesn't get as soggy."

"It's fine," Bessie assured him, taking a big bite of the crunchy sandwich and finding that she quite liked that as well. "You've picked up a lot of new cooking skills since the last time you stayed with me," she remarked.

"Oh, aye, Grace likes to stay in and cook most nights, and it's cheaper than eating out as well. She's taught me a lot and she has some really good cookbooks as well. They're really fun to go through. Even if you don't like the recipes, sometimes you can get ideas from the books."

Bessie nodded. "I often buy cookbooks, but I rarely try the recipes. I just enjoy looking at the photographs."

Bessie let Hugh have a few more cookies after he'd cleared both his plate and bowl, but she put the rest away for the guests she was expecting throughout the afternoon.

"I'd better hide a dozen for tonight or John and Doona will have to settle for ice cream on its own," she told Hugh.

"Just don't hide them in the sitting room with me, or you won't have any for tonight for sure," Hugh laughed.

Bessie was pleased to see him laughing and more importantly, eating again. He still looked tired and as if he was under considerable stress, but he'd improved dramatically since he'd arrived on her doorstep.

"I'm going to get back to my case files," he told Bessie after he'd done the washing-up. "There's a lot I want to talk to John about tonight with regard to, well, all of them."

"I'm glad you've found something useful to do to keep you busy," Bessie said.

The telephone rang again as Hugh left the room.

"Bessie? It's Elizabeth. I just wanted to see if you'd solved it all yet or if you still want to talk to the others."

"I'm nowhere near solving anything," Bessie told her. "I'm really just trying to gather background information in the hopes that that might help John."

"Well, I'm sure Bruce was full of loads of that sort of thing," she drawled. "He loves talking about everyone and he never holds back."

"He was very informative," Bessie agreed. "But I'd still like to see everyone else. Oh, but I did speak to Sarah this morning, so I don't need to see her again."

"Yes, she mentioned seeing you on the beach before seven. I can't imagine why she was even up, but that's Sarah for you. Okay, I'll find an excuse to send Nigel next. It will be nice to have him out of the house for a while as well."

On that curious note, Elizabeth disconnected. Bessie was left to wonder what trouble Nigel was causing at Thie yn Traie as she waited for him to arrive.

CHAPTER 10

*W*hen the knock on her door came, not much later, Bessie took a deep breath before she opened it.

"Hullo, I hope I'm in the right place. You're Bessie Cubbon, right?" Nigel asked, looking as if he didn't much care who she was.

"I am, yes," Bessie answered.

"Elizabeth asked me to bring this to you," he told her, handing her a small box.

"Oh, good, yes, thank you," Bessie said, taking the box. She set it on the counter behind her, curious as to what was in it, but unwilling to open it in front of Nigel. Whatever it was, it had worked as an excuse to get the man to Treoghe Bwaane.

"It's Nigel, isn't it? Why don't you come in for a cuppa?" Bessie suggested. "I'm sure you won't mind a few minutes away from Thie yn Traie."

"More like they'll be glad to have me out of the way for a while," Nigel muttered, but he stepped inside the cottage.

"I should imagine everyone is getting quite fed up, being stuck here at the moment," Bessie said as she refilled the kettle. "I shouldn't be surprised if you're all bickering with one another."

Nigel barked out a short laugh. "Mostly they're fed up with me," he said. "But I can't help how I feel. Gennifer was my soul mate and I'm lost without her."

Bessie busied herself with getting out plates and teacups rather than respond immediately. From what she'd seen of the couple, she certainly wouldn't have described them as soul mates.

Nigel remained silent until Bessie sat down opposite him, after she'd delivered tea and snickerdoodles to the table.

"We fought a lot," he said before picking up a cookie and giving it a suspicious sniff.

"That must have been difficult for you," Bessie said, keeping her tone neutral.

Nigel took a bite of his cookie and then washed it down with tea. "I can see why Howard was raving about these," he said. "The woman who is cooking for us up at Thie yn Traie keeps making Eton mess for pudding. I suppose that's because I went to Eton, but it gets a bit dull after the second day. These make a nice change."

He nibbled his way through his first and then took a second cookie. Bessie deliberately remained silent, waiting to see what he'd say next.

"I'm usually the life of the party," he told Bessie after a while. "But I just can't do anything right now but sit around and miss Gennifer. She was, well, she was the most beautiful woman in the world."

"She was lovely," Bessie agreed.

"And she understood me," Nigel continued. "We barely needed to speak to one another. We just understood each other's thoughts."

As they'd been barely speaking to one another at the party, perhaps that was a good thing, Bessie thought.

"You seemed very upset with her at the party," she remarked casually.

"Oh, I was. Gennifer didn't like the island, you see, and she blamed me for our being here. She was getting back at me by pretending to be interested in other men. It didn't mean anything."

"What brought you all over here, anyway?"

"Howard," Nigel laughed. "He's been sort of involved with Elizabeth for a while now, but since she's moved back here he hasn't seen much of her. I gather she'd been nagging him to visit for months. This way, he was able to bring us all with him, so he didn't have to be alone with her."

"Oh, dear, that doesn't sound good," Bessie exclaimed.

"It's just that he isn't serious about her, that's all. If he came for a weekend and it was just the two of them, well, she might start getting ideas."

Bessie stopped herself from asking what sort of "ideas" Howard was worried about. "But Gennifer wasn't happy?" she asked instead.

"That's an understatement," Nigel replied. "She changed her mind about coming when we arrived at the airport and she saw the tiny plane we'd be travelling on. I managed to talk her onto the plane, but she complained about everything, just about nonstop, from the time we left until, well, you know."

Bessie nodded. "I'm sorry. You must be heartbroken."

"I am, yes. No one else here understands how I feel. They're all still just seeing one another casually. They don't understand that Gennifer and I were serious. Her parents didn't get it either. They thought I was just another of Gennifer's friends. I tried to explain things to them, but they, well, they wouldn't listen, really."

"I'm surprised you didn't ask her to marry you," Bessie said as she reached for a cookie.

"Marriage is for our parents' generation," Nigel told her. "Gennifer and I had a connection that went beyond what a piece of paper can provide."

Bessie nodded. "How long had you been together?" she asked.

"Not long enough," was Nigel's vague reply. "Anyway, it doesn't matter if it was two hours or two days or two years. We were perfect for one another and we would have been together forever, if, well, if."

"So who do you think killed her?" Bessie asked.

The man looked at her in surprise. "How should I know that?" he demanded.

"Surely you've given the matter some thought," Bessie replied. "You were the person who was closest to her. Did you get the idea that she was afraid of anyone or worried about anything?"

Nigel shook his head. "There wasn't anything. If I'd known that she was in danger, I would have stepped in and protected her, obviously. Anyway, I thought the police had a suspect, one of the men she was talking with early in the evening? Someone told me that."

"As far as I know, the police haven't arrested anyone," Bessie said. "I suppose it's fortunate that you have an alibi."

Nigel looked surprised again and then nodded. "Yes, Emma and I were together," he said.

"That's odd, considering how involved you were with Gennifer."

Nigel flushed. "It wasn't anything," he said quickly. "I mean, me and Emma, it was just a, well, just a, I was pretty drunk, you see. She's been chasing after me for years, and I was drunk and just angry enough with Gennifer to, well, whatever."

"Did Emma realise it was just a one-off experience, or was she hoping for more?"

"You'd have to ask her that," he said, staring down at the table.

"I shall have to do just that," Bessie murmured.

"I don't suppose you saw Gennifer after she left the great room, then?" Bessie asked.

"No, I left right after she did, but I couldn't find her anywhere. Emma followed me out and helped me look and then, well, then we went back to her room for a while."

"And you didn't return to the party until nearly midnight."

"Yeah, I wanted to make sure I was there at midnight to kiss Gennifer. When I couldn't find her in the crowd, I went back out to look for her."

Bessie frowned, thinking about poor Emma.

Nigel seemed to read her expression. "Emma knew the score," he said defensively.

"And do you have any future with Emma, do you think?"

Nigel laughed. "No, I can't imagine that I do," he said. "She's a sweet girl, but not my type at all. Anyway, I can't possibly think about such things at the moment. It will be a long time before I start thinking about replacing Gennifer."

"I wonder if Emma is hoping for a different outcome," Bessie said, hoping the man might try to see things from the girl's perspective for a change.

He shrugged. "She ought to know me better than that," he told Bessie. "Anyway, when we get out of here, I'm off to New York for a few months for work. She'll probably forget all about me while I'm away. Who knows, maybe I'll meet a gorgeous fashion model and she'll mend my broken heart."

"Good luck with that," Bessie said.

"Anyway, I suppose I should be getting back. Thank you for the tea and the biscuits. I'm actually feeling better, having been able to talk about how I feel for a bit."

"I'm glad I could help." Bessie walked the man to the door and watched as he went out and climbed into his car. She recognised it as one of the fleet that George and Mary owned. Shutting the door, she turned to the small box that Nigel had given her.

"What's that?" Hugh asked from the doorway.

"I'm about to find out," Bessie said. "Nigel brought it. It's from Elizabeth, apparently."

She opened the box and pulled out something wrapped in tissue. Unwinding the tissue revealed a small figurine of a cat playing with a ball of yarn.

"It's cute," Hugh said unenthusiastically.

Bessie laughed. "It is rather cute, I suppose. I assume Elizabeth will want it back at some point, but for now it can live by the sink."

She set the ornament next to the bottle of washing-up liquid and then shrugged. "No doubt it was just an excuse to get Nigel to visit, but it does look nice there."

"You should have a cat," Hugh said. "I can just see one curled up in your sitting room, keeping your books company all day."

"It's a lovely idea, but I really don't like cats," Bessie replied. "My older sister was badly scratched by one when we were young and the whole experience put me right off the idea of ever owning one myself."

"Maybe you should get a dog," Hugh suggested next.

Bessie sighed. She could tell he was warming to the subject. "I'm quite happy on my own," she told him. "I enjoy being free to come and go as I please and would hate to be responsible for looking after any living thing, really."

"Fish?" Hugh asked.

"Not even fish," Bessie said firmly.

Hugh might have argued further if someone hadn't knocked on Bessie's door just then. Relieved to be done with that conversation, Bessie was feeling inclined to like her next visitor, whoever it might be. She swung the door open and smiled at Emma Taylor, who was shivering on the doorstep.

"Do come in. You look as if you're freezing," she exclaimed.

"I'm fine," Emma said, her teeth chattering slightly. "Only I thought I would walk over, and it's a lot colder than I realised."

Bessie shook her head. "Sit down and I'll make you some tea. That will soon warm you up."

Emma sat in the chair that Nigel had just vacated, and Bessie started more tea. "So what brings you here?" she asked the girl after a moment.

"Oh, Elizabeth needs to borrow some flour and sugar," Emma said. "She's going to try her hand at baking some biscuits for us, but apparently the kitchen is short on ingredients."

"Do you know how much of each she needs?" Bessie asked.

"Yes, I have a note." Emma handed Bessie a slip of paper that was covered in a nearly illegible scrawl.

Her recent class in paleography sometimes came in handy in unexpected ways, as Bessie worked out what Elizabeth needed. "I'll just measure everything for her when you've had your tea," she told Emma as she handed her a cup. "Have a cookie as well," she suggested, gesturing towards the plate that was still in the centre of the table.

"Oh, thank you," Emma said. She took one of the snickerdoodles and broke off a tiny bite. "It's very good," she said in a polite monotone.

"How are you holding up?" Bessie asked as she sat down across from her.

"Oh, I'm okay, just anxious to get home, you know."

143

"Yes, I'm sure you must be. Still, at least you have Nigel to keep you company," Bessie said, watching the girl closely to see her reaction.

"Nigel?" Emma blushed brightly. "I mean, we're all keeping each other company. We've no choice, really."

"Yes, but I thought someone told me that you and Nigel were a couple. I must have misunderstood." Bessie tried to look like a confused and harmless lady in her late middle age.

Emma blinked and then shrugged. "We're not," she said flatly. "He's taken Gennifer's death badly. He'll need some time to recover before he's ready for a new relationship."

"Oh dear, I have mixed it all up, haven't I?" Bessie exclaimed. "I thought someone told me that you and Nigel were already involved before Gennifer died. I thought I'd heard that you two were together while Gennifer was missing."

Emma blushed again. "We were," she muttered, looking down at the table. "But, well, that doesn't mean anything. Nigel was just mad and trying to upset Gennifer, that's all."

"But you care about him a great deal, don't you?" Bessie asked softly.

"Of course not," Emma scoffed, still staring at the table. "He's just one of the group, you know? We've all been friends for years and I think it would be best if we all just tried to stay friends instead of people getting romantically involved with one another."

Bessie nodded. "That's a very sensible attitude," she said. "Of course, Elizabeth and Howard are a couple."

"But they aren't serious," Emma told her. "They're just having fun together. Howard went out with Gennifer for a while, too, but that was casual as well."

"And Sarah is quite smitten with Bruce, isn't she?" Bessie asked.

"What a good word," Emma said, smiling. "Yes, Sarah is very smitten with Bruce, but he wouldn't sleep with her if she were the last woman on earth. It's quite sad, really. I keep encouraging her to move on, but she won't listen."

"I got the feeling that Bruce was too enamoured of Elizabeth to look at other women."

"Another excellent word," Emma said. "Yes, Bruce has been chasing after Elizabeth for a while now, but she barely notices him." She sighed. "Listen to me, I make our little group sound like a sad bunch of people chasing unrequited love. We really do enjoy each other's company, you know, at least usually."

"I'm sure it's very difficult at the moment," Bessie said.

"Yes, it is definitely that," Emma agreed. "Anyway, I should be getting back," she said. "Elizabeth is waiting for me so she can start baking."

"Oh, of course," Bessie said. She pulled flour and sugar down from the cupboard and found her scales. "So," she said causally as she worked, "who do you think killed Gennifer?"

Emma's teacup clattered into its saucer as the girl gave Bessie a shocked look. "How could I possibly know?" she asked.

"Oh dear, I didn't mean to upset you," Bessie said. "I just assumed that you'd given the matter some thought. It must be worrying sleeping at night, knowing that there is a murderer somewhere on the island."

"She must have slipped and fallen by accident," Emma said a touch desperately. "I can't believe she was murdered."

"I think the police are quite certain about it," Bessie replied. She carefully measured out flour and then poured it into a small plastic bag. "I might have suspected Nigel, if he didn't have an alibi," she said conversationally.

"Nigel wouldn't have harmed a hair on her head," Emma said bitterly.

With the sugar measured and sealed into another bag, Bessie put both items into a large bag and handed them to Emma. "There you are, I hope I've understood Elizabeth's handwriting correctly."

"I'm sure it will be fine," Emma said. "Thank you for the tea."

"You're welcome any time," Bessie told her. "If you need someone to talk to, I'm nearly always here."

"That's very kind of you, but really I just want to go home. I'm sure things will be much better at home."

"Perhaps there's still a chance for you and Nigel," Bessie said gently.

Emma shook her head. "Whatever he thought about Gennifer while she was alive, he's convinced himself now that she was the perfect woman. I don't think anyone will ever be able to take her place."

"You're all so very young," Bessie said. "You and Nigel both have a long life ahead of you and plenty of time to meet the right other person."

Emma shrugged. "What if the right other person doesn't even know you exist?" she asked in a sad voice.

Before Bessie could reply, Emma had taken the bag that Bessie had prepared and was letting herself out of the cottage. Bessie followed to lock the door behind her, her mind turning over the girl's last words in her head. Who had Emma been referring to in that comment? Surely, it couldn't have been Nigel, not after all their years of friendship and especially not after their time together on New Year's Eve. Shaking her head, Bessie turned around in time to see Hugh sneaking another snickerdoodle.

"Hugh Watterson, you'll spoil your dinner," she said sharply.

"But the sitting room still smells like cinnamon and these cookies are all I can think about," Hugh said sadly. "I can't even focus on my cold case files. I love the smell and the taste of cinnamon."

"Cinnamon on its own isn't very good," Bessie told him. "It needs sugar mixed with it in order to taste nice, although it does smell wonderful."

"I wasn't suggesting I wanted to try cinnamon on its own," Hugh replied. "Just that I need to take a few of these back with me when your next guest arrives."

Bessie thought about arguing, as she didn't want the man to fill up on biscuits before tea, but she was so pleased that he was eating anything that she gave in. "Take a small plate and take two or three cookies with you, then," she said. "But that's all until after the pizza."

"You're the boss," Hugh told her, giving her a grin.

Hugh filled his plate and carried it through to the sitting room, then he rejoined Bessie as she waited for her last guest. He was just nibbling his way through a snickerdoodle, under Bessie's glare, when the knock came.

"Jeremy? What can I do for you?" Bessie asked the young man at her door.

"Elizabeth has sent me a list of a few other things she needs," he said apologetically. "Apparently, she forgot to read the whole recipe before she sent Emma."

Bessie laughed. "Come in and have some tea while I see what I have," she suggested.

Jeremy handed her another nearly indecipherable list and then sat down. Bessie switched on the kettle before she tried to read it.

"Two eggs, I can certainly do that," she said. "Butter I have, and I think I have plain chocolate chips as well. What is she trying to make?"

Jeremy shrugged. "I haven't the foggiest idea. All I know is that she'd already sent everyone else down here for some reason or another, so she had to ask me this time."

Bessie laughed. "She'll have to come over herself if she's forgotten anything else."

"We're all just happy to get out of the house for a while," Jeremy told her. "It's huge, but it feels quite claustrophobic when you feel as if you're stuck there."

"I can't imagine," Bessie said. "I do hope you aren't too upset about poor Gennifer?"

"I'm sad, obviously. She could be, well, difficult to get along with at times, but no one deserves to die."

"No, of course not," Bessie replied. "I don't suppose you've given any thought as to the identity of the killer?"

"That's a job for the police, not me," he told her firmly. "They're the experts at that sort of thing. I'll stick to what I do best."

"I hope Nigel is okay," Bessie said, trying a different approach. "He seemed very upset when he was here earlier."

"He's taking Gennifer's death very badly. While they fought a great deal, it seems he had real feelings for her."

Bessie assembled all of the needed ingredients into a bag and then poured tea for her guest and herself. She sat down opposite him and patted his hand. "It can't be easy for any of you," she said softly.

"No, we're all upset, and of course, eager to get home."

"At least Nigel has Emma. I understand they're involved in some way," Bessie said, trying her confused expression on Jeremy.

He gave her a considered look before he replied. "You must have misunderstood," he said. "They were together during the party, but they aren't properly involved, at least not as I understand it."

"Perhaps they'll end up together, now that Gennifer is gone," Bessie suggested.

Jeremy shrugged again. "It isn't my place to speculate on that sort of thing," he said.

"Emma seems like a lovely girl," Bessie said.

"She's very nice, if a bit, um, well, she does rather fade into the background, at least around women like Gennifer and Elizabeth."

Bessie nodded. "And Sarah is hopelessly in love with Bruce, and he couldn't care less."

"You know quite a lot about our little circle," Jeremy replied.

"I've had a chat with just about all of you," Bessie said. "Some details, like that one, are pretty obvious."

"Yes, Sarah does wear her heart on her sleeve. I'm sure one day she'll realise she needs to move on."

"What about you? Are you secretly in love with one of the group, or is that too nosy of me?" Bessie asked.

"I'm more or less engaged to a young lady in London whom I've known since birth," he told her. "For the moment, we're keeping our relationship quiet, but some sort of formal announcement will probably be made before the year is out."

"Congratulations," Bessie said. "I'm surprised she didn't come with you to the island."

"She's in New York City with her family. They like to spend the holidays there. I was going to have a quiet night in for New Year's Eve, until Howard rang at the last minute and invited me here. I didn't see any harm in coming, although I'm quite sorry I did now, of course."

"And the others don't know about her?" Bessie checked.

"I don't like to talk about my personal life," he said stiffly. "I'm not sure why I told you about her, but I certainly haven't mentioned her to that lot." He inclined his head towards Thie yn Traie. "I used to be good friends with Howard, but we'd grown apart in the last six months. I was surprised when he invited me to the party, but as I said, I didn't have anything better to do."

Bessie nodded. "We're all hoping the police will have everything sorted very soon," she said. "I know you've all been questioned about your movements that night and whether you saw Gennifer after she left the party."

"We have," Jeremy agreed. "And for what it's worth, I stayed at the party after Gennifer left, except for a visit to the en-suite attached to my bedroom. I didn't see Gennifer anywhere."

"No one seems to have seen her after she left the party," Bessie remarked.

"Except, of course, for her killer," Jeremy intoned seriously.

"And of course he or she isn't admitting to anything."

"I did hear that one of the empty guest rooms was used by someone that evening," Jeremy said. "I don't suppose you know anything about that?"

"I was actually one of the people who discovered it, while we were looking for Gennifer," Bessie told him. "I know the police had a crime scene team go through it, but I don't know what they found."

Jeremy frowned. "Maybe that's where Gennifer was during the hour or so that she was missing."

"Or maybe someone used the room some time back and no one noticed until that night," Bessie suggested. "George and Mary haven't moved in yet, and Elizabeth is only using a few rooms. I can't imagine anyone has been checking on empty rooms on a regular basis."

"Again, none of this is really our concern," Jeremy said. "I'm quite happy to let the police do their job and work it all out. I just wish they'd do so a little bit more quickly."

"Yes, well, I'm sure they're doing their very best," Bessie said, saying what was expected, rather than what she actually believed.

"I'd better get that bag up to the house so that Elizabeth can get started," he said, getting to his feet. "She's promised us something delicious for pudding tonight and we're all looking forward to it."

Bessie walked him to the door. "I hope whatever Elizabeth bakes, it was worth the trouble," she said.

"Really, at this point, anything would be a nice change," Jeremy said. "The cook we have is very good at meals, but hopeless at puddings. Anyway, it was nice for all of us to have a chance to get out of the house. Thank you for your hospitality."

Hugh was in the kitchen almost before Bessie had the door shut behind the man. "So that's everyone," he said. "Have you worked out who the murderer is yet?"

Bessie shook her head. She knew Hugh was mostly joking, at least she hoped he was. "John and Doona will be here soon," she said. "Maybe between us we'll be able to solve the case."

"I hope so," Hugh said. He picked up another cookie so casually that Bessie could almost believe it wasn't deliberate.

"Put it down," she said in her sternest tone.

Hugh flushed and dropped the snickerdoodle. "How many did you save for later?" he asked.

"Probably not enough," Bessie sighed. "Come on, then, you can help me make another batch, assuming, that is, that I still have enough ingredients. I've sent an awful lot up to Thie yn Traie today."

Hugh was quiet as Bessie weighed and measured ingredients and mixed up a second batch of cookies. He found things in the cupboards for her and did some washing-up, but he didn't speak. When Bessie finally put the first tray of dough balls into the oven, she gave him a hug.

"Hang in there," she said. "It's all going to be okay in the end."

"I'm sorry," he said miserably. "Sometimes I feel like that, but sometimes I start to worry. One of my mates at the station rang earlier. He thinks Inspector Lambert is nearly ready to arrest me."

"Then she's considerably less intelligent than I'm prepared to give her credit for," Bessie said. "She's a senior police inspector. She won't arrest anyone until she's absolutely certain they're guilty. As you didn't do it, you're in the clear."

"I wish it was that easy," Hugh said.

"It is that easy," Bessie insisted. "John and Doona and I are going to look after you and get this case solved. You just need to be patient."

"I really miss Grace."

"Maybe you should ring her," Bessie suggested.

"I can't. Not with this hanging over my head. She has enough to worry about anyway, without wondering if I'm going to get arrested at any moment."

"You know she's worried about that anyway."

"Yeah, but I'd rather not get arrested in front of her," Hugh said.

Bessie nodded. She could understand his reasoning, and it made her sad. "You could still ring her, just to say hello," Bessie said.

"I'd never want to hang up," Hugh said. He sighed and sat down at the table. This time, when he reached for a cookie, Bessie didn't stop him.

"I was thinking," she said, deliberately changing the subject. "What if we put the rest of the dough away for now and put a tray in to bake while we're having our pizza. I thought maybe a fresh hot snicker-doodle might be extra nice with cold vanilla ice cream on top of it."

"Maybe you could put one underneath and one on top, like a sandwich," Hugh said, brightening slightly.

"Yes, that's an idea," Bessie said. She took the tray of hot cookies out of the oven and switched the oven off. "I'll do the rest when John and Doona are here. They're best hot anyway."

"They are, at that," Hugh said, eyeing up the tray in Bessie's hand.

"You may have one more," she relented. "But only one."

CHAPTER 11

*H*ugh was still wiping the crumbs from his lips when someone knocked. Bessie fancied she could smell the pizza through the door as she opened it. Doona and John came in with pizza boxes and bags, leaving Bessie inhaling the rich smells of garlic and tomato as she gave them each a hug.

As she'd gone to open the door, Hugh had jumped up to get plates and glasses ready. By the time Bessie had locked up behind her guests, Hugh had everything organised on the counter behind her.

"Hugh, do help yourself," Bessie suggested as she considered the two different types of pizza and the garlic bread that was on offer.

"You should start," Hugh said. "It's your cottage, after all."

Bessie didn't bother to object. It's difficult to speak when your mouth is watering.

Within minutes the foursome was sitting around Bessie's small kitchen table with steaming plates of food and cold drinks.

"This is very good," Bessie said after a few bites.

"It's from the new place that just opened up near the station," Doona said. "I hope they stick around longer than the others have. It seems like something new goes in there every month."

"I'll eat there every day," Hugh said. "Once I'm back to work, that is."

"That won't be long," John said. "The investigation is moving along very quickly. Anna's under a lot of pressure to get this solved."

"Pressure from where?" Bessie asked.

"Gennifer's parents are friends with their local Member of Parliament," John said. "He's rung our Chief Constable and suggested that perhaps the Chief Constable himself should be conducting the investigation."

Bessie laughed. "I'm sure Anna loved hearing that."

"He's given Anna until Tuesday morning to have a full report on his desk, preferably with the killer clearly identified. Otherwise, he'll be taking over the case," John reported.

"I don't like Anna Lambert, but I almost feel sorry for her," Bessie said.

"I would, if I didn't think she was getting ready to arrest me," Hugh said glumly.

"You're not to worry about that," John told him. "We won't let that happen."

"It isn't like you could stop her," Hugh pointed out.

"But once we solve the case, she won't have any reason to arrest you," Doona said with determination in her voice. "We'll work it out tonight, after we finish off the last of that garlic bread."

"Don't fill up on garlic bread," Bessie cautioned. "I'm going to put some snickerdoodles in the oven in a minute. I think they'll be wonderful served hot with vanilla ice cream."

"Should I ask what a snickerdoodle is?" John asked.

"It's just a sweet cookie that's rolled in cinnamon and sugar before it's baked," Bessie explained.

"They're amazingly delicious," Hugh added. "I've probably eaten two dozen of them so far today and I can't wait for more, and I'm still not even all that hungry."

Bessie glanced at Hugh's now empty plate. He'd started with four slices of pizza and three pieces of garlic bread. Clearly his appetite was returning.

"Maybe we should get started on everything we have to discuss," John suggested as Doona cleared away the dinner plates and Bessie got a tray of cookies ready for the oven.

"There does seem to be rather a lot to go over," Bessie replied. "Why don't you start?"

"I spent a good deal of today with George Quayle," John said. "He was kind enough to agree to have a chat with me about his friends and business associates who were at the party on Thursday evening."

"Was it just Thursday?" Doona asked. "It seems longer ago than that."

"It seems like forever since I saw Grace," Hugh said.

"It was just Thursday night and Friday morning," John said. "Anyway, George shared the guest list with me and gave me some background on each of the guests. He was incredibly helpful, as I have no official standing in the case."

"He's a good person, really," Bessie said. "Just a bit loud and, well, you can tell he was a salesman his entire life, can't you?"

"Definitely," Doona said. "He's also a little too friendly, but he was better at the party."

"I suspect Mary gave him strict orders about his behaviour that night," Bessie said. "She tries to keep him in line."

"Not a job I'd be interested in," Doona muttered.

"Sorry, we're wandering off topic," Bessie said to John. "Did you learn anything interesting about George's guests?"

"Not really," he said with a sigh. "For the most part, I've at least tentatively crossed them all off the list of suspects. One of them might have had some sort of history with Gennifer that I don't know about, but I'm not in a position to dig that out right now. I'm sure Anna has a team working on that very thing."

"I wouldn't bet on it," Hugh said darkly. "She'd rather just pin it on me and close the file."

"She's a good investigator," John insisted. "You don't have to like her as a person to believe that."

Bessie exchanged glances with both Hugh and Doona. She knew

they were both biting their tongues to avoid further criticising the woman.

"Did George have anything else interesting to say?" Bessie changed the subject.

"We went over the list of staff who worked at the party. I simply can't imagine any motive for any of them. Every one of them was born and raised on the island and as far as I know, this was Gennifer's first visit," John said.

"Maybe she just made one demand too many and someone snapped," Hugh suggested.

"That can't be ruled out," John agreed. "But I would be surprised if that was what happened. According to the party planner that Mary was using, everyone on the staff was accounted for all evening and none of them disappeared, even for a short time, and came back with wet hair."

"So we cross them off, at least for now," Bessie said with a sigh. "Does that just leave us with Elizabeth and her friends, then?"

"There were a few other guests around, like Liz and Bill Martin," John said.

"But, of course, they didn't do it," Bessie said dismissively.

"I'll agree to draw a pencil line through Liz and Bill on my list of suspects," John said. "But only pencil. As for the other handful of guests, Mary and I discussed them and none of them seem at all likely. She was sitting with many of them for quite a lot of the time that Gennifer was out of the room, and she's certain that none of them were away for more than a few minutes here or there."

"So, we're back to Elizabeth and her friends," Bessie concluded.

"It looks that way, at least for now," John agreed.

"Maybe we should discuss them in turn," Bessie said. "I spoke to each of them individually today."

"Before we start on them, let me tell you what I've learned," Doona said.

The oven timer interrupted, and Bessie was quick to jump up to remove the cookies from the hot oven. She slid two for each person onto individual plates and then added large scoops of vanilla ice cream to the plates as well.

"Here we are," she said. "What do you think?"

Hugh immediately slid his ice cream onto one of the cookies and put the second one on top. He squeezed the whole thing together and then took a bite. Ice cream oozed out from everywhere, but he grinned at them. "Good, but I have to eat fast as the hot cookies are melting my ice cream."

It seemed only a moment later that his pudding was gone. Bessie and the others ate at a more leisurely pace before the conversation resumed.

"Okay, so I rang a few of the guys down at the station and found out a few things," Doona said, glancing over at John nervously. "I can't tell you who I spoke with, but well, I'm sure they told me things they shouldn't have and I don't care. They are as concerned as I am about poor Hugh."

"Under normal circumstances, I wouldn't be happy hearing that my constables are sharing information about an ongoing investigation," John said. "But in this case, and under these conditions, I'm prepared to ignore it."

Doona blew out a relieved breath. "Right, so as I understand it, they've been working on recreating everyone's movements around the house that night based on all of the statements, but that's proving virtually impossible."

"I can't even imagine," Bessie murmured.

"What's more interesting is what they found in the room that had been disturbed," Doona reported. "It appears that Gennifer had a physical encounter with someone in that room."

"Someone male?" John asked.

"Yes, they found, um, traces of a male partner," Doona replied.

"Can't they get a DNA sample from something like that?" Hugh asked.

"Yes, but they still need someone to compare that sample with," Doona said. "They can't ask for DNA samples from every man at the party, not without being able to connect that room with the murder in some way."

"At this point, we can't be certain that whoever was with Gennifer in that room had anything to do with her murder," John conceded.

"What about fingerprints?" Bessie asked. "Surely they can take everyone's fingerprints and match those to the ones in the room?"

"Gennifer's were scattered around the room, but they didn't find any from her partner," Doona said.

"Someone was being very careful," Hugh suggested.

"Or they simply didn't touch any surfaces that might take fingerprints," Doona replied. "Gennifer opened the door. Her prints are on the knob. They might have gone straight to the bed and done the deed. Gennifer's prints are on the knob on the inside of the door as well. She must have let him out, either before or after she used the en-suite."

"But he didn't," Bessie sighed.

"Not unless he did so without touching anything in the room," Doona said.

"So he was careful or lucky," Hugh concluded. "But who was it?"

"It must have been one of Elizabeth's group of friends," Bessie said. "Gennifer wouldn't have been intimate with one of George's guests, would she?"

"None of them were away from the party for long enough to make their wives suspicious," John said. "I think we should focus on Elizabeth's group as the most likely place to find both the killer and the lover, whether they are the same person or not."

"So let's start with the men," Bessie suggested. "We know the, um, lover was a man, whichever the killer was."

"It seems the most obvious candidate for that would be Nigel, as he was Gennifer's boyfriend," Doona said.

"But he was with Emma, doing much the same thing, during the time Gennifer was missing," Bessie replied.

"Are you certain?" John queried.

"Both Emma and Nigel told the same story," Bessie said. "I suppose they could both be lying."

"You said all of the young people visited you today. What was your impression of Nigel?" John asked.

"He's arrogant and self-absorbed, but he seems really upset by Gennifer's death, as well," Bessie replied.

"How so?" asked Doona.

"He told me they were soul mates. He seemed genuinely distraught, at least as much as a rather shallow person can be."

"But he was with Emma on New Year's Eve?" John wondered.

"Yes, that confuses me as well," Bessie admitted. "He said it didn't mean anything, his time with Emma. According to him, he was drunk and upset, Emma has been chasing him for years, and he finally just gave in."

"Do you think he knew Gennifer was with another man?" Hugh asked.

"He certainly didn't say anything to suggest that he knew," Bessie said. "He and Emma were in her room, which is on the opposite side of the house from the wing where Gennifer and her, um, friend were."

"Do we know anything about his background?" John threw the question out to everyone.

"Elizabeth said he comes from old money, but that there may not be that much of it around, actually. He certainly seems to think he's something quite special, though," Bessie said.

"Yes, and he was very possessive of Gennifer," John said. "He did threaten her at the party."

"They definitely weren't getting along," Doona said. "I don't think it's very likely that he was the man with Gennifer in that empty room."

"Which makes him seem all the more likely as the murderer," Hugh suggested.

"Except according to Emma, he was with her from right after Gennifer left until just before midnight," Bessie said.

"That seems a little too convenient to me," John said. "Would she lie to protect him?"

"Absolutely," Bessie said. "She's crazy about him. As I understand it, he's never given her a second look, at least not before the party."

"That alibi is looking shakier and shakier," John said. "I'm going to put Nigel on the top of the list as potential murderers, but I do agree that it seems unlikely he was the man with Gennifer earlier in the evening."

"Doesn't it seem more likely that the killer and the lover are the same person?" Hugh asked. "I mean, we aren't talking about a very long time. If the two aren't the same person, they must have almost collided in the corridor when the lover was leaving the room where they'd had their tryst."

"I don't suppose the coroner could work out an exact time of death?" Bessie asked.

Doona shook her head. "He couldn't narrow it down any closer than what was already known from people's statements. She was last seen right around eleven and found not long before one. That was actually a shorter time frame than what the coroner could determine from the body. It was bitterly cold, windy and raining, and the body landed in a large pool of water. All of those things complicate matters when it comes to determining time of death, apparently."

"Anyone else have anything to say about Nigel before we move on to the next suspect?" John asked, having made a few notes in his notebook.

"He scared me when he was shouting at Gennifer," Doona said. "It wouldn't surprise me to learn that he was the killer."

John nodded. "If she'd just been pushed off the cliff, I'd be inclined to agree with you. The fact that she was stabbed first, though, suggests more intent. Nigel seems like a bit of bully with a temper. If they fought and he got mad enough, I can picture him giving her a shove, not realising, perhaps, that there was a huge drop behind them. But I'm having difficulty seeing him stabbing her first. He may have cared about her too much to have done that."

"Maybe," Doona said. "But he's still on the top of my list."

"He's on the top of mine, too," John told her, holding up his notebook. Nigel's name was printed neatly on an otherwise blank page.

"Right, off we go, then," Hugh said. "What about Howard? He's Elizabeth's boyfriend. How did he get along with Gennifer?"

"Elizabeth told me that he went out with Gennifer in the past, briefly at least," Bessie said.

"And what did he say about that when you asked him?" John wondered.

"That it wasn't anything serious. He said something about wishing it could have been, but that Gennifer wasn't the type for a serious relationship," Bessie replied.

"But maybe he's still carrying a torch for her," Hugh suggested.

"He doesn't seem that broken up by her death," Bessie said. "But he might be a really good actor, I suppose."

"So he could have been the man with Gennifer in the unused room," John said.

Bessie thought for a moment. "I think if Gennifer had offered, he would have taken her up on it. He and Elizabeth both said that their relationship isn't anything serious. Why would he turn her down?"

"If he was the mystery man, is he also the killer?" Doona asked.

Bessie shrugged. "I suppose he might be," she said. "Although I'm not sure why he'd kill her if he'd just been intimate with her."

"Maybe she laughed at his performance," Doona said. "Or maybe he thought that she wanted to get back together and she said no. Or maybe they fought about the time he left the cap off the toothpaste when they were together." Doona sighed. "Couples don't need much of any excuse to argue, and I suspect Gennifer was even more argumentative than most."

"Boy, marriage is sounding better and better," Hugh muttered, helping himself to another cookie.

Everyone laughed, and Bessie slid the last tray of cookies into the oven. With Hugh's appetite coming back, she was probably going to need them.

"From where did the killer get the knife?" Bessie asked as the thought popped into her head.

"It came from the kitchen at Thie yn Traie," Doona told her. "There was a large block of knives on the counter right inside the kitchen door. According to the head of the catering staff who was running the kitchen, no one was paying any attention to the block; they were far too busy. He couldn't even tell police how many knives were in it at the beginning of the evening, so no one knows how many are missing."

"And the kitchen is only a few steps away from the great room," Bessie said.

"According to the same man, just about every guest stopped in at the kitchen at some point during the evening. It wouldn't have been difficult to slide a knife out of the block and into a pocket or hand-bag," Doona said.

"I didn't go near the kitchen," Bessie said.

"I did," Doona said sheepishly. "There were these little cheese and onion tarts that were delicious, and I went into the kitchen to ask if they had any more. I must say, I didn't notice the knife block, but then, I wasn't looking for a knife."

"I spent a few minutes in the kitchen, too," Hugh told the others. "When I first left the great room, I thought I might hide from Gennifer in there, but it was too busy, with the staff rushing about and chefs shouting orders at one another. I didn't notice the knives, either, but I was only watching for Gennifer."

Bessie looked at John curiously. He met her gaze and chuckled. "No, I didn't go into the kitchen during the party. But I did go in there while we were hunting for Gennifer. I did see the knife block and I noted that at least five knives were missing from it."

"It's a wonder we weren't all murdered," Doona muttered.

"I expect most of those were being used for food preparation," Bessie said.

"When the kitchen staff finished washing up, they were still two knives short. One was obviously in the body, but the second is still unaccounted for," Doona told her.

"Of course, Elizabeth and her friends are all staying at the house," Bessie said. "They could have pocketed a knife at any time."

"Which suggests serious premeditation," John said.

"And that doesn't sound like young Howard, at least to me," Bessie said. "I can just about imagine him being the man in the room with

Gennifer, and even see him fighting with the woman, but I can't picture him stabbing her. If she'd just been pushed, maybe."

"What does he do for a living?" John asked.

"He works in the City," Bessie told him. "Apparently he does very well for himself."

"And his relationship with Elizabeth isn't serious?" Hugh checked.

"They've both said that," Bessie said. "In fact, Howard said something about probably not seeing her again once he goes back, as she doesn't want to move back to London and he can't be bothered to visit her here."

Doona winced. "That's rather cold," she said.

"I don't get the feeling Elizabeth will mind," Bessie replied.

"Is there anything else to say about Howard?" John asked now, making a note in his book.

"At this point I'd put him second, after Nigel, on my suspect list," Doona said. "If Nigel's alibi holds up, we should take a closer look at Howard."

John nodded. "What about Jeremy Lee?"

Everyone looked at Bessie, who shrugged. "He seems very nice," she said. "No one had anything bad to say about him except for Bruce, who didn't have anything nice to say about anyone."

"What didn't he like about Jeremy?" Hugh asked.

"Oh, just that he was nice to everyone, but Bruce thought it was fake," Bessie answered. "He reckons Jeremy has a dark soul."

"What did you think of him?" John queried.

"He certainly has the nicest manners of anyone from that group," Bessie said. "But I can see Bruce's point. There is something superficial about the man. On the surface he's kind and sweet, but, I don't know, maybe he isn't as nice as he appears."

"What about him and Gennifer?" asked Doona.

"Elizabeth told me that she used to try to get him into bed, but he always politely refused," Bessie answered.

Hugh frowned. "Was he interested in any of the other girls?"

"He told me that he's nearly engaged to a woman he's known since childhood, but that the others don't know about her," Bessie reported.

"Interesting," John said. "Why wouldn't he want his friends to know about her?"

"He said he isn't really that close to the group, that he hasn't been spending time with them lately. Apparently the invitation to the island was rather last-minute, and he didn't have anything better to do because his girlfriend is in New York with her family."

"Could he have been the man with Gennifer?" Doona suggested.

"I hope not," Bessie said. "Not if he has a serious girlfriend elsewhere."

"Maybe he wanted one last fling; lots of men do," Hugh said.

Bessie gave him a look that had him blushing. "Not me," he said hastily. "Grace is the only woman I want, but I've heard that some men, well, they get engaged and then panic about never being with another woman and they, well, behave badly."

"But then they worry that their girlfriend might find out, so they murder the poor girl," Doona added.

"Possible, but unlikely," was John's verdict on the matter.

"Again, I can see him as the man in the room much more readily than as the murderer," Bessie said. "We keep coming back to that knife. Stabbing someone must take incredible nerve, mustn't it?"

"Or incredible anger," John replied.

"What would Jeremy have been angry at Gennifer about?" Bessie wondered.

"Again, maybe things didn't go as planned in bed and she made fun of him or something," Doona suggested.

Bessie shook her head. "He's a distant third on my list of possible murderers," she said. "Although all three men are joint first as the possible mystery lover."

"This isn't going well," Hugh muttered as he reached for another cookie.

Bessie took the last tray of cookies out of the oven and offered everyone a fresh cookie with more ice cream. Hugh was the only one who took her up on the offer. When she'd finished preparing his treat and sat back down, John spoke up.

"The only man we've missed is Bruce Durrant. Tell me about him."

"He's not a nice person," Bessie said. "He was here for over an hour, spreading all manner of nasty gossip about his friends, although I hesitate to use that word, considering."

"Is any of it worth repeating?" John asked her.

"Not really, at least not as far as I can tell," Bessie said. "He told me all about Howard and Gennifer, but I already knew about them. He had several nasty things to say about Nigel and his string of female friends, but none of them are on the island, so I can't see how that's relevant. I've already told you what he thinks of Jeremy."

"What did he think of Gennifer?" Doona asked.

"He didn't exactly say it, but I got the impression that he thought she deserved what happened to her," Bessie said, shivering slightly. "He didn't like her and he didn't try to hide it."

John looked up from his notebook. "Any idea why?"

"Someone suggested that he'd pursued her, but she ignored him," Bessie said. "I suppose that would explain his dislike of her."

"What did he have to say about the other girls?" John wondered.

"He knows Sarah is in love with him and he mocked her for it. He didn't have much to say about Emma, mostly that she's bland and that he was surprised that she managed to get Nigel into bed. The only person he didn't say anything horrid about was Elizabeth. I got the impression that he's very taken with her, actually."

"Lucky Elizabeth," Doona said sarcastically.

"This might sound odd, but I can almost see him as the murderer, more than the man in the room with Gennifer," Bessie said after a moment's thought. "He didn't like her and he seems like he might have a temper. If she said the wrong thing to him, I can see him stabbing her."

Doona shivered. "How horrible."

"You don't think Gennifer would have taken him to bed?" John asked.

Bessie shook her head. "No, not even if there weren't any other men at the party. I think she would have made up with Nigel before she'd have given Bruce the time of day."

John made a few notes. "What does Bruce do for a living?"

"Apparently he works for his father's chain of grocery shops. Someone suggested that he doesn't really do much of anything, which I can believe."

"His not liking the girl seems a fairly weak motive for murder," John suggested.

"As I said, they might have had a fight. Maybe he propositioned her and she laughed in his face or something," Bessie replied.

"I'm going to put him down as the last on the list for being the man in the unused room, but maybe a bit higher on the list of possible murderers," John concluded.

"Which takes us to the ladies," Doona said. "We know none of them were in the room with Gennifer, so now we're just looking for a killer."

"I can't prove it, but I like Elizabeth too much to believe that she'd ever kill anyone," Bessie said.

"What if Gennifer went after Howard?" Hugh asked.

"I don't think Elizabeth would mind that much," Bessie replied. "She told me they weren't serious, even before Gennifer died."

"Let's leave her for now," John suggested. "I have to say she's fairly low on my list of suspects for a number of reasons. Tell me about Sarah."

"She's not the brightest person in the world," Bessie said. "And she's crazy about Bruce, which just proves it, I suppose."

"Ouch," Doona winced.

Bessie sighed. "I shouldn't be mean about her, but really, she's wasting her life running after a man who isn't interested."

"She isn't the first woman to do that," Doona pointed out.

"No, I suppose not. But regardless, I can't see where she had any motive for killing Gennifer," Bessie said.

"What if she found Gennifer in bed with Bruce?" Hugh asked.

Bessie thought for a moment and then shrugged. "I suspect she wouldn't have been surprised, really. She'd have been hurt, but I can't see her going into a murderous rage over it."

"But it's possible," Hugh said.

"What does she do?" John asked.

"I gather she has her own little retail shop in London, although from what I've heard, it's her parents who keep it running," Bessie told him.

"She's still on the list, but only just," John said tiredly.

"That just leaves Emma. Let's talk about her quickly or I'm going to need coffee," Bessie said.

"She's very quiet and shy," Doona said. "I barely noticed her at the party."

"Don't they say you have to watch the quiet ones?" Hugh asked.

"Everyone says she's madly in love with Nigel, although she denies it," Bessie said.

"I would too, if I were her," Doona said. "If it's true, it gives her a strong motive."

"From where I was standing, it looked as if Nigel and Gennifer were breaking up," Bessie pointed out.

"Yes, but if she killed Gennifer, she wouldn't have to worry that they might make up," Hugh said.

"Except she also has an alibi," Doona mused.

"If we can believe it," Hugh said. "It seems strange that they suddenly fell into bed together just in time to provide an alibi for one another."

"It is strange," Doona agreed.

"And what does Emma do back in London?" John asked.

Bessie thought for a moment. "I don't know," she said eventually. "No one mentioned it and I didn't think to ask. She does rather blend into the background, even in my head."

"I don't know where to put her on my list," John said. "It's hard to picture her, as tiny as she is, stabbing a much taller woman and pushing her off a cliff, but I suppose she could have managed it if suitably provoked."

"Maybe she caught Gennifer with Nigel and just snapped," Hugh suggested. "Maybe Nigel is providing her with an alibi because he feels guilty about the whole thing."

"That's one possibility," John said, taking more notes.

"Is that everyone?" Bessie asked, yawning as she finished speaking.

"I certainly hope so," Doona laughed. "Before you fall asleep on us."

"I still haven't caught up on my sleep properly from the party," Bessie explained. "I'm not sleeping very well at the moment." She didn't want to mention Hugh's snoring, but it was definitely a factor.

"Well, we'll get out of your way," John said. "I want to let all of the pieces settle in my brain overnight. Maybe we can do this again tomorrow night and get even further."

"Perhaps we should try working out where everyone was throughout the evening," Bessie suggested.

"I'm not sure we'd be able to get anywhere close," John said. "I can tell you when people left and came back, but not where they went when they were out of the room. Beyond that, Anna is relying on people's own statements. Clearly at least one person is lying, and possibly two or more are."

Doona quickly helped Bessie clear up the kitchen as John and Hugh talked about several of the cold case files that Hugh had been studying.

"Once we're both back at work, I want to tackle some of them seriously," Hugh told his boss.

"I think that's a great idea," John said. "I was hoping to do that myself, but every time I try to get started, something else comes up that takes priority."

John and Doona left together, as John had driven them both down to the cottage. Bessie headed up to bed as quickly as she could, hoping to be fast asleep before Hugh began to snore.

"I'll be up in an hour or so," Hugh told her. "I'm just going to go through one more file."

Bessie managed to get about ninety minutes of solid sleep before the snoring began.

CHAPTER 12

Feeling as if she'd accomplished nothing more than a bit of random dozing once Hugh began his noisy onslaught, Bessie rolled out of bed at six and rubbed her eyes. She was more tired than she had been when she'd gone to bed, so she stood in the shower for several extra minutes, hoping the hot water would wake up her body, if not her mind. After absentmindedly patting on some dusting powder and mechanically getting dressed, she headed downstairs to start a pot of coffee.

Bessie was unable to muster up any enthusiasm for her morning walk once she noticed that a heavy rain was falling. Instead, she sat at her kitchen table breathing in coffee fumes and waiting for the pot to finish brewing. As soon as she possibly could, she poured herself a cup of the hot liquid and took a very careful sip. By the time the cup was empty, she was feeling more like herself.

After pulling on Wellington boots and a heavy raincoat, she walked briskly up the beach as far as the holiday cottages and then returned home. A second cup of coffee left her feeling even better. After a quick look in the cupboards, she realised that she needed a trip to the grocery shop. With a hungry Hugh in residence, she needed to stock up. She was debating whether or not to leave Hugh a note and just go when she heard the shower turn on. A short while later, Hugh stumbled into the kitchen.

"Do I smell coffee?" he asked.

Bessie handed him a cup and he drank eagerly. "I didn't sleep well," he told Bessie between sips. "I kept having the most horrible dreams."

"I am sorry," Bessie replied. "Perhaps you should take a nap this afternoon."

"I'm terrible at napping. I'll just have an early night. The coffee is helping, anyway."

"I'm afraid there isn't much in the house for breakfast," Bessie said apologetically. "There's some bread for toast or a few boxes of cereal, although they've been in the cupboard for a while. I'm not sure they haven't gone stale."

"Stale cereal is my normal breakfast," Hugh told her, pulling open the cupboard and helping himself to the nearest box. He poured some flakes into a bowl and added a healthy dollop of milk. "It's fine," he told Bessie after his first bite.

Bessie made herself some toast with honey and drank another cup of coffee. "I need to get to the grocery shop," she told Hugh. "We haven't anything for lunch or dinner today."

"I can drive you," Hugh offered. "Did you want to go into Douglas or Ramsey?"

"I always shop at the ShopFast in Ramsey," Bessie told him. "On the odd occasion when I stop in the Douglas one, I can never find anything."

Hugh laughed. "I know what you mean. The Douglas shop is much larger, but I just find all the extra choice unnecessary. They had twenty or thirty different toothpastes that last time I was there. I just want something that will clean my teeth, you know?"

Bessie nodded. "If you don't mind driving me, a trip to Ramsey is just what I need. We can just go to ShopFast, or we can spend a bit more time there and visit a few more shops."

"Well, if it's all the same to you, I'd rather just go to ShopFast and get back here," Hugh said. "I feel as if the whole island thinks I killed Gennifer since I've been suspended from work. I'd rather not see more people than I have to."

"ShopFast it is," Bessie agreed. "Whenever you're ready."

Hugh went back upstairs to finish his morning routine while Bessie made a quick shopping list. Her normal shopping day was Friday, but she'd missed it this week because of everything else that had happened. Her cupboards were a great deal more bare than normal today.

"Off we go, then," Hugh said. Bessie wrapped up in her warmest coat, tutting at the man, who threw on a light jacket.

"It's very cold out there," she cautioned him.

"I'll be fine," he insisted. "We won't be out in the weather for long."

Hugh drove steadily and Bessie found herself remembering what he'd been like as a child as they went.

"When you were six, you wanted to be a race car driver," she reminded him as he negotiated around a bend.

Hugh laughed. "I did, you're right," he said. "I can't believe you remember that."

"You used to tell me all about it when I saw you on the beach," Bessie recalled. "I think you spent as much time on Laxey Beach that summer as I did."

"Aye, I was there nearly every day, usually all day. Mum used to like to come and sit on the sand and read her romance novels. By the end of the summer, she knew enough other folks that went regularly that she would just drop me off and know that someone would look after me."

"There was a real community feel to the beach in those days," Bessie said. "That was before the holiday cottages went in, of course."

"I was going to be a race car driver and have a different girlfriend for every day of the week," Hugh remembered. "At six, I couldn't imagine what I would want them for, so I just thought we could play games and things."

Bessie laughed. "It wasn't long after that that you decided you wanted to join the police," she said.

"When Uncle Jack had that car accident, the constables that came to tell my aunt and my grandmother were wonderful," Hugh said. "And I thought their uniforms were really neat." He laughed. "Now I know that they're uncomfortable and really hot in the summer, but at the time, I was impressed."

"You're a very good constable," Bessie told him. "And I'm very proud of you."

"Ah, Bessie," Hugh said, swiping a hand at his eyes. "That really means a lot to me, you know."

Bessie patted his arm and then let him focus on his driving. They were in Ramsey only a moment later.

"If you really want to visit a few more shops, you go ahead," Hugh said as he found a parking space. "I can just wait here for you."

"No, I think ShopFast is enough for today. I'm quite tired, really. Let's get some shopping done and get home."

Hugh was out of his seat and holding Bessie's door for her a moment later. "Let's each get our own trolley," Hugh suggested. "I'll want a bunch of snacks and things and I should pay for them myself."

Bessie didn't object. Inside the shop, she worked her way through her list as quickly as she could, nodding and smiling at the acquaintances she saw, but not stopping to speak. She wasn't as lucky with Maggie Shimmin.

"Bessie, I wondered if I'd see you in here today," Maggie said in her booming voice. Maggie was married to Thomas and the couple owned the holiday cottages just down the beach from Bessie.

"Hello, Maggie," Bessie said. "I'm just dashing about grabbing a few things."

"Yes, but what's going on at Thie yn Traie?" Maggie demanded. "I mean, it was bad enough that man from there getting killed last March, but now, just when new owners are moving in, another murder? That house must be cursed."

"Now, Maggie, no one has actually died in the house, you know. If anything is cursed, it must be the beach, surely? Anyway, that's all nonsense. People die every day, all over the island and all over the world. It's just an unfortunate coincidence that those two had a connection to Thie yn Traie."

"Well, you wouldn't catch me going in there," Maggie said. "Oh, me and Thomas were invited to that New Year's Eve party, but I told Mrs. Quayle that we'd be having a quiet night in, I did. And it's a good thing, too. I'd hate to be all caught up in a murder investigation. Why, look at you, you clearly haven't slept since the body was discovered. I can't have that sort of stress in my life, oh no."

"It's all very sad," Bessie replied. "But the police will have it sorted in no time, I'm sure."

"I understand young Hugh Watterson is the chief suspect," Maggie said in a very loud whisper. "He always seemed shifty to me, he did."

"Hugh wouldn't hurt a fly," Bessie snapped at her. "And you should be very careful what rumours you spread around the island. Young Hugh has quite enough to deal with at the moment, without having to worry that some ignorant people are thinking he's a murderer."

Maggie flushed and then looked away. "Well, that's what I heard," she said after a moment.

"Clearly, your sources are wrong this time," Bessie said. Before she could continue, Hugh turned the corner and greeted them.

"Bessie, I'm just about finished. Mrs. Shimmin, it's very nice to see you today."

Maggie turned an even brighter shade of pink. "Ah, you too," she muttered. She glanced at Bessie and then turned and rushed away, pushing her shopping trolley in front of her.

Bessie chuckled. "That was fun," she said to Hugh.

"I could hear her accusing me of murder from three aisles away," he hissed in her ear.

"Never mind," Bessie said, patting his arm. "Let's just get finished and get home."

Hugh insisted on paying for his own shopping and half of Bessie's. "I'm going to be eating at least half of what you've bought," he pointed out. "I should probably just pay for the whole thing."

Bessie knew the young constable didn't make much money, and hopefully, he had a wedding to pay for in the future, so she insisted that he pay no more than half. The drive back to Treoghe Bwaane seemed to take no time at all, and Hugh was quick to help put the shopping away after he'd carried all of the bags into the house.

"It's nearly time for lunch," Bessie exclaimed as she looked at the clock. "The morning has completely rushed away."

"Can I help you make something?" Hugh asked.

"No, no, you go and work on your cold cases," Bessie suggested. "I'll make spaghetti Bolognese. That doesn't take too long and it sounds good on a cold day."

"It does," Hugh agreed.

Bessie set a pot of water on to boil and began to fry some mince. When it was brown, she added some sauce from her freezer and waited for it all to heat through. When it was nearly ready, she dropped some dried pasta into the boiling water and called Hugh.

"Lunch in about ten minutes," she said.

Bessie set out a large bowl of salad and some crusty bread with butter. Hugh joined her a moment later and the pair worked their way through salad, bread and spaghetti in a companionable silence. Bessie simply didn't have the energy to start a conversation and Hugh seemed distracted. When Bessie put out a few leftover snickerdoodles, he apologised.

"I haven't even told you how good everything was," he said. "I'm just lost in one of the case files, you see. It seems as if several mistakes were made during the investigation, and I can't stop thinking about how differently we would do things today, if we had the chance."

"You go and get back to it, then," Bessie said. "I'm quite happy to sort out the washing-up myself."

Hugh objected, but only for a moment. Bessie smiled to herself as he left the room. John had provided the perfect distraction for the man while he was suspended from work.

She'd only just finishing putting the last cleaned and dried plate back in the cupboard when someone knocked on her door.

"Ah, Miss Cubbon, I hope I haven't come at a bad time," Anna Lambert said from the doorstep.

"Do come in," Bessie invited the woman. The rain was still falling;

there was no way she could make anyone, not even Anna Lambert, stand in the pouring rain.

"Thank you. I can't stay long, but I wanted to speak to you about a few things," Anna told her.

"Sit down. I can make some tea, if you have time."

"Oh, no, I don't have time. I'm on my way to Thie yn Traie. That's what I wanted to discuss with you."

Bessie forced herself to remain silent, waiting for Anna to tell her to stay away from the mansion and its occupants.

"We've been having some difficulty in working out everyone's movements on New Year's Eve," Anna surprised her by saying. "I've had three different constables working on a timeline and trying to move the various sus, er, party guests around the house according to their statements, but they simply keep getting muddled up. Of course, we know at least one person is lying, but no one has been able to determine which person or persons that might be."

"I see," Bessie said, not seeing at all.

"Yes, so what we've decided to do is to reconstruct the entire thing," Anna told her. "I'm going up to the house now to start getting everything ready. We need all of the party guests to arrive at the same time tonight as they arrived on New Year's Eve."

"And then what happens?" Bessie asked.

"We're going to go through the evening, minute by minute, and see where everyone goes," Anna explained. "Mr. and Mrs. Quayle are allowing us to install cameras in the corridors so that we can monitor everyone's movements."

"With an eye towards accomplishing what?" Bessie wondered.

"We're hoping to sort out at least a few of the discrepancies we've found in people's statements," Anna said. "People's memories are faulty. If we completely reconstruct the evening, maybe someone will remember seeing someone who was somewhere they weren't meant to be. That's the goal, anyway."

"It sounds like an interesting challenge," Bessie said. "Everyone was drinking and no one was paying much attention to anyone else. I hope it proves helpful, though."

"Thank you," Anna said stiffly. "Actually, you're one of the more important guests. Not only were you there from the beginning, but I doubt very much that you were drunk, even if you were drinking."

"I don't ever drink very much," Bessie replied. "I had some wine before the party started, but I think I only had two glasses of champagne after that."

"I'm going to be counting on you to help us out, then," Anna said, frowning.

Bessie could tell that the woman wasn't happy to have to admit to that. "I'll do my best," she replied. "Obviously, I'm as eager as anyone to see the killer caught."

"Yes, well, if you could please make your way to Thie yn Traie at the same time tonight as you did on New Year's Eve, that will be a good start."

"I arrived not long after four," Bessie told her. "Do you really want me there that early today?"

Anna nodded. "As I said, we're trying to run the reconstruction as closely as we can to the actual timings. We thought about doing it twelve hours out, but we want the lighting and everything else to be as close to exact as it can be."

"That's going to make for another very late night," Bessie remarked.

"Unfortunately, that's an unavoidable consequence," Anna said. She walked to the door and then turned to face Bessie again. "If at all possible, we'd like everyone wearing the same clothes and having their hair and makeup and everything exactly the same as they had them at the party."

Bessie stared at the woman for a moment and then shrugged. "I'm not sure I remember exactly how I did my makeup," she said. "I'll do my best."

"Excellent," Anna said crisply. "Now the only other thing I must ask you is to please let Hugh know what's happening and ask him to attend, preferably in the same suit."

Bessie nodded and watched, wordlessly, as the woman let herself out. It shouldn't have surprised her to learn that Anna knew Hugh was staying with her, but it did. She shook her head. Knowing Hugh's whereabouts was, no doubt, part of her job in investigating the murder.

"I heard her voice and hid," Hugh said from the doorway behind Bessie.

Bessie crossed the room and quickly locked the door. The last thing she wanted was the inspector walking back in unannounced.

"Did you hear what she said?" Bessie asked.

"I couldn't. I snuck upstairs and hid next to the wardrobe in the spare room."

Bessie couldn't stop herself from laughing. "What did you think she wanted?" she demanded.

"I thought maybe she'd come to arrest me," Hugh admitted.

"If she had, she would have found you easily enough," Bessie pointed out.

"I suppose," Hugh shrugged. "But I felt better hiding anyway."

"Well, you can't hide tonight," Bessie said.

"What's tonight?"

"Inspector Lambert is having everyone back to Thie yn Traie to stage a reconstruction of the party. We're all to dress in the same clothes and arrive at the same time. She's going to try to go through the whole evening, minute by minute, to see who's lying about where they were at any given time."

"Say that all again, slower," Hugh asked, shaking his head.

Bessie explained again. "I have to get upstairs and get ready," she added at the end. "I was at the party not long after four."

"I don't want to put that suit back on," Hugh complained. "It needs to go to the dry cleaners, I just haven't had time to take it yet."

"I'm sure you won't be the only one in a crumpled suit," Bessie said. "My dress probably needs a clean, too, but we must try to do what we can to help Inspector Lambert."

"I'm not sure why," Hugh muttered.

"The more I think about it, the more sense it makes, actually," Bessie said. "Everyone has given separate statements to the police, but actually matching everyone's statements in every instance must be impossible. She might be right; this might just clear up a few things."

"I hope she's right," Hugh said. "I want to get back to my job."

A knock on the door preempted Bessie's reply.

"Bessie, I assume you've heard about Anna's plans?" John asked from the doorstep.

"I have," Bessie agreed as she let him and Doona into the cottage. "I was just about to go and start getting ready, actually. I need to be at Thie yn Traie not long after four."

"My dress is at the cleaners," Doona said. "I'll have to wear something else."

"I wish I'd thought to take my suit in," John said. "I'm sure it's a mess after being out in the rain and all. By the time I got home that night, I just wanted to go to bed, and I think the suit is still in a ball in the bottom of my wardrobe."

"No one is going to look their best," Bessie said. "But I can see exactly why the inspector wants us dressed the same. It's much more likely to jog our memories that way, isn't it?"

"Yes," John said. "It's actually a very good idea and I think it might yield some good results if everyone cooperates."

"If they don't, that might be even more telling," Bessie suggested.

"What was Anna's deadline?" Doona asked. "I thought the Chief Constable was taking over today."

"He gave her until eight o'clock tomorrow morning," John said. "It looks as if she's trying to squeeze out every second of investigating that she can."

"I'd be more enthusiastic about this if I weren't so tired," Bessie said.

"I'd be more enthusiastic if I thought there was going to be lovely food again," Doona told her.

"Oh, I hadn't thought of that," Bessie exclaimed. "And I won't get any dinner either, going up so early."

The phone rang and Bessie answered it without thought.

"Bessie? It's Mary," the familiar voice said.

"Oh, I was just going to get ready to come and see you," Bessie replied.

"Now I'm meant to be saying exactly what I said on Thursday," Mary told her. "I think it was something like, 'I'm fine, but you know how nervous I get before parties. Could you possibly be persuaded to come over a bit early, as we're only just down the beach from you?"

"Surely the exact words for this conversation don't matter," Bessie said. "And I'll be on my way as soon as I can be."

"Thank you, Bessie. You're a dear," Mary told her. "Although I'm rather certain I didn't say anything like that last time."

Bessie could hear Mary speaking to Anna Lambert, but she couldn't hear with the policewoman was saying. After a moment, Mary sighed. "I don't suppose you remember exactly what I said," she asked Bessie.

"No, and I don't remember what I said, either, but I'm sure we only talked for a moment or two. I'm going to hang up now and go and get ready, otherwise I'll be late."

"See you soon, then," Mary replied. She put the phone down quickly, no doubt happy to end the call that was being so closely monitored.

"It seems the reconstruction has begun," Bessie said. "I'd better get moving. I don't want to be late, although what Mary and I shall do for the next three hours is beyond me."

"You're meant to do exactly what you did on Thursday," John reminded her.

"Sit around and nibble on the hors d'oeuvres? But there won't be any of those, I'm sure. Mary didn't have time to organise another party, after all."

Still wondering how she and Mary were going to fill their time until the rest of the guests began to arrive, Bessie headed up the stairs and pulled her dress out of the wardrobe. It was wrinkled and it still smelled a bit damp, but she had little choice but to climb into it, all the time wishing she'd had time to take it to the dry cleaners. In the bathroom she combed her hair and had another go at her makeup.

"Even more smudgy than last time," she laughed at herself.

Back in the kitchen, Hugh, Doona, and John were talking.

"You look much better than I will," Hugh told Bessie.

"I'm not sure that isn't faint praise," Bessie replied. "But all things considered, I'll take it."

"I'm going to drop Doona off at home and then go home myself," John told her. "We'll see you at the party at the appropriate times."

"You're welcome to come back here to wait if you want," Bessie said. "I went to the shops today, so the cupboards are full. You can make yourselves something to eat and be close by when it's time for you to join the party."

Doona and John exchanged glances. "That's a great idea," John said. "I'm sure Hugh won't mind some company while he waits."

Bessie glanced at Hugh. He was quite pale and looked miserable. "Hugh, what's wrong?" she asked.

"I'm going to have to see Grace," he said. "And relive those awful moments when I made her so angry with me."

Bessie gave him a hug. "It will all be worth it in the end," she whispered. "Just hang in there and keep a stiff upper lip."

Hugh nodded, but Bessie could see how upset he was. "Really, you must be brave," she insisted.

"I will be," he told her in a soft voice.

Bessie pulled on her Wellington boots and her raincoat.

"Why don't I drop you off on the way," John suggested.

"I arrived that night on foot and I should do the same tonight," Bessie replied. "It's fine, it's only a little rain."

As John and Doona got ready to leave, Bessie pulled open the door. She gasped when she realised someone was standing on her doorstep.

"Grace? How lovely to see you," she said, pulling the girl into the cottage.

"Oh, Bessie, hello," Grace stammered. She glanced over at Hugh and turned bright red.

"Of course, you arrived at the party with Hugh," Bessie said.

"Yes, and the inspector was insistent that we do everything exactly the same," Grace said, staring at the floor.

"John and Doona are just going to get changed and then they're going to wait here with Hugh until they have to go to Thie yn Traie," Bessie told her. "So, of course, you're more than welcome as well."

"Thank you," Grace said quietly.

"You're going to be late," John pointed out quietly.

Bessie glanced over at Hugh, who was studying his shoelaces, and then at Grace. She was busy staring at her hands.

Bessie sighed and shook her head. "You two should talk while I'm gone," she suggested. "And eat something before you head up to the party."

"Doona and I will bring back something from somewhere," John said vaguely. "But we all have to get moving."

Bessie let John and Doona precede her out of the house. As she pulled the cottage door shut behind her, she frowned.

"They aren't going to speak to one another, are they?" she asked Doona.

"Probably not," Doona agreed. "Maybe John and I can help things along when we get back."

"Do hurry," Bessie suggested.

Doona nodded and then followed John to his car. Bessie listened to the sound of the engine getting further away as she began her walk along the beach. When she reached the bottom of the steps that led up to Thie yn Traie, she was met by a young constable.

"Inspector Lambert said to expect you a few minutes ago," the man told her.

"I must have walked faster on New Year's Eve," Bessie replied. "I hope I haven't caused you any trouble."

"No, it's fine," he replied. "I'm stuck out here all night anyway. I'm not sure why, but Inspector Lambert says so."

"Good luck to you," Bessie said. "It's very wet."

"I don't mind the rain as much as the cold. But I don't have a choice with either."

Bessie nodded and began a slow and careful ascent towards the mansion above her. While she agreed that the reconstruction was a good idea, she was already feeling quite nervous about it.

"I just hope Inspector Lambert knows what she's doing," Bessie muttered as she headed towards Thie yn Traie. Tonight the mansion looked dark and ominous, and Bessie was reminded of Maggie Shimmin's words earlier. Thie yn Traie couldn't possibly be cursed, could it?

CHAPTER 13

essie pressed the bell and waited anxiously for someone to open the door. Only a few seconds later, the door swung open and Bruce smiled out at her.

"The party doesn't start until seven," he told her.

Bessie smiled back. "Do we have to go through that whole conversation again?" she asked.

"Hello, Bessie," Elizabeth said in a quiet voice from where she was standing behind Bruce. "The inspector wants us to try to recreate everything as exactly as we can, even the conversations."

"Yes, well, I can't remember one word of what was said when I arrived," Bessie told her. "So she'll just have to settle for my being here."

"Two minutes late," the inspector's cool voice seemed to echo around the corridor.

"I am sorry," Bessie said sweetly. "The wind is stronger than it was that night. I did my very best to walk as quickly as I could, though."

Anna Lambert frowned at her and then shrugged. "Do try to remember at least some of your conversation, please," she said.

Bessie glanced at Bruce and Elizabeth and then shrugged. "I'm sure I said something about how nice it was to see you," she told Elizabeth.

"You did, and then you explained that mum had rung you," Elizabeth replied. "Then I told you that you were very clever to walk over in Wellies, and introduced you to Bruce."

Bessie changed out of her boots and into the same black shoes she'd worn to the party as Elizabeth introduced her to Bruce again, then she took the arm that Bruce offered and the trio headed down the corridor, with Anna on their heels.

In the great room, which was once again decorated for New Year's Eve, Mary was on her mobile. Bessie realised, as she entered, that Mary was only pretending to use it, though.

"I have to go," Mary muttered into the device. "I'll see you in a little while." She crossed to Bessie and greeted her with a hug.

"I hope that wasn't an important phone call," she said, winking at Mary.

Mary laughed. "Just George," she said. "He wants help selecting the perfect tie, but I've told him I'm too busy to dash down to Douglas just now."

"I'll go and help daddy," Elizabeth offered.

"Take some of your friends with you," Mary suggested. "They'll just be bored here."

"I'll go," Bruce offered.

"Oh, no, you stay here and relax. I'll take Howard," Elizabeth replied. She headed out of the room and then stopped in the doorway. "And then I went down to Douglas with Howard," she told Anna. "I'm not sure what you want me to do now."

"You can sit in the room we've designated for waiting," Anna told her. "There's a constable in there and he has copies of everyone's statements, in case you can't remember what time you arrived back."

"Is that where you've stashed daddy?" Elizabeth asked.

"That's where your father is waiting, yes," Anna told her. "You should go and find Howard, just like you did that night, and then the pair of you can wait in the room until whatever time you returned here. There's a constable in the corridor who can accompany you to wherever you found Howard."

"Fun, fun, fun," Elizabeth said brightly as she turned and left the room.

"Sorry for the interruption; do carry on," Anna told Bessie and the others now.

"I think this is where I said something about having nothing to do," Bruce said, frowning.

"I believe you're right," Mary replied. "I suggested you take a car into Douglas or simply go for a drive."

"Yeah, and then I went back to my room and watched some telly until time for the party," he recalled. "Am I to wait in my room tonight or am I to wait in the designated waiting room?" he asked the inspector.

"You should wait in your room," Anna told him, sounding impatient. "The waiting room is only for people who left Thie yn Traie at any point during the evening and then returned. Everyone else should do exactly the same things they did on New Year's Eve."

"Got it," Bruce said with a snappy mock salute. He turned on his heel and marched out of the room, pausing in the doorway to wink at Bessie and Mary.

"And once he'd left, I had a good moan about how Elizabeth had invited an entire group of people to the party without warning me," Mary said.

"And you told me a little bit about them all," Bessie remembered. "Although I'm not sure that I can remember anything specific that you said, especially now I've met them all myself and formed my own impressions of them."

"Yes, well, I probably said I didn't like Nigel or Gennifer and that Sarah was sweet and Emma was quiet," Mary said. "I'm sure I didn't say anything nice about Howard, mentioned Jeremy's lovely manners, and told you something or other about Bruce, but I can't imagine what."

"I can't recall a word you said," Bessie told her. "But that all sounds about right, anyway."

"And then we chatted about all the lovely people that I'd invited before we headed over to the kitchen to get food and drinks," Mary said.

"That part I do remember," Bessie said with a laugh.

"Do you recall what time you left this room?" Anna asked before Bessie and Mary moved.

Bessie looked at her friend and they both shrugged. "I wasn't paying that much attention to the time," Bessie said. "I knew it was hours until time for the party to start, so it didn't seem to matter much."

"I didn't notice either," Mary said apologetically.

"Where did you go from here?" Anna asked, glancing at the pile of papers she was holding.

"The kitchen, to get food and wine," Mary replied.

"Off you go, then," Anna said.

Bessie and Mary turned and walked the short distance to the kitchen. Bessie shook her head at the chaos there that looked strikingly similar to what she'd seen the night of the party.

"They've done a wonderful job in here," Bessie said. "This is exactly how I remember it, with people rushing about everywhere."

"My friend and I would like a bottle of wine, please," Mary said to a passing woman. "And maybe a sample of the food?"

"Yes, of course," the woman replied.

It seemed to Bessie to take a little bit longer this time, but within minutes she and Mary were heading towards the office with their tray of food and bottle of wine. Anna Lambert followed them into the room and then, after Bessie and Mary were settled, sat in the second small desk chair.

"I didn't realise there would be food again tonight," Bessie said, helping herself to a few of the tastier-looking samples.

"We're trying to be as exact as possible," Anna reminded her.

"Still, catering for this many people is expensive," Bessie said. "Or are the police paying for it this time around?"

"George and I don't mind," Mary said quickly. "We're just hoping that the murderer will get caught tonight and that our lives can get back to normal."

"And what did you two talk about when you were in here?" Anna asked, glancing up from the pages in her hand.

"Goodness," Bessie exclaimed. "What did we talk about?"

"It was just small talk, wasn't it?" Mary asked her. "The weather and local politics and that sort of thing."

"I don't remember talking all that much," Bessie said. "We were doing a lot of eating and drinking, though."

Mary poured Bessie a glass of wine. "It's non-alcoholic," she told Bessie as Bessie reached for the glass. "The inspector thought it might be better if we used non-alcoholic drinks tonight, instead of the real thing."

"That's probably very wise," Bessie said. "Although it would be more realistic if half the party were drunk by midnight."

"More realistic, but possibly less helpful," Anna said. "I'm hoping someone will suddenly remember something that points us in the right direction. That seems less likely if people are intoxicated."

"Did Elizabeth's friends complain much when you told them?" Bessie had to ask.

"They're all so eager to get off the island that they probably would have agreed to just about anything," Mary replied. "Besides, Elizabeth promised them champagne once the reconstruction is finished, whatever time that is."

"Let's hope we'll have something to celebrate," Bessie murmured.

Bessie and Mary chatted self-consciously about the food, the wine and the weather, painfully aware of the inspector's presence.

"There's more than enough food for you to have some," Mary offered the woman after a while.

"No, thank you," Anna replied.

"Would you like some wine?" Mary asked. "As it isn't really wine, you could have some."

"No, I'm fine," Anna said, making another note on the sheet in her hand.

Mary exchanged glances with Bessie and then shrugged.

"So, tell me about the grandchildren," Bessie suggested.

Mary could talk happily about her grandchildren for hours and

Bessie was more than happy to listen. Bessie drank half of the bottle of wine and ate at least as much of the food as she had on the night of the party.

"The wine is good," she told Mary. "It tastes very like the real thing. I'm enjoying it and staying quite sober, which seems slightly odd."

"I often drink this when we have a party," Mary told her. "It's so much like the real thing that no one knows I'm not drinking, but I don't have to worry about having too much. It's a good thing, too, as we had a couple of cases of it in Douglas that we could use for tonight. I'm not sure I could have arranged to get sufficient supplies quickly enough, otherwise."

Bessie found herself watching the clock on the wall, wondering if it was possible that it was broken. Time seemed to be almost standing still. Bessie usually enjoyed talking with Mary, but tonight it felt like hard work, in spite of the food and wine.

"I'm fairly certain this is about when George came in," Mary said after a while. "Isn't it?" she asked Bessie.

"It feels about right," Bessie agreed.

"According to my notes, we have another ten minutes to wait," Anna said.

"Goodness, I can't possibly sit here for another ten minutes," Mary said. She flushed. "I'm sorry, but this is incredibly difficult." She got to her feet and began to pace around the small room.

"Things should move much more quickly once it gets to seven o'clock," Anna replied. "When the guests start arriving, there will be a lot more happening."

"Yes, that should help," Mary said thoughtfully. "The night of the party, I really enjoyed having this quiet time with Bessie, but tonight I'd much rather just get things moving."

The knock on the door had Mary scurrying back to her seat. She'd only just sat down when George walked in.

"Hello, hello," he said in his booming voice. "I can't recall a word I said in here, but here I am."

"It's lovely to see you again," Bessie said, standing up and getting a

187

hug. "I think you said something quite unkind about spinach," she
added as she returned to her seat.

"Oh, yes," George exclaimed, his eyes on the half-eaten tray of
food. "I mustn't eat those green ones, as they are full of slimy spinach.
I remember that now."

"You were only here for a few moments before we were told that
guests were arriving," Mary reminded him.

As if on cue, someone knocked on the door. The same man in the
same black suit announced the arrival of the first guests.

"So I went to finish getting ready while George went to greet
everyone," Mary told Anna.

"And what did you do, Miss Cubbon?" she asked.

"Oh, I just sat here and drank wine and nibbled on the food until
Mary came back for me," Bessie said.

"Right, off you go, Mr. and Mrs. Quayle. Miss Cubbon and I will
wait here," Anna said.

Bessie resisted the urge to make a face as she settled back in her
chair. She sipped her wine and watched the clock again, wishing Mary
would hurry. Fifteen silent minutes later, Mary was back.

"The guests will think I'm terrible for not being there to greet
them," she told Bessie.

"It's a party," Bessie reminded her. "I'm sure no one will have even
noticed."

The pair left the office and headed to the great room. Bessie forced
herself to ignore the police inspector who was on their heels. In the
doorway of the great room, Bessie looked around. Everything looked
almost exactly the same as it had on New Year's Eve. Bessie took a
glass of champagne from a passing waiter and headed towards the
corner. For a little while at least, she could simply watch the show.

She was even more relieved tonight than she had been on
Thursday when Doona arrived. Bessie smiled as her friend
approached. Doona had clearly taken the police instructions seriously,
as her hair and makeup had been done as carefully tonight as they had
been at the actual party. She greeted Bessie with a hug and then
looked around.

"It's creepy," she whispered. "I feel as if I've walked into my own past or something. Everything is exactly the same."

"So we have to chat for a few minutes and then join Elizabeth and her friends," Bessie said.

"Yes, that's right," Doona agreed as the pair took glasses of champagne from the passing waiter.

"No alcohol tonight," Bessie said.

"It still tastes good, anyway," Doona replied after her first sip.

"How did things go between Hugh and Grace?" Bessie had to ask.

"They still hadn't said one word to one another before I left," Doona told her, frowning. "I just hope everything gets worked out tonight so they can sort themselves out."

"The reconstruction isn't going to help," Bessie said. "It's just going to remind Grace of why she was so upset to begin with."

Doona shrugged. "I hope it all works out eventually," she repeated herself.

"Me too," Bessie replied.

"So let's go and join Elizabeth and her friends, then," Doona said loudly, glancing sideways.

Bessie looked over to see what Doona had seen and met Anna's amused eyes. "Pretend I'm not here," she told Bessie.

Bessie smiled tightly and then she and Doona crossed the room towards Elizabeth.

"Ah, Bessie, do come and meet my friends," Elizabeth said, her voice dull.

As Elizabeth once again introduced Bessie and Doona to her group of friends, Bessie found herself wondering what was going to happen when they reached the point in the evening when Gennifer arrived. She was getting ahead of herself, though, as John Rockwell was the next to arrive.

"Oh, there's John," Doona exclaimed.

"We must go and talk to him," Bessie said.

They walked over to the man, and after exchanging hugs that felt forced because of the circumstances, stood around awkwardly. Hugh and Grace arrived only a moment or two later. Bessie could tell, from the strained looks on both of their faces, that they still weren't speaking.

Bessie hugged them each in turn and then smiled as brightly as she could. "And then we stood around and chatted for a bit," she said.

"Yes, and then Hugh wandered off to the buffet table," Doona added.

"Did I?" Hugh asked. "I suppose I should do that, then."

He glanced at Grace, but she was staring at her shoes. Bessie gave his arm a small squeeze, which earned her a half-hearted smile before he walked away.

"And then Elizabeth came over," Doona recalled, looking at John.

"Oh, yes, er, maybe we could skip that part," John suggested.

"We're meant to do everything exactly the same," Bessie reminded him.

"Hello, again," Elizabeth cooed. "I know this is meant to be helpful for working out what happened to Gennifer, but it isn't going to be at all good for my ego, watching you run away from me again," she told John.

"It wasn't you," John said. "It was the offer of food, that's all."

"Really?" Elizabeth asked, taking a step closer to him.

John turned bright red and quickly grabbed Doona's arm. "Time for us to head over to the food, isn't it?" he asked.

Elizabeth laughed as they walked away. "I don't know about him," she said. "He's a big bad police inspector, but he seems frightened of me."

Before Bessie could reply, Nigel appeared in the doorway and shouted for champagne. Elizabeth sighed. "Here we go," she muttered.

She walked over to Nigel and then spoke briefly. A moment later the whole room seemed to freeze as everyone waited to see what would happen next. Bessie felt as if she were holding her breath, almost hoping that Gennifer might appear. Instead, Anna Lambert stepped through the door.

"If I could please have everyone's attention for a moment," she said. "I just have a few things to say to everyone before we continue."

Bessie heard a few whispers around the room, but they didn't last long under Anna's icy glare.

"You all know why we're here tonight. I'm hoping that by midnight I'll have a much better idea of exactly what happened here on New Year's Eve. You've all been very cooperative about dressing in the same clothes and arriving at the same time, and your cooperation is greatly appreciated. Now I have to ask you for one extra piece of assistance." She paused and looked around the room.

Bessie felt a chill down her spine as she made eye contact with the woman. If she'd been guilty of anything, Bessie felt sure she'd have confessed on the spot.

"I can't make the timeline work from the statements I've been given. There are gaps and overlaps and all sorts of contradictions. What I need each and every one of you to do is help me clear these up. That means if you see someone in the room at a time you don't think they were here, please let one of the constables know. If you go to the loo and the person in the queue in front of you isn't the same one as on Thursday, let us know. Those are the sorts of things we need to help clear up the timeline. Ninety per cent of the discrepancies will, no doubt, turn out to be minor issues due to people forgetting they stepped outside for some air or wandered into the kitchen for a fresh glass of champagne. Everyone needs to help us work out exactly what happened on Thursday."

Bessie glanced at Grace, who looked pale. No doubt the woman was thinking about the ten per cent of discrepancies that weren't minor at all. That was certainly what Bessie was focussed on. If everyone did as Anna asked, she might just be able to work out who killed Gennifer.

"I thank you all again for your participation tonight," Anna said now. "Again, please alert anyone on my staff to any minor issue. Now we'll carry on with the evening. This is Constable Amanda Evans from the Douglas Constabulary. She will be standing in for Gennifer for the rest of the evening."

Anna stepped aside as the young woman walked into the room. She was shorter than Gennifer had been and she was wearing much more sensible shoes. Her dress was white, but it was considerably more modest than Gennifer's tiny sequined number had been. Bessie wasn't sure that the red wig was flattering on the girl, but she supposed it was necessary, as her hair had been one of Gennifer's most striking features.

"I believe I began the evening by complaining about the party?" she said tentatively.

Elizabeth sighed. "You did, and then you asked for champagne."

Bessie looked over at Grace and shrugged. "We headed for the food next," she reminded the girl.

"Yes, I know," Grace said flatly.

They joined the others as they had done at the party, and the group stood awkwardly together, waiting for "Gennifer" to join them.

Bessie watched as the girl wandered through the party, chatting with each of Elizabeth's friends in turn. As far as Bessie could recall, she was following in Gennifer's footsteps exactly. Anna followed close behind her, with her notes in hand. As she approached Bessie's group, Bessie saw tears in Grace's eyes.

"I know I came over and talked to you for a while," the fake Gennifer said. "So, how are you all enjoying the party?"

"You're supposed to be following the script," Anna told the girl. "We have the conversation that took place here from several different witnesses."

"Yes, well it wasn't a very nice conversation," the girl replied. "I don't intend to try flirting with Hugh. We trained together and he's far too nice a guy to have to suffer through that sort of thing twice. And then I'm meant to fight with poor Nigel, who's been through a lot this week. Surely the timing of everything matters more than exactly what was said?"

Anna glared at her and Bessie worried for a moment that the girl might get fired on the spot. Nigel arrived before Anna spoke.

"I'm here," he said dramatically. "And now we must shout at one another and I must make vague threats that were probably a great deal more impressive than I remember."

The fake Gennifer giggled. "I'm meant to laugh at you and be mean, so please pretend that I am."

"After this is all over, you are going to join us for champagne, right?" Nigel asked her. "I'd love a chance to talk to the real you."

The girl flushed. Anna opened her mouth to speak, but she was interrupted by George's arrival.

"And here I am to drag young Gennifer away to meet Robert," he said loudly. "Come along, my dear, off we go."

The girl nodded, took a step and then turned back and whispered something in Hugh's ear. He flushed and looked down at the floor.

"Now I'm supposed to try to apologise for Gennifer, but end up saying nasty things about her," Elizabeth said. "Which I feel horrible about now, because she did end up dead a few hours later." With that, Elizabeth rushed away behind the retreating Nigel.

"What an unpleasant couple," Bessie said, pleased that she'd remembered her words from Thursday.

"They deserve each other," Doona said, giving Bessie a grin.

The awkward silence that followed Doona's words reminded everyone what had happened next.

"I think this is about when Grace went over to look out the window," Bessie said, trying to soften the uncomfortable moment.

"I think you're right," Grace said in a small voice. She went and sat with her back to them while Hugh looked sadly after her.

"I can't go and talk to her," he said.

"No, but the others are about to join her," Bessie reminded him.

Bessie watched as more people arrived. She chatted with a few, doing her best to speak to them in the right order and in the right location. She was corrected a couple of times by one of the constables, who seemed to have extensive notes on everything that had happened.

"I think you're meant to be by the buffet table just now," one said to her as she stood in the centre of the room, feeling a bit lost. Bessie was about to move that way when Liz and Bill arrived. She could remember exactly where she'd been when she'd greeted them, so she quickly crossed to them, giving Liz a hug.

"How are you?" she asked.

"We're good," Liz replied.

Bessie studied her friend intently and felt relieved to see that the girl looked better tonight. Liz was holding Bill's hand tightly, and she didn't drop it when she saw the fake Gennifer.

"Who's playing Gennifer, then?" she asked.

"A police constable from Douglas," Bessie told her. "She actually seems very nice."

"And here she comes," Bill said.

"Ah, good evening," the fake greeted them. "I'm now meant to be horrid to you, aren't I? This is very hard work, being mean all the time."

"I thought we agreed that you'd stick to the script," Anna hissed from her side.

"I just can't flirt with the man," the girl protested. "He's clearly madly in love with his wife, and she's adorable."

"Just do your job," Anna snapped.

The girl looked at Liz and Bill and shrugged. "You used to be such fun," she said to Bill. She leaned over to whisper something in his ear and then walked away.

Bessie watched her go and then looked curiously at Bill, who was chuckling. "What did she say?" she asked.

Bill watched until both the fake Gennifer and Anna Lambert were some distance away before he spoke. "She said she thought her boss would have been better at pretending to be Gennifer than she is," he said, laughing.

Bessie and Liz laughed as well and then Bessie went back to watching the crowd. A moment later, "Gennifer" walked out of the room. Bessie glanced at her watch. They were doing a good job keeping to the timeline, she thought. It was almost exactly eleven.

After thinking for a moment, Bessie began a slow walk towards the bar. That was where she'd encounter Hugh, who was the next person she'd spoken with. She resisted the urge to sigh as she watched one of the constables check his notes. This playacting was exhausting her and they'd only just reached the time when things could get interesting.

Hugh arrived right on schedule, dripping wet, with a constable on either side of him. They were also dripping wet, which made Bessie smile.

"It's just as bad tonight as it was on Thursday," Hugh told Bessie. "Maybe even worse."

He got his pint and headed off to try to talk to Grace. "This is a total waste of time," he muttered. "I know she isn't going to speak to me."

"I'll help you sort everything out on that front once the case is solved," Bessie promised him.

Hugh nodded and walked away. Bessie watched him go and then turned again to look around the room. She watched George and his crowd of friends leaving, presumably on their way to the wine cellar. Elizabeth's friends seemed to be moving in and out of the room every other minute. Bessie watched as two different constables checked their notes and then spoke to Sarah. The girl nodded and then got up and left the room.

"Pardon me, but I believe you went to the loo around this time," a voice near Bessie's ear said.

Bessie jumped and nearly spilled the champagne that she had been carrying around for much of the evening. "I beg your pardon," she said to the young constable.

"According to my notes, in your statement you said that you went to the loo around now," the man told her.

Bessie sighed. "I suppose I must have," she said. "If it's in your notes."

He nodded, clearly missing the sarcasm in her tone. Bessie sighed and then headed out of the room. The loo wasn't a bad idea; if nothing else, it would be a change of scenery. Besides, he was probably right. She'd guessed at the timing when she'd given her statement, but she couldn't have been more than a few minutes off, as she'd been keeping a fairly close eye on the clock, waiting for midnight so that she could go home.

She joined the queue, noting that the woman in front of her was the same as previously.

"This is crazy," another woman said. "There must be loos all over this house, as big as it is. I'm going to find one."

She stomped off down the corridor, with a constable right behind her. Bessie was temped to follow, but she hadn't done so previously so she knew she couldn't tonight. Shifting her weight back and forth and wishing she'd worn more comfortable shoes, she waited patiently for her turn. When it finally came, she felt painfully aware that at least one police constable would be timing her visit. Now she couldn't remember if she'd combed her hair or touched up her lipstick previously. She wanted to get the timing right, but she simply wasn't certain. With a sigh, she made a face at herself in the mirror and walked back out into the corridor.

The woman who had gone hunting for another loo was just coming back down the hall. She smiled at Bessie and then at the police constable at Bessie's elbow.

"That woman, the one who dragged us all here, she said we should report anything that's different, right?" she asked the man.

"Yes, that's right," the man replied. "Has something happened that's different to what you remember?"

"Yes, but it's only a tiny little thing," she said.

"It could still be important. What is it?" he asked.

"Well, I went off in search of more loos and I found a nice one near the front door. On the night of the party, after I'd, um, finished, when I opened the door, there was a man walking down one of the corridors towards me. I, well, I stepped back into the loo and shut the door. I didn't want him to see me, in case I wasn't meant to be there," she explained, blushing.

The constable looked at her and raised his eyebrows.

"My husband is trying to get an huge investment from George Quayle," she said defensively. "He told me I had to be on my very best behaviour, and I'd already had too much to drink, which meant I couldn't wait patiently for a loo. He'd have been furious if I'd have been found in a part of the house where guests weren't meant to be."

The man nodded and made a note. "And that person wasn't in the corridor tonight?" the constable asked.

"No, he wasn't," the woman replied.

The man nodded. "Wait here a minute," he told the woman.

She sighed deeply. "Maybe I should have kept my mouth shut," she muttered. "My husband isn't going to be happy about this."

"But if you help the police catch the killer, George and Mary will be delighted," Bessie told her.

The woman brightened noticeably. "They probably wouldn't even mind that I was in the wrong place," the woman said.

"I'm sure they won't," Bessie told her.

The constable arrived back with Anna Lambert in tow. It only took the woman a moment to repeat the story for her.

"Did you recognise the man?" Anna asked.

"I'd seen him at the party, but I don't know who he is," the woman replied.

"Can you point him out to me?" was Anna's next question.

"Certainly," the woman said.

Anna and the woman walked towards the great room with Bessie close behind, trying to look as if she were just strolling back to where she belonged. In the great room, the woman glanced around and then pointed.

"It was him," she told Anna. The band finished a song just as the woman spoke again. "That's the man I saw in the empty corridor."

A hush fell over the room as all eyes turned towards Jeremy Lee.

CHAPTER 14

*A*fter a moment of stunned silence, the man, who was sitting on a couch next to Elizabeth and Howard, rose to his feet.

"Am I being accused of something?" he asked in his polished voice.

"The night of the party, you were in a corridor down by the front of the house," the woman with Anna said.

The band played the first few notes of the next song and were suddenly silenced by a look from Anna. Someone giggled nervously and someone else coughed.

"Now that I think about it," Elizabeth said. "You weren't here with us all the time," she said. "You were just sitting quietly and I wasn't paying attention, but at the party, you were gone for a while."

"I went back to my room to get some headache tablets," Jeremy said.

"That isn't in your statement," Anna told him.

"It must have slipped my mind," Jeremy replied with a shrug. "I wasn't away from the party for long."

"You left right after Gennifer did," Howard said. "I remember watching you go and hoping you weren't mad at her, too. She'd whispered something in your ear before she left and you looked upset about whatever it was."

"It was nothing," Jeremy said. "Just Gennifer being Gennifer."

"But you did follow her out," Howard insisted.

"I didn't follow her," Jeremy replied. "I may have left the party not long after she did, but that was just because my head was pounding and I thought I should take some tablets. If it had been any other day of the year, I would have simply gone to bed, but you can't do that on New Year's Eve, can you?"

"So you left the party right after Gennifer did and went straight to your room?" Anna asked.

"Yes, that's right," Jeremy said. "And then, after I'd taken some tablets, I came back. I may have taken a rather more circuitous route back, though. I was trying to walk off the headache before I rejoined the party. That must be where you saw me." He addressed the last remark to the woman who was still standing next to Anna.

"Where did you see him?" Anna asked the woman.

As the woman described where she'd been, Bessie realised that the corridor the man had been coming down could only be the one that she and Doona had explored while looking for Gennifer. Bessie could see the same realisation on the inspector's face. Could Jeremy have been the man with Gennifer in the bedroom at the end of the hall?

"The thing is, Mr. Lee, none of the wings in this house link up, aside from in the centre of the house. There isn't any circuitous route that would have taken you from your bedroom to that particular corridor. Unless, of course, you'd been outside?"

"Of course not," he snapped. "You're starting to sound like you're accusing me of something," he added, his usual polite composure gone.

"What time did you arrive back at the party?" Anna asked him.

"I've no idea," he said. "And it makes no difference, anyway. I did not kill Gennifer."

"Maybe not," Anna agreed. "But you may well have spent some time with her in an empty guest room."

Several people gasped as Jeremy turned bright red.

Elizabeth chuckled. "Jeremy? I thought you were immune to Gennifer's charms. You're just like every other man after all."

199

"I am not," he said haughtily. "She was nothing but a cheap tramp. I would never have..." he trailed off and shook his head.

"Perhaps you'd be willing to allow us to take a DNA sample?" Anna asked. "Something that we could compare with what we found in the room in question?"

"I absolutely will not allow that," Jeremy told her. "In fact, I don't think I'll answer any more questions, either. If you want to arrest me, I'll wait for my solicitor, thank you."

He sat back down, clearly upset. Anna smiled humourlessly. "Perhaps Elizabeth could suggest a good local advocate," she told the man. "One of my constables will take you down to the station for questioning once we're finished here."

"You can't do that," he said, jumping back up. "Do you know who my father is?"

"No, I don't," Anna said calmly. "But I'll make sure I ask you in our interview later, okay?"

"I'm not going anywhere," the man said. "You can't make me."

"Actually, I can," Anna told him. "I'd rather you cooperate, but if you don't want to do that, I can arrest you and take you in."

"I haven't done anything wrong," he shouted.

"You gave the police a false account of your activities on the night of Gennifer Carter-Maxwell's murder," Anna retorted. "Your lying has impeded our investigation. I have reason to believe that you're not being totally honest about what you did during the time you were missing from the party. I believe you may have been intimate with Ms. Carter-Maxwell not long before her death. The fact that you are so loath to admit to that intimacy suggests that you might have also had a motive for murdering the woman."

"I didn't kill her," Jeremy yelled. He looked around and seemed to notice for the first time that everyone in the room was watching him. "Look, let's just go out into the corridor and chat," he suggested to Anna. "I can clear everything up. We don't need an audience."

"Actually, before I take your statement, I'd like to finish the reconstruction," Anna said. "If you didn't kill Gennifer, someone else did."

Jeremy glared at her. "I didn't kill Gennifer," he said insistently.

"Then our work here isn't finished," Anna said. "It's ten to twelve. Let's restart the reconstruction."

The band began to play again and people began to move towards the large television again. Mary switched it on and Bessie was surprised to find that it was replaying the countdown. Someone must have videotaped it, she decided. As she headed towards her friends, she noticed Jeremy talking to John. That hadn't happened at the party, but she didn't interrupt.

"I didn't do anything wrong," the young man was insisting. "I'm getting married soon. It was one last fling, if you like. You understand, but that policewoman won't."

John didn't reply. After a moment, Jeremy continued. "Anyway, there's no law against having sex with a willing woman during a party. The policewoman can't arrest me for that, can she?"

"The inspector can arrest you for withholding vital information during a murder investigation," John told him. "If I were you, I'd tell her absolutely everything you can remember about that night. Maybe you can help her work out who killed Gennifer, and then she might not be so unhappy with you for lying to her."

Jeremy nodded. "That's what I'll do," he said. "I'll tell her everything."

"Only a few days too late," John muttered to Bessie as Jeremy walked away.

"That's one mystery solved, anyway," Bessie said. "Do you think he killed her, as well?"

"He'd be at the top of my suspect list now," John replied. "But his wouldn't be the only name on the list."

Bessie looked around the room, trying to remember how things had looked at the party. Everything seemed just about right. She turned and watched the countdown a second time. While there were just as many horns and party poppers this time as previously, the celebration at midnight was much more subdued.

Bessie hugged John and Doona and smiled as she watched Liz and Bill greet the year with a proper kiss this time. This time Elizabeth and Howard did little more than share a perfunctory kiss and then they joined the others in their group hug. As Sarah clung to Bruce yet again, Bessie noticed Emma's long blonde hair. There was something different tonight, she thought.

"Has anyone seen Gennifer?" Nigel demanded from the doorway. Everyone turned to look at the man who was staring angrily at Jeremy.

"You killed her, didn't you?" Nigel demanded. "Did she laugh at you? Wasn't your performance up to her standards?"

Jeremy laughed. "She didn't have standards," he snarled. "She slept with you, didn't she?"

"I loved her," Nigel said angrily. "I loved her and you killed her."

"I didn't do anything to hurt her," Jeremy snapped back. "Yes, okay, I'll admit it. I had sex with her. It was just one of those things. She'd been chasing after me for years and I just got tired of turning her down."

"And what happened when you'd finished?" Nigel asked.

"I left," Jeremy replied. "I wanted to get back to the party before anyone noticed that I was gone. She said she was going to have a shower and that she'd see me back at the party. We agreed to pretend that nothing had happened."

"You'd say that now," Nigel said. "No matter what really happened."

"I think that's enough," Anna said in a no-nonsense voice. "We're still trying to reconstruct events here. Mr. Lee, I have a number of questions for you, but they can wait until later. Let's get back to the reconstruction for now."

"Now is when we organised the search party," John said. He walked past Bessie and stood near the door to the room. "I asked where George was and also asked for volunteers to help me look for Gennifer."

"That's when I came back in," George piped up from behind John.

"I sent one of the staff to check Gennifer's room," Mary reminded everyone.

"And when she came back to say that Gennifer wasn't there, the search party headed out to look for her," John said.

"Right, can all of the volunteers who offered to help with the search come forward?" Anna asked.

Bessie and Doona joined the others as they made their way towards John. Bessie frowned as she looked at Emma. Something teased at her memory.

"And then we went out and the others went back to their celebrations," John told Anna.

"Emma?" Bessie said. "You're wearing your hair down."

The girl looked at her, startled. "Yes, I nearly always do," she said softly.

"But the night of the party, it was down at the beginning of the evening, but up in a clip by the end of the night," Bessie said.

"Was it?" the girl frowned. "I don't recall," she said after a minute.

"I do," John said. "Well remembered, Bessie."

"I remember as well," Doona chimed in. "The clip was really pretty. It was very sparkly and it looked nice against your blonde hair."

"Thanks," the girl blushed. "I must have pinned my hair up when I went back to my room with Nigel."

"Nigel, do you remember her putting her hair up?" Anna asked the man.

He shook his head. "I wasn't paying attention," he said, staring at his hands.

"You'd just been intimate with the woman," Anna said. "Surely, you'd notice something like what she did with her hair."

"Maybe she did it after I left," he said.

"According to your amended statement, you and Emma returned to the party together before you went back out to look for Gennifer," Anna said. "Was that not the case?"

Nigel looked up and shrugged. "I don't remember," he said.

"Perhaps you don't remember because it isn't true," Anna suggested.

"I just don't remember," Nigel muttered. "I was drunk."

"Drunk enough to go to bed with a woman you've spent years avoiding," Anna suggested. "Much like Mr. Lee. Of course, Mr. Lee is single. You've said you were in love with Ms. Carter-Maxwell."

"I was in love with Gennifer," he said.

"But you were still intimate with another woman," Anna pointed out.

"No, I wasn't," Nigel exploded.

"Nigel," Emma called. "Think."

Nigel looked at her and smiled. "I know you're trying to protect me, but I didn't kill Gennifer. Thank you for trying to provide me with an alibi, but I can't lie anymore. I spent most of the time after Gennifer left the party trying to find her. I walked all over this stupid house and even went outside for a while, but I couldn't find her anywhere."

"So you weren't with Ms. Taylor at all?" Anna asked.

"No, I wasn't," he replied.

Anna nodded. "Ms. Taylor, would you like to explain where you were during Ms. Carter-Maxwell's absence?"

Emma swallowed hard. "Me?" she asked. "Why, I was at the party for most of the time. I did go back to my room for a little while, to, um, freshen up."

"And why did you lie about being with Mr. Hutton?" Anna asked.

"I wanted to protect him," Emma said bitterly. "I thought he might appreciate my kindness."

"I do," Nigel said. "But I'm a terrible liar. It's better the police know the truth. I know I didn't hurt Gennifer."

"So when did you put your hair up?" Anna asked Emma.

"When I went back to my room," Emma told her. "I was just playing with it and threw the clip in and then decided to leave it in for a while."

"Where is the clip now?" Anna asked.

"In my room, I suppose," Emma answered, flushing under Anna's watchful eye.

"I think I'd like to see it," Anna said. "Miss Cubbon, could you join us for a moment?"

Bessie nodded and then followed the pair out of the room, nearly bursting with curiosity as to what was going to happen next. Anna and Emma walked together down a long corridor with Bessie behind them. Behind Bessie were three uniformed constables and behind them, John Rockwell followed, a serious expression on his face.

"Here we are," Emma said after she'd let them all into her room. She stood in front of a mirror, holding up the clip that Bessie remembered from the party.

"Is that the right clip?" Anna asked Bessie.

"I believe so," Bessie said. "I didn't do much more than glance at it."

Anna nodded and looked disappointed. "Let's get back to the party, then," she said. They turned to leave the room, but Anna held up a hand.

"Hang on a minute," she said. "Your hair was up by this time, right? Go ahead and put it up now."

Emma nodded and turned towards the mirror. She gathered her hair into a knot and tried to slide the clip in. Several strands of hair slipped out on either side. Emma removed the clip and tried again, but again the hair simply wouldn't stay in place.

"It would work better if your hair was wet," Anna commented quietly.

Emma gave her a horrified look. She turned away and then nodded. "Of course, that's right. I forgot. I came in to, um , that is, while I was here I thought I might as well do something special with my hair, so I wet it in the sink and then twisted it up."

"In the sink in there?" Anna asked, pointing to the door to the en-suite.

"Yes, in there," Emma answered quickly. "I didn't have time to redo my makeup or anything, so I just wet my hair."

Anna nodded. She crossed the room and pushed open the door to the en-suite. "Perhaps you could demonstrate for me?" she asked the girl.

Bessie could see just enough of the room to realise that the very fancy vessel sink was far too small for anyone to get their head into.

Emma crossed the room and stopped in the doorway between the rooms. She looked at Anna and then shook her head. "I must have just used a wet comb or something," she stammered. "I mean, I stuck my head in the shower, that's what I did."

"Or maybe you were caught in the rain," Anna suggested.

"Yes, that's it," the girl replied. "I was caught in the rain. I went out to get some fresh air and it was raining."

"Did you happen to see Gennifer on your walk?" Anna asked.

"No, I mean, well," the girl looked around the room and then back at Anna. "I did see her. She was walking along and then she, well, she jumped off the cliff. I didn't want to tell anyone, because I didn't want her family to think she'd killed herself, but that's what happened."

"I see," Anna said. "Is there anything else you'd like to tell us about that night?"

The girl sighed and looked down at the floor. "She had a knife in her hand and she stabbed herself before she jumped. She must have wanted to be absolutely certain that she killed herself."

Anna nodded. "Well, that's all very interesting," she said briskly. "We'll have to have the rest of this conversation at the station, however."

"You can't possibly be arresting me," Emma said.

"I'm taking you to the station so that you can help us with our enquiries," Anna told her. "There are quite a few contradictions in your version of events and I'd like to give you a chance to explain them to me."

"I can explain everything," the girl said.

"Excellent," Anna replied. She had a few words with one of the uniformed men, and then two of the constables escorted Emma out of the room.

"She killed Gennifer?" Bessie asked, feeling stunned.

"It certainly seems that way," Anna told her. "No one knew about the knife, except the person who used it."

"And it couldn't have happened the way she said? Gennifer couldn't have stabbed herself and jumped?" Bessie wondered.

"Not according to the coroner," Anna replied. "I suppose the defense will argue that it was possible, but it doesn't seem very likely. That's for the advocates, though. I've done my job."

"She seems like the type who will fall apart under questioning," John said. "I suspect you'll have a confession within the hour."

"I agree," Anna said. "Let's hope we're both right."

"She seemed like such a nice girl," Bessie said.

"She was clever, too, providing Nigel with an alibi, which also gave her one," John said.

"If he'd stuck to his story, you might never have caught her," Bessie exclaimed.

"That's what makes reconstructions like this so helpful," Anna told her. "Even when people aren't watching one another, they notice things, like Jeremy being in the wrong corridor and Emma's hair clip."

"Well, it was certainly successful tonight," Bessie said. "I've never been through one before, but I am impressed."

"Maybe you'll have more faith in my abilities going forward," Anna suggested. "I'm good at my job."

"We were all just worried about Hugh," Bessie said, blushing.

"I have very high expectations for the men and women who work under me," Anna said. "Mr. Watterson is going to have start working a lot harder if he wants to earn my respect. Having said that, I never thought he killed Gennifer, but by suggesting I did, I was able to get everyone to let their guard down, at least a little bit."

Bessie pressed her lips together before she said something she'd regret later. Poor Hugh had suffered a great deal from being seen as the chief suspect in the case. While the tactic had paid off in the end, the price that Hugh had paid was a large one.

"I need to get down to the station and start questioning my suspect," Anna said. "John, did you want to come and observe?"

"I would, rather," John answered.

"Let's go, then," Anna said.

Bessie watched the pair as they walked away. Anna stopped and had a word with one of the uniformed constables in the corridor and then she and John continued on their way.

"If you'd like to come with me," the constable said to Bessie, "I'm going to make an announcement and then everyone can go home."

Bessie nodded and followed the young man back to the great room. The constable stopped in the doorway and let Bessie into the room. She looked at her friends, who were all watching anxiously to see what might happen next.

"Ladies and gentlemen, Inspector Lambert has asked me to thank you all once more for your participation tonight. Mr. Lee, the inspector would appreciate it if you'd come down to the station now to amend your statement."

Jeremy frowned and shook his head. "It's late and I want to go to bed," he complained. "I'll do it in the morning."

"I'm afraid the inspector didn't offer me any options," the man told him. "Constable Clucas will take you down now, please."

Jeremy stood up as another constable approached him. "I don't have a choice, then?"

"No, sir," the man replied.

"I want my solicitor," Jeremy snapped.

"You're welcome to ring him once you arrive at the station. I'm not sure how long you might have to wait for him to join you, but I'm sure he or she will get here eventually."

"I didn't do anything wrong," Jeremy insisted. "I'm being treated like a criminal."

No one spoke as the man and his escort left the room.

"May I ring for a local advocate for him?" Mary asked. "He should have someone on his side at the station."

"You may," the constable replied.

"You might want to get someone for Emma as well," Bessie said, frowning as everyone turned to stare at her. "She's been taken to the station as well," Bessie explained.

"Has she?" Mary demanded. "Emma?"

"Yes, she has," the constable confirmed.

The room was quiet as Mary made a phone call. Bessie knew that she'd be ringing Doncan Quayle, who was the best advocate on the island, at least in Bessie's opinion. He didn't do much criminal work, but he would be able to find the right person to help both Jeremy and Emma, at least until their own solicitors arrived from London. After Mary disconnected, everyone turned back to the young man in the doorway expectantly.

"Ah, yes, well, as I said, the inspector thanks you all for your cooperation. Everyone is free to leave. A great deal of new information was gathered tonight and we're confident that we'll have the case wrapped up very quickly. Someone will be interviewing each of you in light of the new information received, but that will take place over the course of the next several days. Thank you again and good night."

Of course, no one was happy with that. The constable did his best to deal with the onslaught of questions he was faced with, but he'd apparently been told to say nothing about the case at all so after a short while he was forced to resort to saying "no comment" repeatedly.

"Bessie, you must know something," Elizabeth said after a few minutes. "What's going on? Don't tell me Emma killed Gennifer. That simply isn't possible."

Bessie shook her head. "I'm afraid I can't comment, either," she said. Although she hadn't been told not to repeat what she'd heard, she didn't think Anna Lambert would appreciate her talking. "I'm sure it will be all over the news tomorrow," was all that Bessie would say.

The room slowly began to empty as George's business associates and their wives gave up on finding out more and headed for home. They left with a great deal of unhappy muttering, but slowly the room began to clear. Elizabeth and those of her friends who were still left all went and sat in a circle. Bessie could see confusion on all of their faces.

"I know you can't tell me anything, but do the police know what happened?" Liz asked Bessie as she and Bill headed for the door.

"I think they have a pretty good idea," Bessie told her. "The investigation should all be over in a day or two."

Liz nodded and patted her tummy. "I shall sleep better tonight," she told Bessie. "Assuming baby lets me."

Bessie smiled at her. "I thought they were only hard work once they arrived," she said.

"Oh, good heavens, no," Liz laughed. "I don't sleep at all well when I'm pregnant. If babies weren't so darn adorable, I'd have never had more than one."

Bessie gave her friend a hug and watched as Liz and Bill walked away, his arm around her shoulders.

"So, what's going on?" Doona demanded when she joined Bessie.

Bessie sighed. "I'll tell you when we get back to my cottage," she told her friend. "Grace, you and Hugh should come, too," she called to the couple who were sitting near one another but not speaking.

"But what happened?" Mary asked as she crossed the room.

"I don't know what I'm allowed to talk about and what I can't say," Bessie replied.

"But the police have arrested Emma?" Mary queried.

"I don't think she's been arrested," Bessie replied. "She's just been taken down for questioning."

"The same as Jeremy," George said as he joined them. "Do the police think one of them killed Gennifer?"

Bessie was saved from answering by a strange and loud sound.

"I think that's your mobile," Doona told her.

Bessie flushed. "I changed the sounds on it again so I could be sure I would recognise it. Clearly, that didn't work." She dug the phone out of her bag and glanced at the display. It was John. The conversation wasn't a very long one, and when she'd disconnected she smiled at everyone.

"Okay, I've been given permission to share some news," she said.

Elizabeth and her friends crossed the room quickly, and Grace and Hugh weren't far behind.

"Emma has just confessed to killing Gennifer," Bessie told them all.

"Emma? But why?" Elizabeth asked.

"She's said it was because she saw Gennifer with Jeremy and felt that Nigel deserved better," Bessie reported.

"Or maybe she just really wanted Nigel for herself," Sarah said sadly.

"I'm sure her father will get her declared mentally unstable and she'll spend the rest of her life in a posh mental facility," Bruce said.

"At least she won't be out on the streets," Elizabeth replied.

"She killed Gennifer over me?" Nigel asked, his face drained of colour.

"I knew she was obsessed with you, but that does take things a bit far," Sarah said. "I mean, I'm pretty hung up on Bruce, but I wouldn't kill for him."

"That's good to know," Bruce commented dryly.

"So, are we all free to go home?" Howard asked.

"The police want one last conversation with each of you," Bessie replied. "But I should think they'll be able to do that tomorrow."

"I can't wait to sleep in my own bed again," Sarah said.

"I'm never coming back to this island again," Howard declared.

"Gee, thanks," Elizabeth snapped.

Bessie turned away from the drama and looked at Hugh. He was staring straight ahead, a strange look on his face.

"Hugh? Are you okay?" she asked gently.

Hugh blinked a few times and then smiled at Bessie. "I'm fine," he told her. He turned around and looked at Grace, who glanced at him and then looked away.

"This is all wrong," Hugh said loudly. "I planned this for months and months and it wasn't anything like this, but I can't wait any longer."

Bessie and Doona exchanged smiles as they realised what was coming. Hugh took a step towards Grace and then dropped to one knee.

"Grace Christian, I've messed this up a dozen or more times, but the thing is, I love you and I want to spend the rest of my life with you. Please, will you marry me?"

CHAPTER 15

Grace blushed and looked at Hugh, a stunned expression on her face. After a very awkward minute, she gasped. "Oh, but, that is, I…" she trailed off and then shook her head.

Hugh's face fell and Bessie felt a huge rush of sympathy for the young man.

"Oh, no," Grace exclaimed. "I didn't mean to shake my head. I'm just so overwhelmed. Of course I'll marry you. You know that."

Everyone cheered as Grace and Hugh hugged and then shared a passionate kiss. Around them, everyone was hugging everyone else, and Bessie noticed that Bruce was the one hugging Sarah, rather than the other way around.

"Champagne," George called, and a moment later several members of his staff were distributing glasses of the ice-cold bubbly drink.

"Congratulations," Bessie told Hugh when the excitement had died down a little.

"Thank you," Hugh replied. He was holding onto Grace so tightly that Bessie wondered if it hurt, but Grace wasn't complaining. "I want to get married next week," Hugh told Bessie. "Do you think that's enough time to plan a wedding?"

Bessie shook her head. "I think you'd better ask Grace," she said. "I'm sure she has her own ideas about your wedding."

Bessie was exhausted an hour later when Doona finally dropped her off at her cottage. Her friend insisted on coming inside to make sure everything was okay.

"I'm too tired to care," Bessie complained as she opened the door. "Just let me get to bed."

"I'll be two minutes," Doona promised. Bessie stood in the kitchen, staring at the blinking light on her answering machine as she listened to Doona walking around the upstairs. By the time Doona came back to the kitchen, Bessie had decided to ignore the messages for now.

"I'll ring you in the morning," Doona said. "Hopefully, I'll be back at work in Laxey tomorrow."

"You and John both," Bessie told her. "And Hugh."

Bessie slept until seven, which left her feeling slightly disorientated and still quite tired the next morning. Doona rang not long after eight.

"John, Hugh and I have all been reassigned to our old positions," she told Bessie. "If you're feeling up to it, we'll be over around six with dinner and pudding so we can talk it all through."

"I'll be here," Bessie told her.

If her friends had asked her when they arrived how she'd spent the day, Bessie might have struggled to remember. She moved through it in a bit of a fog, simply marking time until six.

"Bessie, you look tired," Doona greeted her.

"I am, but I'll have an early night," Bessie replied. "I'll sleep better once I know that everything is all wrapped up."

"It is," John assured her as he unpacked cartons of food. "Emma has given a full confession in the presence of her solicitor. Her father is demanding that she be transferred to a hospital for the mentally ill, and it looks as if he's going to get his way."

"Is she mentally ill?" Bessie asked.

"I watched Anna question her," John said. "Her grasp on reality seemed quite shaky. She kept telling Anna that Nigel was going to

213

come and get her and they were going to get married and live happily ever after. I think she might actually believe that."

"The poor girl," Doona murmured.

"Apparently she had a breakdown a few years ago over some other man with whom she was obsessed," John said. "She was treated and released and her family thought she was fine."

"Poor Gennifer," Bessie said. "She didn't deserve to die."

"What about Jeremy?" Doona asked. "Is he facing any charges?"

"I don't think there's any point in pressing charges against him," John said. "He lied in his statement, but even if he'd told the truth, nothing he knew would have helped solve the murder. I think he'll be in enough trouble with his fiancé anyway. Apparently, Nigel rang her up while he was at the station last night."

"I thought Jeremy said no one knew about her?" Bessie asked.

"I understand Bruce knows all about her," John said. "I got the impression that he enjoys poking into his friends' private lives."

They settled in to eat their dinner, with chocolate fairy cakes for pudding.

"So, Grace and I have set a date for the wedding," Hugh announced after his second fairy cake.

"That was fast," Doona said.

"Yes, well, I wasted too much time waiting to ask her at just the right moment," Hugh said, blushing. "Now neither of us wants to wait at all."

"So what date have you chosen?" Bessie asked.

"Valentine's Day," Hugh said.

"This year?" Bessie asked.

"Yes, this year," Hugh laughed. "I know it's only about six weeks away, but we don't want to wait."

"You're sure Grace is okay with marrying so quickly?" Doona asked. "People will talk."

"I don't care what people say," Hugh replied. "Grace and I are doing what we want to do."

"Good for you," Bessie said. "I just hope that's enough time for Grace to get everything organised."

"I'm going to help as much as I can," Hugh said. "It won't be a big wedding. Her parents can't afford much and neither can I."

"Small weddings usually lead to happier marriages," Bessie told him. "At least you're focussed on what really matters, the getting married part, rather than on the big fancy ceremony."

"Yes, well, as her family is all in Douglas, we'll be having the ceremony and the reception there," Hugh said. "But you'll all be there, right?"

"Of course we will," John said.

"I shall need a new hat," Bessie said happily.

"Oh, maybe I'll wear one, too, if you're going to," Doona said. "I've always wanted to wear a hat to a wedding, but no one really does anymore."

"I shall be wearing one," Bessie told her. "And you should wear one as well. It's the proper thing to do."

With that pronouncement, the foursome happily discussed weddings and happily ever afters for the rest of the evening, putting all of the unfortunate events of the past week firmly out of their minds.

GLOSSARY OF TERMS

MANX TO ENGLISH

- **fastyr mie** — good afternoon
- **kys t'ou** — how are you?
- **moghrey mie** — good morning
- **ta mee braew** — I'm fine

HOUSE NAMES – MANX TO ENGLISH

- **Thie yn Traie** — Beach House
- **Treoghe Bwaane** — Widow's Cottage

ENGLISH TO AMERICAN TERMS

- **advocate** — Manx title for a lawyer (solicitor)
- **aye** — yes
- **biscuits** — cookies
- **car park** — parking lot

217

- **chemist** — pharmacist
- **crisps** — potato chips
- **cuddly toy** — stuffed animal
- **cuppa** — cup of tea (informally)
- **estate agent** — real estate agent (realtor)
- **fairy cakes** — cupcakes
- **holiday** — vacation
- **loo** — restroom
- **midday** — noon
- **mince** — ground beef (hamburger)
- **pavement** — sidewalk
- **pudding** — dessert
- **starters** — appetizers
- **supply teacher** — substitute teacher
- **telly** — television
- **trolley** — shopping cart
- **uni** — university

OTHER NOTES

CID is the Criminal Investigation Department of the Isle of Man Constabulary (Police Force).

When talking about time, the English say, for example, "half seven" to mean "seven-thirty."

With regard to Bessie's age: UK (and IOM) residents get a free bus pass at the age of 60. Bessie is somewhere between that age and the age at which she will get a birthday card from the Queen. British citizens used to receive telegrams from the ruling monarch on the occasion of their one-hundredth birthday. Cards replaced the telegrams in 1982, but the special greeting is still widely referred to as a telegram.

When island residents talk about someone being from "across," they mean that the person is from somewhere in the United Kingdom (across the water).

Plain chocolate in the UK is (more or less) semi-sweet chocolate in the US.

In the UK, rather than use measuring cups for dry ingredients, they use scales and measure the ingredients in ounces or grams.

Ronaldsway is the location where the airport on the island is located. While it is officially called the "Isle of Man Airport," locally it is referred to as "Ronaldsway."

Eton College is (arguably) the best-known boys' boarding school in the UK. (Such schools are called public schools there.) Eton mess is a pudding made with strawberries or bananas, cream, and pieces of meringue, all mixed together.

ACKNOWLEDGMENTS

Thanks, as ever, to

Denise, my amazing editor.

Charlene, Janice, Ruth, and Margaret, my incredible beta readers, and

Kevin, the brilliant photographer whose photos grace Bessie's covers.

Most importantly, thank you, readers, for coming along on this journey with Bessie and her friends. Please get in touch at any time to share your thoughts!

Bessie's adventures continue in
Aunt Bessie Likes
An Isle of Man Cozy Mystery

Aunt Bessie likes weddings.

Elizabeth Cubbon, known to everyone as "Aunt Bessie," is delighted to see two of her friends being united in marriage. But before the wedding, there's a cold case that has the whole island talking.

Aunt Bessie likes helping Hugh Watterson and John Rockwell with their investigation.

But when the three girls who went missing decades ago turn out to have been murdered, Bessie isn't as happy to be involved. When one of the main suspects turns up dead, things look increasingly complicated.

Aunt Bessie doesn't really like surprises.

But she's determined to give the happy couple the best possible surprise she can arrange. She just has to find time to plan that while hunting down a killer.

ALSO BY DIANA XARISSA

Aunt Bessie Assumes

Aunt Bessie Believes

Aunt Bessie Considers

Aunt Bessie Decides

Aunt Bessie Enjoys

Aunt Bessie Finds

Aunt Bessie Goes

Aunt Bessie's Holiday

Aunt Bessie Invites

Aunt Bessie Joins

Aunt Bessie Knows

Aunt Bessie Likes

Aunt Bessie Meets

Aunt Bessie Needs

Aunt Bessie Observes

Aunt Bessie Provides

Aunt Bessie Questions

Aunt Bessie Remembers

Aunt Bessie Solves

Aunt Bessie Tries

Aunt Bessie Understands

Aunt Bessie Volunteers

Aunt Bessie Wonders

The Isle of Man Ghostly Cozy Mysteries

Arrivals and Arrests

Boats and Bad Guys

Cars and Cold Cases

Dogs and Danger

Encounters and Enemies

Friends and Frauds

Guests and Guilt

Hop-tu-Naa and Homicide

Invitations and Investigations

Joy and Jealousy

Kittens and Killers

Letters and Lawsuits

The Markham Sisters Cozy Mystery Novellas

The Appleton Case

The Bennett Case

The Chalmers Case

The Donaldson Case

The Ellsworth Case

The Fenton Case

The Green Case

The Hampton Case

The Irwin Case

The Jackson Case

The Kingston Case

The Lawley Case

The Moody Case

The Norman Case

The Osborne Case

The Patrone Case

The Quinton Case

The Rhodes Case

The Isle of Man Romance Series

Island Escape

Island Inheritance

Island Heritage

Island Christmas

Have you tried Diana Xarissa's Ghostly Cozy Series?
Turn the page for a sneak peek at the first book.
Arrivals and Arrests
An Isle of Man Ghostly Cozy

Fenella Woods has only met a few people during the twenty-four hours she's been in Douglas, the capital of the Isle of Man. She's shocked when she discovers one of them dead in an alley behind her apartment building.

Struggling to adapt to her new life in a foreign country seems easy compared to coping with finding herself in the middle of a murder investigation.

Nearly fifty and newly single, Fenella meets a handsome police inspector, a dashing new neighbor, and a sophisticated businessman, all of whom have her questioning her determination to remain unattached.

Having a ghost for a roommate and a kitten as an uninvited house-guest has her questioning her decision to start a new life on the small island in the Irish Sea after all.

CHAPTER 1 - ARRIVALS AND ARRESTS

*I*f they could put a man on the moon, why couldn't someone find a way to make plastic shopping bags comfortable to carry, Fenella Woods thought to herself as she walked through the alley behind her apartment building. She'd bought far too much, really, and now the six bags, three in each hand, were cutting off the circulation to her fingers.

It didn't help that it was raining, a cold and steady rain that made Fenella sorry she'd ever left her warm apartment. That there wasn't a single thing to eat in that apartment was what had driven her out into the rain in the first place. A gust of wind blew her shoulder-length hair into her eyes and made her mutter under her breath.

Why would anyone be lying on the ground outside in the rain, she wondered to herself when she saw the man lying just a few steps away from the building's back door. He looked vaguely familiar, which surprised Fenella. She'd only been on the island for twenty-four hours. The man, who was lying on his stomach anyway, couldn't possibly be anyone she knew.

"Hello?" she said cautiously, not wanting to startle the man, who must have suddenly taken ill. He hadn't been there when she'd left an hour or so ago. She was sure she would have noticed. "Hello? Are you okay?"

The man didn't respond. Fenella sighed and switched all of her bags to one hand. The hand protested, sending shooting pains through Fenella's arm. Flexing her fingers repeatedly on her now empty hand to try to restore circulation, Fenella bent down over the man and tapped him on the shoulder.

"Hello?" When she saw the knife in the man's chest, Fenella wondered for a moment if she were on some sort of hidden camera show. She looked around the alley, hoping to spot a camera and some B-list celebrity hiding behind one of the dumpsters. When she didn't spot anything other than a few seagulls, she pulled out her new mobile phone.

She punched in 911 and held the phone to her ear. She heard nothing but silence. The woman in the shop had assured her, only forty minutes earlier, that the phone was ready to use. Deciding she must have done something wrong, Fenella began to dial again.

"The emergency number in the United Kingdom is 999, not 911," a voice in her head told her. Fenella frowned when she recognized the voice. At least some of the endless lectures and hectoring she'd received from the man she'd left behind were proving useful, she told herself as she tapped in 999.

"Isle of Man Emergency Services, what is your emergency?" a female voice asked.

"Oh, yes, well, I've found, that is, there's a man here and I think he might be dead," Fenella said.

"Can you give us a location, please? I can dispatch an ambulance."

"I'm behind the Promenade View Apartments building in Douglas," Fenella replied. "In the alley that runs behind the building."

"And the man you're calling about is in the alley?" the woman asked.

"Yes, he's just lying on the ground here."

"I'll send an ambulance," the woman said. "If you could just wait with the man, please."

"Oh, I think you'll want to send the police," Fenella replied. "I think the man has been stabbed."

"Do you?" the woman sounded shocked. "Well, I'm sure the paramedics can ring for the police if they think they need to. Please just wait with the man until they arrive. Have you tried talking to him or shaking him to wake him up?"

"Yes, I've tried both," Fenella said. "When I tapped him on the shoulder, that's when I saw the knife, you see."

"Okay, is there anyone else there with you?"

"No, I'm alone in the alley," Fenella replied. As soon as the words left her lips, she felt terrified. Someone had stabbed this man and left him in the alley. Goodness only knew where the killer had gone next.

"I'm going to send the nearest constable. He should be with you in a minute or two. In the meantime, keep talking to me."

"I don't want to talk to you. I want to take my shopping up to my apartment and put my ice cream in the freezer. I have six bags of shopping that are spoiling while I'm standing here. Yeah, maybe I bought too much stuff, but I was hungry and there isn't a single thing to eat in my apartment, nothing."

"I am sorry about that. I'm sure someone will be with you soon. Do you recognize the man in the alley?"

"He looks very familiar, actually, although he's lying on his stomach, so I can't see his face. Maybe it's his clothes that look familiar. I can't possibly know him, though. I've only been on the island since yesterday afternoon. I don't know anyone."

A head suddenly appeared around the side of the building. Fenella jumped and shrieked. "There's someone else here," she said in a loud whisper.

"Hello," the man called. "I'm from Manx Ambulances. We received a call about an injured man."

Fenella nodded. "He's here," she said, staring hard at the man, as if that would help her work out if the new arrival really was who he claimed to be. A moment later a second man joined the first and the pair walked the short distance to where Fenella was standing. They were both dressed like paramedics, at least, which made Fenella feel a little bit better.

"You can tell the operator that we're here now," one of the men said. "And you can hang up."

Fenella felt curiously reluctant to disconnect from the voice on the other end of the phone. In a strange place and under incredibly odd circumstances, the woman on the other end of the phone felt like the only friend Fenella had.

"That's the paramedics, then?" the voice asked.

"Yes," Fenella agreed. "Thank you."

She disconnected the call and dropped the phone back in her pocket. As she took a step backwards, she switched all of her shopping to her now free hand. Feeling as if the other hand might never recover, she took another step backwards. The two paramedics were bent over the man, speaking quietly with one another.

"I'll just go and get my shopping put away," she said in a voice that sounded weirdly strained to her. "Thanks."

"I think you'd better stay here," one of the men said. "We've rung for the police."

"I told the woman on the phone that she should send the police," Fenella replied.

"Yes, well, they'll be coming now for sure," the man said.

She nodded and then glanced over at the man on the ground. "He's dead, then?"

"Not officially, not until the coroner gets here," she was told.

Fenella shifted three of the bags back into her other hand. That way she was balanced and both hands hurt equally.

"I see, well, I hate to be demanding, but I'd really like to get my shopping put away," she said tentatively. "I've spent a lot of money on far too much food and it's all getting ruined out here in the rain," she said.

"You'll have to stay to talk to the police," the taller of the two men said. "Maybe they'll let you take your shopping inside before they question you."

"I can't possibly tell the police anything," Fenella argued. "I only arrived on the island yesterday. I don't know a soul."

"Is that a fact?" The question came from behind her and Fenella spun around so quickly that she nearly lost her balance as her shopping bags spun with her.

"Yes," she said with more certainty than she felt. There was still something naggingly familiar about the man on the ground.

The man smiled at her and Fenella found herself smiling back. He was probably approaching fifty, with light brown hair and hazel eyes. He was taller than Fenella's five feet, seven inches, by at least another half a foot. Fenella sucked in her stomach as she noted that his body looked fit and firm under his dark raincoat. She was conscious of the ten extra pounds she was carrying. To her mind they were relics of the extravagant fortieth birthday vacation she'd taken eight years ago.

"I'm Inspector Daniel Robinson," the man said. "Douglas CID."

"It's nice to meet you," Fenella replied. She looked down at her shopping bags and then shrugged. "I'd shake hands if I could," she told him. "I'm Fenella Woods, anyway. I moved to the island yesterday and this was my first trip out of my apartment. Now I've tons of food to get put away. I do hope you don't mind if I take the shopping upstairs?"

The man frowned. "As soon as one of the constables gets here, I'll have him or her escort you to your flat," he said. "They can wait with you until I'm ready to question you."

Fenella was going to argue that questioning her was a complete waste of time, but she bit her tongue. Instead she watched as the man approached the body. As he leaned over the man, Fenella's tired brain suddenly made the necessary connection.

"It's Alan Collins," she gasped.

ABOUT THE AUTHOR

Diana grew up in Pennsylvania, moved to Washington, DC, and then found herself being swept off her feet by a handsome British man who was visiting DC on vacation. That was nearly nineteen years ago.

After their wedding, Diana moved to Derbyshire, where her new husband had his home. A short time later, the couple moved to the Isle of Man. After more than ten years on the island, now a family of four, they relocated to the outskirts of Buffalo, NY, where Diana keeps busy writing about the island she loves and driving her children everywhere.

She also writes mystery/thrillers set in the not-too-distant future under the pen name "Diana X. Dunn" and fantasy/adventure books for middle grade readers under the pen name "D.X. Dunn."

She would be delighted to know what you think of her work and can be contacted through snail mail at:

Diana Xarissa Dunn
PO Box 72
Clarence, NY 14031

Find Diana at:
www.dianaxarissa.com
diana@dianaxarissa.com